AMERICAN ODYSSEY

AMERICAN ODYSSEY

MAX McCOY

PINNACLE BOOKS
Kensington Publishing Corp.
www.kensingtonbooks.com

For George,
who knows the song of the river otter

The mountains do not need other mountains, but people do need other people. —Basque proverb

We men are wretched things. —Homer

1 *The Last Perfect Day*

Jack Picaro would not know it for many years, but the day the aspens turned to gold on the side of the mountain behind the lodge would be the last happy day of his life. There would be other days, to be sure, in which he would find gratification in food or drink or women, fleeting amusement at the turn of a card, or some grim satisfaction in placing a rifled ball through the heart of an enemy. He would be free, and he would be feared, but never again would he be happy.

In seasons to come he would think about that day and count the details, each of which seemed mundane when lived but which would turn a distant gold in memory. He had awakened in the cool and dark of early morning, with Sky sleeping beside him beneath the elk robes, and he had reached for her warmth and drawn her close. She had protested the awakening, in a sleepy mixture of French and Arikara, but had slowly yielded. He would recall the smell of her hair, and softness of the skin on the nape of her neck, and the roundness of her breasts. He was gentle, for she was with child.

After, he sat up and rested his elbows on his knees and stared into the shadows.

"Qu'est-ce que c'est?"

Sky reached out and touched his cheek.

He flinched.

"Toothache," Jack said.

She asked him to show her where. He took her hand and guided her fingers to his upper jaw, below his right cheekbone. The flesh was swollen and warm.

"It must come out," she said.

There were many long moments during which Sky listened to his breathing in the dark.

"No," he said with finality.

Jack said he would pack the cavity with a pinch of gunpowder and the pain would go away and things would be all right. Sky made some small disapproving sound and gathered herself and said she was climbing downstairs to sit inside the circle of stones she had placed in front of the lodge and watch the sun rise over Stinking Water River.

"Stay," Jack said. "It's cold outside. It is warm here."

"I'm being cooked," Sky said. "You place twice as much wood as is needed to bank the fire for the night. You make the place into a sweat lodge. That is the problem with your kind."

"My kind?"

"The *waisachu*," she said. "You are a wasteful people."

"But you are mixed blood," Jack said. "You slander only yourself."

Jack could feel Sky's frown in the darkness.

"It was not my choice," she said.

"And it *was* my choice?" Jack laughed.

"You shift between nations as it suits," she said. "Now you are Basque, then you are French, but always you are American. You have American hungers and yet you choose to live here at the world's edge far from the feasts of any nation."

"My hungers are dangerous."

"You are a wicked man," Sky said. "But I love you still."

Then she placed the fingertips of her right hand upon his thigh, as she had done a thousand times before in the morning.

"I traveled," she said.

"Tell me of your dream," Jack said as he always did.

"Lost in a sea of white sand," she said. "It was not a place I have been, but a place I heard of once. It is far from here, along the black road, and nobody lives there, at least not anymore."

The black road was the road to the west, to death.

"The setting sun had come to earth and everything was burned by its fire—the trees, the animals, even the rocks, which were melted."

"Were you burned?"

"I was a ghost and could not be burned."

"You were too warm in the night," Jack said. "It was only a nightmare."

"No," Sky said. "I was a ghost."

"You're not a ghost," Jack said.

"We will all be ghosts, soon enough," Sky said. "But you had somehow made the sun come to earth and made ghosts of us all."

"How?" Jack asked, suddenly interested.

"You had found the number of it."

"That makes no sense," Jack said.

"Dreams have their own truth," Sky said. Then she again gathered herself to watch the sun rise and listen to the birds.

"Stay here," Jack said. "It's cold."

"I'm being roasted," Sky said. "And living in this box makes me ill. Shadows gather in the corners and it makes me ill to look into them."

"You'll freeze."

"I need the embrace of the roundness of the world."

"You will be seeking warm corners again when the cold bursts the trunks of the trees."

"That is moons away," she said.

"As you will," Jack said. "But you will miss me when you begin to shiver."

"You weave words like the baskets my people make to trap fish," Sky said, pausing at the top of the rough-hewn ladder to downstairs. "But there is none here but ourselves and no strange fish to snare. Speak truly to me, Jack, for we are at the edge of the world with only each another for the long winter."

"People mean trouble."

"People mean coffee and whiskey and salt and powder and lead," Sky said as her bare left foot touched the top rung of the ladder that led below. "And all of the other things we cannot make for ourselves."

"We have meat year-round and fruit in the summer and warm robes in winter," Jack said. "And we are free. That is enough."

He could hear her hands and feet on the ladder and the loft seemed suddenly darker.

"Sky?" he called. "What was the number of the sun?"

But she had already gone.

Jack stared into the darkness for a long while after she had gone, feeling the throbbing in his jaw. He wished there were whiskey, or even tobacco, but those things were weeks or months away, likely bundled on the back of a mule trailing behind some free trapper hundreds of miles beyond the mountains. The early morning was so quiet that Jack could hear the blood pulsing in his ears, and the sound reminded him that for every human being there is a finite yet unknowable number of beats. The thought of an unwinding clock at the center of his chest made him melancholy, and he pondered the echo of measures long past, the beats that marked times and faces he would never see again. This stirred a deep agitation within him, because memories were painful. Twelve years ago, when he had made his retreat to this spot along the Stinking Water, he had vowed to leave the past buried with the unreachable dead.

"Enough," he said, although it was more of a growl than a word.

He stretched out his right hand, and his fingers found the polished grip of the single-shot pistol that was always nearby while he slept. His fingertips traced the lines of the walnut and across the chill of steel and brass and on to the roughness of flint. He picked up the gun and, still on his back, pointed it aloft, his hand trembling with its weight. His mind went back to a night many years before, not long before he quit St. Louis, when he dueled at a place called Bloody Island. Then, even though drunk, he had brought expertise and dash to the affair of honor. Now, he aimed at nothing and everything in the darkness, wishing that one could kill one's own demons with the same tools used to dispatch enemies. But that was only possible as a world-ending act of annihilation.

"Damn it, Jack."

He lowered the gun.

He sat up and flung the robes from his naked body. There was much to be done before winter came clawing at the lodge door, and perhaps today he would go to the snow-covered meadow beyond the boiling springs and seek a fat elk. The animals would be in rut and not yet scattered to the lower elevations to escape the cold of the mountains. But first, he required coffee.

When the coffee pot was boiling furiously, Jack used a piece of hickory notched on one end to catch the bail and removed it from the oven-like hearth. Then, using a scrap of leather to protect his fingers, he tipped the pot and poured a cup almost to the brim. The coffee bubbled and swirled in the tin cup, and the comforting aroma of coffee filled the kitchen. Then Jack sat down at the stout table, the coffee at his elbow. A sliver of early sunlight had found a crack in the wall, and it rippled like fire across the floor, up onto the table, across his arm, and danced upon the cloud of steam rising from the cup. Jack stared at the beam, transfixed by its beauty and transience, and for a moment he felt his soul as that scimitar of light cleaving the morning dark in the kitchen of the lodge.

He had recreated this traditional Basque wood-and-stone combination house and barn from his childhood memory, adding his own touches as needed for life along Stinking Water River in the Rocky Mountains. He had named the lodge Hell's Gate, because the richest man in the world, John Jacob Astor, who had made his fortune in the fur trade, had an estate in New York called "Hell Gate." Jack laughingly said that *he* felt like the richest man in the world, because he lived as he pleased, so his lodge would have a similar name—and because the Stinking Water Valley was the entrance to a mysterious region of geysers and boiling springs that sometimes stank of sulphur.

The first floor of the building was stone, the walls fitted together like a jigsaw puzzle from boulders found nearby, and the top floor—where they slept—was timber. Attached to the rear of the first floor was a small wooden stable, and Jack's workshop and forge. A wide porch with a stone floor ran three-quarters of the width of the front, which faced the river below. The pitch of the cedar-shingled roof was steeper than those he knew as a child, so that snow in the depth of winter would not easily collect and crush the roof. Still, once or twice during the coldest months when the snow clung to the roof, he had to clamor about with a long cord, with Sky holding the other end, to cut the snow in chunks, and let it slide to the ground. It had taken ten years to build the lodge, and still it was unfinished. Jack had rebuilt the workshop three times already, attempting to improve on the bellows in order to get a hotter fire, and the fireplace twice, to give it a better draw and improve the niche for an oven. All he needed was the iron door, which he might someday be able to trade for—or forge himself, given enough scrap.

One day, he imagined, he would buy, or trade for, yeast starter and real flour made from wheat or oats. Until then, he could only dream of rising bread. It was the smell of his grandfather's kitchen; it was the smell of home.

Beneath the lodge was a dugout cellar, where they stored smoked meat and sometimes fish and vegetables in season. It was also the place where Jack had instructed Sky to hide if strangers came.

When the coffee had cooled enough to drink, Jack pulled a ledger book from a shelf that was within arm's reach of the table. He had traded the book for some repairs to the lock of an ancient musket a Crow warrior had brought him years ago, and he did not ask about the drops of blood that flecked the book's cloth cover. Crows and the Blackfeet warriors and sometimes the Shoshones who were often at war in the Stinking Water Valley and beyond, and trappers and others of European stock, generally avoided the area, but Jack managed a delicate neutrality by providing gunsmithing services to all without favoritism. But now it had been fourteen months since a visitor had come to the lodge, and their supply of the things they could not make or gather for themselves was nearly exhausted.

In the book he sketched, first in pencil and then in ink, details of mechanisms he could only imagine because he did not have the materials necessary to make them reality. The plan he had been working on for the last month was of a mechanism for a repeating rifle. Such firearms were not unique in Europe, although most were impractical because of complicated recharging mechanisms that required arm power to cycle and reliance on flint or wheel ignition, which did not lend itself well to multiple shots. The best of the repeating arms relied not on gunpowder but on the power of compressed air—even Lewis and Clark relied on one. This had gotten Jack to thinking about the massive spring-like power of suddenly expanding air, and while he had no interest in a firearm that did not use gunpowder, it occurred to him that every firearm, when fired, had a considerable force of expanding gas in its breach that could be used to actuate a reloading mechanism. As Jack sketched how he imagined the articulating lever would function inside a receiving chamber, he did not hear Sky enter.

"We have enough coffee for two or three more pots," she said. "After that you will have to rely on sumac tea."

Jack made a face.

"Some trapper will come along soon with goods to trade for a few small repairs," he said. Jack knew he was low on powder and lead as well, but did not mention it. "Or they may have tea. Proper tea, not undrinkable stuff made of leaves."

"Or you may have to learn to do without."

"A trapper always comes," he said.

"How long has it been since the last?"

"Long," Jack said. "Months. Eight or nine months, perhaps."

"It's been fourteen months," Sky said.

"No . . ."

"I have counted the moons," she said. "It has been fourteen months. That is a very long time to be without, by ourselves. We have been without flour for more than a year. The coffee only lasted so long because I am very good at rationing."

He put his right arm around her waist and pulled her to him. Her hip fit comfortably against him and her unbound hair brushed his cheek. The sun had moved, and the shaft of light that had split the kitchen was forever gone now.

"I have no aptitude for doing without," he said.

"What has made you so moody?" Sky asked.

Jack ignored the question.

"You have been too long with only me for company," she said.

"What nonsense."

She looked at the open ledger with its drawings and calculations and notes written in Jack's precise hand. She ran her left hand over the page, as if her fingertips could read the language of ideas.

"This is something new," she said.

"It is only a sketch," he said. "Something I dreamed."

She looked at him with unblinking eyes.

"The things you dream are more real to you than I am," she said. She started to turn the pages. Jack put his hand on hers.

"Don't," he said. "There are things not yet to be revealed."

"I will never be able to compete with the visions inside your head," she said flatly. "You carry an entire world inside you that I will never be a part of, never even able to glimpse except in the shadows of your sketches."

"None of us share that," he said. "I cannot peer into your mind."

"You do not need to," she said. "You have seen every mile of my world, from the rivers and the villages to the places where the old ones have gone to die. My world is the mountains and the sky and the autumn breeze among the aspens. Your world is beyond where the sun rises and I will never know it, in this life or the next."

"You could," Jack said. "We could follow the Yellowstone to the broad Missouri and put in a pirogue and drift all the way to St. Louis before the river freezes. You speak English and French better than most of the people I knew there and you would find many other Catholics, like yourself, and they would take you in."

"And you would be arrested the moment you set foot in the city and be hanged for murder," Sky said. "That is the truth, is it not? So for you to give me your world you must sacrifice yourself and leave me with strangers. No, I will stay here at the gates to the mountains with you and your life in the city named for a king will forever be a mystery."

"There is no mystery to it," Jack said. "The city is a cruel and brutish place."

"All places are cruel and brutish," Sky said. "It is the nature of the wolf to kill and the antelope to submit. So it is that some men are wolves and others antelopes. You are, and have always been, the wolf."

Jack smiled.

"Then how can you love me?" he asked. "Your religion teaches that killing is a sin, that it is better to turn the other cheek, that the wolf shall live with the lamb.

I have killed many men, I have never turned my face away from anyone, and I am fond of mutton."

It was an old argument, and Jack enjoyed it.

Sky shook her head.

"You are a rebellious child," she said. "A dangerous one, but a child still."

That is not what his joints told him on the coldest mornings, Jack thought.

"I will go out today and bring back meat," Jack said. "Come with me and we will linger where the boiling spring meets the river, as we once did. After resting for as long as it suits, we'll continue to the upper meadow to hunt. It is easier to dress the animals when you help."

"It is already too late in the day," Sky said.

"The day has hardly begun."

"To hunt the upper meadow, you should have been moving by first light."

"We have our robes, and the canvas," Jack said. "The weather is yet tame. We could spend the night away, as we used to."

"The cliffs scare me," Sky said. "They belong to the twilight nation."

"You speak of them as if they live still."

"They are neither alive nor dead, but shadows upon the earth."

"Come," Jack said. "You can sleep away from this wooden box. We will take meat and drink warm blood and remind ourselves that we are not yet shadows upon the earth. We will celebrate the coming of another winter, together."

"We will need gifts for the people of the cliffs."

"Then gather your gifts," Jack said.

Shortly after, when Jack was outside preparing to saddle the animals, as the sun warmed his face and the breeze carried the scent of pine, he felt the passage of the years and the slow drawing of the curtain that revealed the mystery of days to come.

2 *An Aching*

A billowing column of steam marked where the boiling spring met the snowmelt-filled river. The bank was low here and rocky, and a spit of gravel curved out into the river and was lost beneath the cloud. Jack had stripped away everything except his blue wool shirt and was waiting, with a rifle held easily in the crook of his left arm, for Sky to join him.

The horses were staked higher up the bank, and Sky was standing between them. Jack's horse was 'Clipse, a coal black stallion. The gray horse was the mare Sky called Smoke. After speaking in low tones to the horses and gently touching the forelock of each, she walked down the bank and followed the gravel bar toward Jack. In what seemed one motion, she removed her belt with the elkhorn-handled knife in its scabbard, the wooden cross hanging from a red and white zig-zag pattern of Arikara beadwork around her neck, and slipped her antelope skin dress over her head. She dropped her clothes on the gravel and stood there with her rounded stomach and smiled. She had a chipped front tooth, an accident from childhood.

"Damn," Jack said, "I never thought I'd ever see anything as pretty as the aspens on the side of the mountain. But I was wrong."

A driftwood log with many branches lay near the end of the gravel bar and Jack nestled the rifle in a pair of forks. Then he took off his shirt and spread it on top of the rifle to keep the sun from glinting on the metal.

Sky touched his chest in the same manner she had touched the horses.

"You are turning gray," she said.

"Men do at this season of life," he said. "I am thirty-three."

"But there's only a touch at your temples," she said.

"It was the same with my father," Jack said, taking her hand in his. They crept barefooted to the edge of the water, testing the temperature. Sky said it was too hot, so they went a few yards downstream, into the cloud.

"Yes," she said.

They waded into the water. A mallard hen scooted noisily from the middle of the cloud to the safety of the grass on the far bank. Sky laughed, then she took another step and her foot didn't find the bottom. She fell until the water reached her chin. Jack lunged and put his arm around her waist and pulled her up to him.

"What would I do—"

She pressed her forefinger against his lips.

"Don't," she said. "Be here, with me. Now."

She kissed him.

Jack drew back slightly.

"The tooth," he said.

Sky frowned.

Jack probed at the molar with the tip of his tongue, then winced in pain.

"You fool," Sky said. "It must come out."

"Not without whiskey," Jack said.

"You are only prolonging your pain," Sky said. "And perhaps hastening your death."

"It's nothing," Jack said.

"That makes you flinch as if burned."

"Later," Jack said. "We'll speak of this later."

"We will," she said. "Or I will take some of your gunsmith tools and pry it out myself, whiskey or no."

She kissed him again, this time more gently.

Jack felt the warm water swirl around his legs and the cool air brush his chest and Sky's moist lips against his. In that moment he forgot the shame of his past and how the coffee was nearly gone at the lodge and his frustration at being only able to sketch the things he wanted to make with his hands. For now, the world they shared was enough and more, and Jack felt his spirit rise and dance with the mist over the river.

Sometime later—it could have been five minutes or an hour, because time had lost track of Jack—the mallard hen made a racket and beat her wings and took off from the water fifty or sixty yards downriver. Then came the sound of the horses shuffling, and Sky gripped his forearm and gave a little shake.

"I hear," he said softly.

"Crows?" Sky asked.

"We would have heard nothing," Jack said. "Some slinking thing. Wolves, perhaps."

Jack started slowly toward the gravel bar.

"Stay here," Sky said.

"We cannot afford to lose the horses."

"'Clipse would kick them to death."

"But not before throwing the stake," Jack whispered. "I'd rather not chase a horse down today. Besides, it might not be wolves."

Sky began making for the bank.

"Stay here," he said. "If there's trouble, swim to the other bank and hide in the trees beyond."

She nodded.

Jack moved slowly through the water and, when he reached the gravel bar, crouched low and inched his way toward the driftwood where the rifle was hidden. He was out of the cloud now but dared not rise up for a look around, for fear of giving away his position. When he came to the driftwood and flattened himself on the river side of it, he carefully reached up and grasped the shirt and the barrel with one hand and began to pull them close. The stock of the rifle caught on a small dry twig that snapped and Jack froze for a moment, listening intently. He was cold now that he was out of the water and began to shiver. He counted silently to thirty and then, his arm shaking, drew the shirt and rifle fully to his chest.

Jack wrapped his right hand around the grip of the rifle and thumbed the hammer back until it locked. Then he folded the shirt until the pocket with the powder horn, patches, and lead balls were within easy reach. He might have to reload in a hurry.

Then he took a deep breath and leapt over the trunk

of the driftwood, his rifle at the ready and his shirt wrapped in his hand beneath the stock. He made for the horses in great strides, the balls of his bare feet slapping the earth, his manhood swinging in time. On the far side of 'Clipse, a figure was moving toward the trees. Jack couldn't make out to which nation the figure belonged, or even if it was a man or a woman.

As Jack drew close to the horses, he watched the figure melt into the trees. He stopped and planted his feet. Jack brought the rifle to his eye and attempted to fix the blade sight on the figure, but there was nothing now to aim at, not a shadow or even a rustling branch.

Jack cursed and carefully uncocked the hammer.

Then he turned his attention to the horses. 'Clipse was still shuffling and making anxious snorting sounds, but his halter rope was still securely staked to the ground. Smoke, the mare, was tied to the ground as well, but acting almost as troubled.

Jack spoke to both horses in soothing tones.

Nothing seemed amiss, nothing had been stolen. Still pondering what the person had wanted, Jack turned and then saw Sky's dress on the ground. It had been taken from where she had discarded it in a hurried heap and was carefully laid out, as if for ironing. The belt was fastened and placed over the waist, and the knife was still in its sheath. But the wooden cross had been placed upside down between the hips of the dress.

Jack shivered, partly from the cold.

"Who would do this?"

Jack knelt on one knee and picked up the items, the cross first, then the belt, and bundled them inside the dress. Then he slipped on his own wool shirt, found his trousers and moccasins, and walked out on the gravel spit and called to Sky.

"Come on out," he said.

In a few moments, she appeared dripping from the cloud.

"What's wrong?" she asked.

"Nothing," he said. "There was someone here, but they ran."

"Crows, you think?" she asked, taking her bundle from Jack. "Snakes?"

"I did not get a clear look," Jack said. "Perhaps it was a member of your twilight nation."

"Not at this time of day," she said, hanging the cross from her neck. "And not this far from the cliffs."

Sky unfolded the dress, gathered it in her arms, and prepared to slip it over her head. Then she paused and looked at a few flecks of crimson on the tan skirt.

"Did you cut yourself?" she asked.

"No," Jack said.

"Then our stranger bleeds," she said. "You knew he touched my things and did not tell me."

"It would have frightened you," Jack said.

"Fear is useful," Sky said. "This gives me a glimpse of the mind of the stranger, and I do not like what I see." She wet her thumb with her tongue and rubbed at one of the flecks. "The dress is forever stained."

"There will be other dresses."

"Did you draw this blood?"

"No," Jack said. "There was no clear shot. I never got close enough to use my knife."

"And nothing was taken?"

"The horses remained staked," Jack said. "Nothing else seems to have been touched."

"My father, perhaps, or a warrior sent by him."

"Lightning Crow is more direct," Jack said. "And I would have been the target."

"Killing you would be quick and unsatisfying," she said. "Humiliating and then killing me would hurt you more."

"I do not think it was Lightning Crow. He doesn't send others skulking to do his business."

Sky sighed.

"There is no point in spinning stories until we know more," she said. "We will wait and watch and be ready if the stranger comes. Let us not waste time by indulging our need to make sense of things, when there is no sense in some things."

3 *The Wind and the Rain*

At the base of the obsidian cliff, Jack walked slowly, inspecting the ground, and paused often to pick up a piece of the shiny black material. He dropped most of the rocks back but every so often would find one that was exceptionally flat or sometimes one that had been in the process of being knapped into a point, and then abandoned because it had fissured in some disappointing way. Rarely he would find an intact point—sometimes a small one, no larger around than a penny, and at other times ones so large they had to be the tips of spears—and he would marvel at how expertly they had been made, and how razor-sharp the edges were still. He slipped the best finds in a leather bag and placed them in the pocket of his shirt. Later, for fleshing game, Sky would mount the larger pieces in wooden handles.

"Don't take too much," Sky cautioned him.

"Just what I need."

"You sometimes confuse your wants and your needs," Sky said. "The Nation that Has No Name still uses the obsidian from this cliff for their needs. We mustn't take what they need."

"You and your ghost tribes," Jack said, shaking his head.

"Not ghosts," Sky said. "They are simply the last of their kind. Their village is somewhere in the Elk Valley of the Yellowstone, but they move often and their numbers are few. Their name is known only to them, because they are the last to speak the language of their ancestors."

She held a bunch of wildflowers in her hand. They were what she could find blooming so late in the year— yarrow and astrid, orange and white—tied with a grass ribbon.

Jack put a hand over his eyes and looked at the cliff, a hundred feet of volcanic glass rising above them. Like many things west of the lodge on the Stinking Water, he had never seen anything to compare to it.

"Why don't the nations come here any longer?" Jack asked.

"The shiny black rocks belong to a past age," she said. "Long before lone man came, the twilight nation traded with the mound builders across the middle world, but no one is alive now who remembers. But we have the stories, and the spear points, which were used to slay the cannibal owl and the wooly beasts and even the thunderbirds. Those were days when there were giants in the earth, the sons of God, as it says in Genesis, and they found the daughters of men to be fair, and took them as wives."

"Well, who wouldn't?"

"Stop it!"

"I'd say you're mixing your cultures," Jack said. "The heathen and the Catholic are having one hell of a duel inside that warm heart of yours."

"I feel the twilight nation all about us here," Sky said. "The centuries judge us."

"It is we who must judge the centuries," Jack said. "For we are yet alive. Others will judge us when we are dead."

Sky walked to the base of the cliff, lifted the hem of her dress, and knelt. She was chanting the words to an old prayer in French. Jack knew the prayer from the cadence alone. *Blessed Mother of those whose name you can read in my heart, watch over them with every care.* Sky reverently placed the wildflowers on the ground. *Dry their tears if they weep; sanctify their joys; raise their courage if they weaken; restore their hope if they lose heart, their health if they be ill, truth if they err, and repentance if they fall.*

"Amen," Jack said softly.

Sky stood, smoothed her dress, and walked back.

"The centuries will not judge," she said. "We are the wind and the rain upon the earth, and when our bones become one with the world, we will live in the memory of but a few. And when they are gone to their ends, so is the last trace of us. Whether my soul rises to heaven or is condemned to oblivion, I am reconciled to the anonymity of the unmarked grave."

"Then I will share that unmarked grave with you."

"No, Jack," Sky said. "You will not."

"Stop talking so," Jack said. "You act as if you see the future."

Sky shook her head.

"I see nothing," she said. "Only the rocks at my feet and the sky above. But the wind whispers to me, and it reminds me that unlike the stones and the sky I am mortal. Human beings differ from animals only in one way, and that is we know we will die. I do not expect to die today, tomorrow, or even thirty years from now. But I know that one day I will die, and that when I die, gravity will return my body to the forgiving and anonymous earth."

4   *The Comet*

They left the obsidian cliff and sought the higher eleva-tions. Jack was riding 'Clipse, the coal black horse he had found a year before in the valley below the lodge, shuffling and dragging its reins in circles around the corpse of its owner, a free trapper who had fallen from the saddle. He had died from a wound to his neck that had gone septic. Jack judged the wound to have been in-flicted by a knife or possibly a hatchet, some days or weeks before. It was impossible to know for sure.

Smoke was a blue roan, and Sky had ridden her for almost as many years as they had lived in the lodge. Jack had traded a bundle of plews for the mare. In those days Jack still set traps in the ice-cold streams for beaver, a demanding trade he had learned as a younger man with the Rocky Mountain Fur Company. He had since stopped taking beaver because his skill as a gunsmith was worth more than any amount of beaver pelts he could gather.

Late that afternoon they stopped short of the high valley and made camp. Here the snow was in patches on the ground and they chose a dry spot for the canvas. Jack hung the canvas over a rope tied between two pine trees that were eight or ten feet apart, and beneath the canvas they made their beds from woolen blankets and elk robes. They unsaddled the horses and tied them to trees a few yards away. Dinner was a mixture of jerked meat, berries, and suet. There was no need for a fire because there wasn't enough coffee left at the lodge to pack. Jack wanted his last cup to be at the stout wooden table with his idea ledger by his elbow.

Still, it was pleasant under the canvas, with just their heads peeking out.

Sky leaned back in Jack's arms and together they watched the night deepen and the stars emerge. There was a smudge of light in the west, and as the sky deepened it became relatively brighter and more distinct from the stars around it. It was a fuzzy point of bluish-green light followed by a curved, fan-like tail. They had seen it in the sky for the past few days, just after sunset.

"What is it made of?" Sky asked.

"What are the stars made of?" Jack asked. "Nobody knows."

"What do you think it means?"

"It's a comet," Jack said.

"I know it's a comet," Sky said. "But my people say celestial visitors such as this portend catastrophe. Famine, sickness, war. Do you think there's a meaning to this visitor?"

In the years to come Jack would think often of this conversation, and it would change slightly in his memory. Once he could remember his true answer as, "No, there is nothing to it." But time and desire and disappointment had made his memory plastic, so that eventually the answer became equivocal.

"I don't know."

After a pause, he continued.

"But my people, too, have a long history of associating comets with events of great portent. Shakespeare said comets mark the passing of princes. The Romans believed the soul of Julius Caesar was born back to Venus on a comet, and that a comet foretold a plague under the rule of emperor Justinian. But later men said they are within the natural order of things. A British astronomer named Halley reckoned that some return at predictable intervals, and he predicted one of the brightest would return in 1758. And it did, or at least that is what the old men said when I was a boy in Carcosa."

"And this one?"

"The same comet," Jack said. "Returning seventy-six years later, as Halley predicted."

"We will not be here to see its return," Sky said.

"Few will," Jack said. "The child, perhaps."

She sighed.

"Is a long life a blessing or a curse?"

"It depends on the life," Jack said.

"Then let us pray it is a happy one."

And this is where Jack's memory found the true path again, urged back by something so woven into his memory at a young age that he could not forget it.

"Happiness is the only thing we can give without having," Jack said. "That's what my grandfather told me. I remember him saying that sitting at his table, so long ago. I must have been seven or eight years old."

"You recall such odd things with perfect clarity," Sky said. "And yet you do not remember things that happened just this week. Do you remember what I said to you the day before yesterday?"

"I remember perfectly," Jack said. "You told me to wipe my filthy feet before entering the lodge."

"That's not what I meant," she said.

"Oh, the name for the baby," Jack said.

"Do not tease me," Sky said.

"I would not," Jack said. "The knife you carry is as sharp as your wit."

"A dull knife is worse than none," Sky said. "So tell me, what kind of name?"

"Whatever suits the child in time," Jack said.

"But your people name their children at birth and those names stay with them," Sky said.

"Mine did not," Jack said. "I left it behind in the states."

"The child's name will stay," Sky said. "So the question is what manner of name? English? French? Basque?"

"Whatever you desire," Jack said.

"This is your child," Sky said. "You must have an opinion."

"If a boy," Jack said, "we should not name him after me. Not Jack, not Jackie, not Jacques."

"It must have something of yours."

"Then he can have Picaro."

"Very well," Sky said. "And if a girl?"

"What does her mother favor?"

"I will dream on it," Sky said.

The sound of the wind sighing in the valley below filled the silence.

"What happens to our words?" Sky asked. "When we die. What happens to the words we speak to one another? What becomes of the many times we've spoken of love and of anger? What will become of the conversation we had tonight, of comets and children? What of our whispers and cries of love from this morning? Where do they go?"

"They are borne forever by the wind, to be heard by those who listen."

"You are a beautiful liar," Sky said.

It was the end of the last perfect day.

5   The Wolf and the Hand

Jack shouldered his rifle and thumbed the hammer back to full cock. He was prone atop a rocky ridge overlooking the high meadow, with his elbows buried in four inches of snow and his belly pressed against a cold flat stone. Behind him the just-risen sun was painting the clouds a cold pink and blue. The meadow was still pooled with shadow, but he could see the shapes of a bull elk and his harem two hundred yards away. He had heard the bull long before he could see it. About twenty minutes before sunup, the bull was bugling, a frightening sound that began as a high-pitched scream and ended in a deep growl. He was proclaiming his territory, the possession of the females—and an invitation to other bulls to fight.

When he could see the bull, he saw a rack so big it looked like the animal was wearing a chandelier for a hat. A half dozen cows milled about him. Jack would have liked to have had the bull for its rack, because many useful things could be made from it, but one of the cows would be easier to butcher. The bull likely weighed seven or eight hundred pounds, with the cows two hundred pounds lighter. Also, during rut, the hides of the bulls were often filthy, caked with the mud and the urine they had rolled in, which made for unpleasant skinning.

Sky was down the slope a hundred yards, holding the horses, ready to help with the butchering. She knew that dawn was the best time to take the elk, and if a shot didn't come within a few minutes after dawn, it would likely be an all-day wait.

As the sun illuminated the snowy meadow, Jack could clearly see the herd, the tracks the animals had left behind in the otherwise unbroken snow, and the tree line beyond. He could see that the bull had rubbed all of the velvet from its rack and was prepared to spar. Every so often the bull would toss its head and smell the air. The elk and his harem had been ambling slowly toward Jack's position, and while they were in range, a bit closer would result in a surer kill. So he decided to wait for just another minute or two, letting the herd get just another twenty or thirty yards closer, before taking his shot.

Then the bull tossed its head and made a confused sort of sound.

At first Jack thought that another, bigger bull had emerged from the tree line and was intent on a challenge. But the shape that was approaching was too small for an elk. It was a gray wolf, trotting unhurriedly across the meadow, sometimes hopping as it encountered deeper snow. The wolf's pack was likely not far behind, Jack guessed.

The bull stood its ground for the moment, but the elk harem began to shift nervously. Jack knew he must take his shot within the next few seconds or not at all, and impulsively he chose the bull. In a moment he had aligned the brass blade of the front sight with the notch of the rear sight and aimed at a spot just behind the shoulder of the bull, at a spot where the ball would pierce both lungs, and adjusted a bit for distance and a slight north breeze. He squeezed the trigger. The hammer fell, sparked the pan, and this ignited the charge. The rifle threw fire and smoke, and the report sounded like an artillery piece in the quiet of the morning and echoed from the sides of distant hills.

Jack rose to one knee, a patched ball already in his mouth and powder horn in hand. The breeze was carrying the smoke clear, and he could see the bull still standing. The cows had spooked and were already dozens of yards away. Jack charged the rifle, but had some difficulty because the little powder left in the horn had drawn moisture and there were clumps among the grain. Jack took the ball and patch from his mouth, and held them in place with his thumb over the muzzle. He tapped the ball a couple of times with the handle of his knife to start it in the barrel, and then with one smooth motion he used the ramrod to push the ball all the way down into the breach. Then he turned the rifle over, charged the pan, and cocked the hammer.

The bull remained standing.

Jack did not shoulder the rifle, because he knew it had been a clean kill. It just took some animals some time to realize they were dead. Suddenly, the bull fell heavily to the snow ground, all four legs giving out at once. The bull had had more meat than they could carry back to the lodge, but Jack would make something clever from the rack—parts for a chair, perhaps. The rest of the meat would not go to waste, as the scavengers would soon go to work on it.

Jack cradled the rifle in his left arm and was about to call for Sky when he noticed the wolf was still advancing. Jack was only mildly surprised, because he knew from experience how fiercely wolves could fight for fresh kills. But wolves gained their courage from the pack, and this wolf was alone.

Then Jack saw the wolf was carrying something tightly in its jaws.

The wolf passed the downed bull and did not pause or even slow. It was still too far for Jack to see clearly what the wolf was carrying, but it seemed a chunk of bloody meat.

Sky was coming up from below with the horses.

"Cow?" she asked, ten yards below the ridge.

"Bull," Jack said. "But wait where you are, so as not to frighten the horses."

"Why?"

"Wolf," Jack said.

"Don't let the pack claim the kill," Sky said.

"It's not a pack," Jack said. "It's one wolf, and it is acting strangely."

"Mad?"

"Perhaps," Jack said, staring intently. The wolf was coming straight across the meadow toward him. Jack squinted, trying to get a better look at what it carried. When he saw what it was, he blinked and looked again.

"What does it have in its jaws?" Sky asked, now standing beside Jack. She had tied the reins of the horses to a tree below.

"A human hand," Jack said. "A right hand."

The wolf was fifty yards away now and gaining speed.

"Get behind me," Jack said.

Sky tugged at his left elbow.

"This scares me," she said.

"It must be killed," Jack said. "Rabid or not, it must die."

The wolf had dropped the hand and charged. The sunlight illuminated its face, the snarling mouth full of teeth and flecks of blood and foam, the bright gray eyes, the tawny fur and the flattened ears. It bounded through the snow. Jack leveled the rifle and aimed down the wolf's throat and pulled the trigger. The hammer fell and the pan flashed, but there was no report. The last of his powder was bad. The gun had misfired.

Jack cursed and shouted for Sky to make for the horses.

He turned the gun around in his hands, so that he was holding the barrel like a bat over his shoulder, and he timed his swing for when the wolf leaped. The broad part of the stock took the animal on the left jowl, and Jack could feel both the stock and the neck bones snap. The wolf tumbled to one side, one hundred fifty pounds of fur and muscle and teeth. Jack was knocked backward into the snow, the rifle with the splintered stock spinning out of his hands to land a few yards away.

Jack drew the knife from his belt and rolled over onto one knee, not sure the fight was over. But the rabid wolf lay dying, bleeding from the mouth, its neck broken and the side of its head crushed, its eyes open but already growing cloudy.

Sky was beside him now, a hand on his shoulder.

"I'm unharmed," Jack said.

"The wolf is dead?"

"Yes, or nearly so," Jack said. "It is quite mad."

Jack stood and slapped the snow from his butt and

legs. Sky brushed clean the back of his shirt. Together, they walked forward, giving the wolf a wide berth, to find the hand in the snow. It was definitely a right hand, detached raggedly at the wrist, with blackened nails. It had not been very long from the body, because they could still tell that it came from a white man.

Sky started to crouch down to examine it closer, but Jack stopped her.

"Best not to get too close," he said.

She nodded.

"Do you remember how my father Lightning Crow lost his hand?"

"A rabid wolf," Jack said.

"What sign then is this?" Sky asked, shuddering.

"I don't know," Jack said. "But I will give you the odds are long against it."

Jack recalled his gambling days before escaping to the river and how his capacity for numbers and ability to calculate odds always gave him an advantage, but he had no mental probability tables for this.

"A man, likely a trapper, dies somewhere nearby," Jack said. "Death is common enough in the mountains, particularly if you don't know the territory or the nations. His body is left to the elements. Then the wolves come along, and they do what wolves do. They take the soft parts first, the genitals, the face, and then the feet and the hands."

"But is it likely the wolf was already mad?" Sky asked.

Jack paused.

"What do you mean?"

"If the wolf was not already sick," Sky said, "then it was the man who was rabid."

The thought made Jack ill in the pit of his stomach.

"Let's leave this place," Jack said.

"What about the elk?"

"I want no meat from here," Jack said.

"There are other animals," she said. "Deer and sheep. You can take them at your leisure."

"No, I cannot," Jack said. "I am out of powder."

"Then we will return to the old-fashioned ways," Sky said. "We will snare rabbits and catch fish from streams. We can make do. But what now of the dead wolf and the, well, the hand?"

"We will leave them where they fell."

"We cannot," Sky said. "Other animals will find them and they will all become mad, and spread it to even more animals. Then it will be unsafe to take any animals for meat. We must burn them, because the ground is too hard for burying."

They began gathering fallen limbs from the wood nearby to make a pyre over the wolf's body. When they were half finished Jack used a forked branch to scoop up the hand and deposit it in the fire. Then they piled an equal amount of wood on top, and Jack used his flint and steel to ignite a handful of leaves and dry grass. When the tinder was burning, he threw it deep in the pile of wood. Even though it had been snowing for weeks at this elevation, the humidity was low and the wood was dry. The pyre caught fire easily enough and within a few minutes was blazing brightly. The smell of burning hair and flesh was sickening, and Sky went back down to the horses to keep from retching. Jack stayed and added more substantial logs to the pyre, increasing the intensity.

"Stay dead," he intoned over the roaring blaze.

Then he retrieved the rifle from the snow, and what pieces of the broken stock he could find. The largest piece still had the butt attached. It was not such a great loss, he thought, and would cause mostly inconvenience in the time it would take to repair the stock. He was worried that one of his two last full charges of powder, however defective, was still in the barrel. The other was in the pistol at the lodge.

6 *Friends in Christ*

At the bottom of the trail from the high meadow, in the middle of their journey back to the lodge, they came upon a white woman staggering barefoot. She was of thirty or thirty-five years, with ragged blond hair streaked with gray, and her ripped calico dress was smeared with grease and dirt and blood. Her face was burned by the sun, and her fingernails were chipped and blackened, as if she had been clawing with her hands at some obstacle. Her eyes were bloodshot and bulging. A gash on her forehead glistened with blood. Her cheeks were coated with what looked like fine, cream-colored dust.

The woman was muttering to herself.

"Harken," she said. "Harken."

Jack dropped the reins and slid down from the saddle in one motion, his moccasins splatting in the snow and mud.

"Stay back," Jack said.

"Don't let her bite you," Sky said.

The woman slipped and fell. As Jack approached, she scrambled forward and clutched his left arm.

"Harken," she said.

"Listen for what?" Jack asked.

"The word of God."

Jack knelt next to her.

"You hear it, do you not?"

The woman had difficulty speaking because her lips were cracked and bruised.

"I hear the wind," Jack said.

"A gentle whisper," the woman said. "And the sound of rushing wind."

"Not so close," Sky said.

"She's not rabid," Jack said, cradling the woman.

"But she is not right," Sky said, remaining in the saddle. "She frightens me."

"Why?"

Sky brushed a wisp of hair from her eyes.

"I've never seen a white woman before," she said. "She is so unlike the men."

"As are all women."

"So many clothes," Sky said. "How do they breathe?"

"Come help me," Jack said.

"She seems washed out, like mud in the rain."

"She's been beaten," Jack said. "And worse."

Sky carefully dismounted, holding her stomach with one hand as first one foot and then the other touched the ground.

"What's your name?" Jack asked.

"Narcissa," she said in an accent that made her English sound soft, even drunken. "Narcissa Yost."

"Where are your people?" Jack asked.

The woman pointed behind her.

"What happened?"

"The will of God."

"Sure it wasn't the Almighty that abused you so," Jack said. "Who did this?"

"Devils," she said.

"Crows?" Jack asked. "White men?"

Her eyes became unfocused, and she gave a low moan.

Jack rubbed her cheek with his thumb to examine the crumbly off-white powder.

"What is it?" Sky asked, leaning over Jack's shoulder.

Jack rubbed the stuff between his thumb and forefinger, then tasted it.

"Flour," Jack said. "Wheat flour."

The woman's eyes fluttered open.

"Narcissa Yost," Jack said. "Stay awake."

"Yes," she said sleepily.

"Your people," Jack said. "How many are there?"

"My husband, Hiram," she said. "Our son, Hawk."

"Are they still alive?"

"Hiram is dead," she said.

The woman's eyes closed again and her head lolled to one side and Jack noticed sunlight glinting from a clear fluid seeping from her ear. Then she began to shake. She coughed and flecks of white spittle ran from the corners of her mouth.

"Take it easy," Jack said.

"She can't hear you," Sky said.

Jack placed her gently on the ground.

"Get away from her," Sky said.

"It's not rabies," Jack said. "Her skull is cracked and her brain is inflamed."

"Will she live?"

"I have seen this type of injury before," Jack said.

"Men who stumbled and struck their heads on the deck of a keelboat or had their heads flattened with a stave during a fight. These injuries are almost always fatal in the strongest of men, and this woman . . ."

"Is barely alive," Sky said.

"But this condition can last for days before death comes."

The woman groaned piteously.

"I don't know what to do for her," Jack said.

"There's nothing to do," Sky said. "Except shoot her. But we are out of powder."

"We can't kill her," Jack said.

Sky was pacing, inspecting the rocks at the side of the path.

"Of course, we can," she said.

"She is a white woman," Jack said.

"And if she were red that would be acceptable?"

"I didn't mean that," Jack said

"Of course, you did," Sky said. "The killing of a Crow woman, or Snake, or Arikaran and there would be no questions. But you're afraid of killing this mad white woman and having to explain to other whites."

"I can't," Jack said.

"It is a kindness," Sky said, using both hands to heft a rock that was the size of a small melon. "It is the only relief from her suffering. Sweet Jesus, get farther away from her."

Sky was striding toward the woman with the rock poised when Jack put a hand on her shoulder.

"No," he said. "Put that down."

"It is necessary."

"Put the rock down," Jack said. "Allow me a gentler way."

Sky brought the rock to chest height and gave it a shove. It thudded heavily into the ground a few feet away. The woman was still moaning, and her fingers were twitching now in an unsettling fashion.

Jack knelt again.

"Can you hear it?" he asked loudly.

There was no response.

"It is the voice of God," Jack said. "He is calling your name."

The woman's shaking became more severe.

"Hiram is here," Jack said.

The woman's teeth rattled as a convulsion washed over her.

"Blink if you understand," Jack said.

Her eyes remained shut.

"Very well," Jack said. "May Jesus and the Goddess Mari greet you."

He reached out and put his right hand over her mouth and pinched her nose shut with his left. The shaking grew worse and her arms flailed without aim. But gradually the movements slowed. After a few minutes, her chest sank and rose no more, and the woman was finally still on the ground.

Jack removed his hands.

"It is the first time I've killed a woman," he said.

"The rock would have been quicker," Sky said.

"Your fierceness sometimes scares me," Jack said.

"It must be the heathen part of me."

"What in the world was she and her people doing

out here?" Jack asked. "There must not be another white woman for three hundred miles."

"Good," Sky said. "They scare me. What about the man and the boy?"

"I will go look," Jack said.

"What if whoever did this is still about?" Sky asked.

"We must learn who did this," Jack said. "Otherwise, our fear will be on every nation and we will be forever without rest. If they are still lurking about, then better to see with my own eyes."

"And if they want to fight?"

"I would rather fight them here, than have them trail me to the lodge—and to you," Jack said. "Return to the lodge, but take the longer path. When you reach home, watch from the woods for long enough to make sure nobody is waiting inside for you. Spend the night outside, if you must, to be sure."

"Happily," Sky said.

"Once you are inside, fetch my pistol from among the robes in the loft. It is charged and ready to fire. If I don't return by sundown tomorrow, then you are to return to your people where the Missouri meets the Heart River."

"You are my people," Sky said. "I have none other."

"You have me and the child in your belly," Jack said. "But you must think only of the child if I don't return."

Sky nodded.

They embraced, then Jack helped her up into the saddle by giving her rump a gentle push.

"Be careful, Jack Picaro," she said. "But do what is necessary."

* * *

A mile down the path, Jack found Hiram Yost. He had been shot in the neck, and had run down the path with the wound gushing blossoms of blood upon the ground, and then had been shot in the back. The ball had struck just below his shoulder blades, shattering the spine, and traveled through one lung before exiting his chest.

Jack remained in the saddle, staring down at the body.

Yost's thatch of sandy hair was riffled by the wind. His clothes were city clothes, poorly suited for the mountains. He retained his breeches and boots, which was unexpected; boots, especially, were worth more in the mountains than silver.

A few hundred yards behind was a wagon on its side. It was a heavy wagon, with a green, boat-shaped body and red wheels, and the spokes of one wheel were broken and the iron rim was on the ground. Also on the ground were the tongue and the trees. There was no trace of the oxen that must have pulled it. The bows that had held the bonnet in place looked like ribs now, because they were bare of canvas. The side of the wagon was scorched, and one of the ribs was burned nearly in two.

Jack rode slowly toward the wagon, being mindful that he was in the middle of an open clearing with no cover except a few scrubby cedars. As he neared the wagon, a pair of crows took flight from the rear of the box, their displeasure expressed in a series of raspy *kruas*.

Jack dismounted.

He expected to find arrows in the wagon, but there were none. He placed his hand on a scorched sideboard. It was cold. On the other side of the wagon, where the contents had spilled on the ground, were mounts of flour from cloth sacks that had been slit open, and splintered wooden crates with books falling from them. Jack reached down and cupped some of the flour in his hand. It had mixed with the ashes of the fire. Jack tossed the stuff to the wind.

He took up one of the books and opened it, then another, and finally a third.

They were all King James Bibles, printed on cheap paper and bound with thin cardboard covers, and each had neatly printed on the first page.

A gift to the Nez Perce and Flathead peoples from their friends in Christ at Ashfield, Massachusetts. Since learning of your request by letter from Capt. Bonneville for religious instruction, we have prayed and worked tirelessly to prepare a missionary expedition to the Oregon lands. May the Lord grant you the wisdom and grace to embrace our messengers in the same spirit they are sent. Blessings upon you.

"Dumb bastard," Jack said, looking down the path to where Yost's body was swelling in the sun. "Did you really think sending books in English was the best way to help these people? You could not have crossed the divide on this route, so what was your immediate goal?"

Jack looked through the other crates, but found only more of the cheap Bibles. There was a newspaper from Independence, dated three months earlier, and Jack folded this and put it in his pocket.

"No guns," Jack said. "No gunpowder."

He went through the toolbox on the side of the wagon. There was a hammer and a few spanners and a screwdriver and Jack wrapped these things in a split flour sack, along with some nails and screws and assorted loose hardware. There were other things that would be useful—what good lumber was left in the bed of the wagon, the steel tires from the wheels, the big grease bucket still hanging from the rear axle, the Bibles for tinder—but he would return for these later. The wagon was too burned for repair. He wished he could locate the ox team, because the animals would be useful at the lodge in pulling up stumps and hauling timbers into place.

He placed the flour sack bundle of scavenged tools on the ground near 'Clipse and went back to the wagon. He was looking for a shovel. He would bury the Yosts together, and their child as well, if the body was nearby. There was a box of clothes, dresses and sunbonnets, but no food to be found. As he stepped over a box of spilled Bibles to grasp the handle of a shovel, his eye caught something to the side. It was a red earth crock.

Jack ignored the shovel and snatched up the pint crock.

He loosened the bale and slid aside the top. The crock was nearly full of bread starter, gray as the mud around some of the geysers beyond Hell's Gate, and pockmarked with slow-forming bubbles.

"Now, here's a blessing," Jack said.

He added the crock to his sack of loot.

"Now if only I could find gunpowder," he muttered.

Jack heard a footstep behind him. He pretended not to notice, keeping his eyes on the contents of the sack, but he inched his right hand toward the hilt of his knife. He allowed the footsteps to draw closer and, when he judged the person to be only a few feet away, pitched and rolled and came up in a fighting stance with the blade in his hand.

A boy of about ten years stared at him. He was alone.

"She didn't tell me you were an Indian," Jack said.

The boy had brown skin and straight black hair and large, sad eyes. He was thin and wore a heavy wool shirt that was much too large for him and, cinched at the waist with a belt, looked like a dress. Atop his head was a large black hat with a flat brim, of the kind flatlanders wore, but his feet were in proper moccasins.

The boy took a few steps backward, preparing to run.

"Don't," Jack called. "I'm sorry."

He sheathed the knife and held the palms of his hands out.

"I mean you no harm," Jack said.

The boy stopped.

"Your name Hawk?"

The boy nodded.

"I suppose you ran off and hid," Jack said. "It was the wise thing to do. Tell me who did this."

The boy began to speak, but in a language Jack had seldom heard before.

"English?" Jack asked.

The boy stared.

"French?"

No reaction.

"Flathead, aren't you?" Jack asked. "They are a fine-looking people, and you have their features. And the other clue is in that tinder yonder. Your nation is in the Bitterroot Range, so you're still far from home. And you're not on the right path to get you there, at least not with that cabin on wheels. This is about as far as you could get, never mind the Divide. What in thunder were you doing here?"

The boy spoke and made some gestures, but Jack

was unsure if he was answering the question or asking one of his own.

"Somebody brought you down from the Bitterroots, didn't they?" Jack asked. "How many auditoriums did you fill as they raised money to send missionaries? But you didn't stay long enough to learn any English beyond your name."

"Nederlands," the boy said.

"Dutch?" Jack asked. "Ah, your adopted parents were Dutch. There's the accent. I'm afraid that's a tongue I do not speak."

The boy understood Jack's tone, if not his words.

"Now what?" Jack asked, holding his hands up.

The boy thought, then pointed at the knife in Jack's belt, and made the motion of being stabbed in the chest.

Jack shook his head.

"No," Jack said. "I'm not going to hurt you."

The boy understood.

He looked from the ruined wagon, then over to Yost's body. He turned back to Jack and held up three fingers.

"Good," Jack said, nodding. "That is something. There were three of them. Were they members of the nations like yourself or were they white? No, I didn't suppose you would be able to jump to that question next, or be able to tell me if you did."

The boy held out his right hand and made a slashing motion at the wrist with the other.

"Ah," Jack said. "One was missing a hand? That cannot be a coincidence."

The boy stood motionless, not understanding.

"Strange how things work out," Jack said. "For fourteen months I've been waiting to talk to a human being other than my wife and I encounter three of them in one day. The first was just a disarticulated hand. The second, a dying woman out of her mind with pain and grief. And now you. Not to say that you aren't welcome company, of course. Isn't that right, Hawk?"

"Hawk," the boy said.

"Let me introduce myself," Jack said, and he squatted down to be at eye-level. "Jacques Aguirre. At least that is how I was known in the states. But you may call me Jack, because that is how I'm called in the mountains."

Jack held out his hand.

"Jack. Say my name."

The boy took his hand, and they shook.

"Jack," the boy said.

"Damn fine handshake," Jack said. "Now there is work to do. We must bury your white parents, and you must help. It will give you a sense of purpose, and perhaps even comfort. Can you find the prettiest spot in the meadow?"

Jack pointed at several locations, then made the motion of digging.

"Some place that has a nice tree nearby to mark the spot, and has a good view of the mountains? I know this place and it is beautiful in every season. In time, there will be no trace of what happened here."

The boy nodded.

Jack walked over to the spilled cargo and grasped the handle of the shovel he had found earlier. He pulled it free of the other things, then walked over and placed it in Hawk's hands.

"Pick a spot and start digging," he said. "I'll go fetch your mother and father and carry them back here, one by one, over my saddle and wrapped tight in strips of canvas from what's left of the bonnet. Damn, finding something to read over the graves won't be a problem. We have a plague of Bibles."

When they finished with the graves, two hours later, Jack took his knife and cut the names of the Yosts into a single slab from the wagon sideboard and drove it into the ground as best he could at the head of the grave. "There," Jack said. "They're facing east. Isn't that the way it is supposed to be?" Then Jack said he wasn't really qualified to read a verse, but would do so anyway. He turned to Jeremiah.

Hawk removed his hat.

"Pursue justice and righteousness," Jack read, freely interpreting. "Free those who have been robbed of their possessions or even their lives from the might of their oppressors. Do not mistreat or do violence to the stranger, the orphan, or the widow. And shed no more blood in this innocent place. Amen."

"Amen," Hawk said.

"Good boy," Jack said. "Now, it's time to leave this place. Daylight lasts long this time of year, but I'm afraid we've just about used it all up."

Jack made the motion for Hawk to follow him to where he had tied 'Clipse to the trunk of a scrub cedar. Jack put his left foot into the stirrup and swung up into the saddle. There were a couple of flour sacks of supplies from the wagon that were tied behind the saddle.

Hawk looked up at Jack with uncertain eyes.

"You don't think I'm going to leave you here, do you?" Jack asked.

Jack reached down and grasped the boy's outstretched hand.

"Watch your hat," Jack said.

He pulled him up onto his lap. Jack judged the boy couldn't have weighed fifty pounds.

"Now, put your legs down. I'll scoot back some and you can have the front of the saddle."

The boy did so, settling easily in the saddle.

"We'll not make home before dark," Jack said, "but it won't be long after."

Jack turned 'Clipse in the direction of the lodge. The horse started off at an easy clip, tolerant of the extra weight. Jack held the reins easily in one hand, his arm circling the boy.

7   A Strange Tongue

The boy sat at the table near the fireplace with a bowl of bighorn sheep stew in front of him and ate carefully, lest a single drop of the stew should escape the spoon. Sky asked in Arikara which Flathead band was his own, but he did not understand her.

"And no French or English?" Sky asked.

"Nope," Jack said. "Dutch, I think."

"That is not a useful tongue in the mountains," Sky said. "Well, he will learn one of our languages naturally enough. We should try always to speak English around him, to make it less confusing for all. When I was a girl, I would have said French would have been most practical, but no longer. Your countrymen are relentless, Jack."

"He won't be here long enough to learn."

"Too late this year to return him to the Bitterroot Range," Sky said. "So, we're looking at spring. Seven months? Eight? Enough time. And Jack, before we return him to his people, he has to be able to tell us where his people are, and if they still live. Smallpox had wiped out entire villages. There may be nowhere for him to go back to."

Sky paused.

"And Jack, he's already lost one set of adopted parents. He might have been orphaned twice. We should not be in a hurry to orphan him a third time."

"I did not choose this responsibility," Jack said.

Sky laughed.

"The universe does not care," she said. "It chose you. You had better be used to the idea of being father to a young boy a little sooner than you thought. He seems a well-mannered child."

"Yes, I suppose we are lucky in that."

Sky shook her head.

"We have to break him of it," she said. "What he learned from the missionaries he can unlearn. He must learn to fight. His survival will depend on it."

"He doesn't seem to have the instinct."

"Perhaps not," Sky said. "But did you at his age?"

"No," Jack said.

"How did you learn?"

"My anger taught me," Jack said.

"Then the boy is fortunate," Sky said. "He will have you to teach him."

Jack nodded.

Sky went to the fireplace and returned with a tin cup of weak coffee. She placed it on the table in front of Jack, then asked about the earthenware crock that was in the sack of things gathered at the wagon.

"It's starter," Jack said. "It makes yeast bread."

"Explain," she said, placing the crock on the table.

"You use this and flour and water and salt and you have bread that rises," Jack said. "But it requires flour made from wheat, or oats, or other grasses. Have you never had a biscuit?"

"I have had crackers," she said.

"No, I don't mean tack," Jack said. "Biscuits rise. They are fluffy, full of air, and delicious. Do you remember the crust we had for the cobbler so many years ago, when we first came here with the supplies brought by the keelboats? It would be like that crust, only bigger."

"What makes it that way?"

"The yeast in the starter," Jack said. "It's alive, and you use a bit of it for each loaf of bread or batch of biscuits. The yeast acts in the flour in the same way that yeast makes beer or wine, it ferments. But the alcohol burns away in the baking and the bread rises because of the release of gases from the fermentation."

She undid the bale and moved the lid aside. She held it low to the floor so she could see inside by the light from the fire.

"It looks like mud," she said.

"You can't see the yeast," Jack said. "It's tiny. You've seen yeast before, or sign of it, on the skin of wild fruit. But this yeast comes from far away, maybe as far away as the Old World."

"You mean your world," Sky said. "My world is just as old as yours. How much bread will this jar make?"

"Countless," Jack said. "As long as you feed it with a bit of flour and water from time to time. It's immortal, or at least the colony is."

Sky frowned.

"This sounds crazy."

"The Egyptians ate leavened bread," Jack said. "So did

the Greeks. The Romans built their empire on it. It's the stuff of civilization."

"Civilization?" Sky asked.

"Society," Jack said.

"Do we have society here, Jack?"

"We have each other."

"And that is not enough, is it?"

She replaced the bale on the crock.

"Where does this civilization in a jar live?"

"Someplace damp and cool," Jack said. "The root cellar, I think. Too hot near the fire."

Sky sighed.

"I grow increasingly uneasy," she said, and pulled her rosary from the pocket of her dress. "The world and its bad luck crowds our door. Tomorrow I will gather sage and sweetgrass and smudge the lodge for protection."

"You're tired," Jack said. "Let's retire to the loft and dream together."

The boy was sitting patiently, the empty bowl in front of him, his hands folded in his lap.

"Where will he sleep?" Jack asks.

"The instruction begins," Sky said. "Let him choose his place. Cuff him about the ears if he tries to sleep near us."

8 *The Doorbreaker*

Warm beneath the elk robes, his hand pulling Sky close to him, Jack surrendered quickly to a deep and untroubled sleep. In what seemed only a few minutes, but during which hours had passed, he was awaked by the boy shaking his shoulder.

"Don't," Jack muttered, slapping the boy's hand away. "Go downstairs."

The boy whispered rapidly in his own language, and it was the urgency in his voice that brought Jack awake.

"What is it?"

Then Jack heard it, a scraping at the exterior of the front door.

The loft was dark, except for a well of golden light where the ladder led downstairs. The fire in the hearth had burned down to embers and flickering flames. Jack sat up and placed a finger against the boy's lips. He nodded his understanding.

Jack found the pistol at arm's length on the floor, then sat up. Sky roused, and Jack leaned close and whispered in her ear to not speak. Then he found her right hand and guided it to the pistol, and she curled her fingers around the butt.

"Bear?" Sky whispered.

Then came the sound of laughter from downstairs, and after that the shaking of the door handle. The wooden latch rattled but held the door shut.

"Damn," Jack exclaimed. "Stay here."

"There's nowhere else to go," Sky said.

"Jump out the loft door."

"You forget the baby," she said. "I cannot."

Jack slipped into his breeches, cinched his belt, and touched the pommel of the knife in its scabbard. His feet and chest were bare. He went down the ladder two rungs at a time until his feet touched the rough floor.

There was pounding now at the door, hard enough to shake dust from the planks.

"Open the damned door," a raspy male voice called. "I know you're in there. Open up and give me what I want. I know you have it. My skin feels like it is on fire. Oh God, how it burns. Why do you torture me so?"

There followed a regularly spaced series of blows, once every other second.

Jack drew the Damascus toothpick and crept to the door.

Keeping the knife in his right hand, he pressed his left shoulder against the door, close to the jam. The jolt of each blow went through the door and through his shoulder.

The blows came harder. The stench of whoever was on the other side seeped through. Jack could hear the planks beginning to splinter.

"Go away," Jack said. "Go away or I'm going to fire through the door."

There was a growl from the other side, so deep that for a moment Jack thought it might indeed be some kind of animal trying to break in.

"You have five seconds to clear out, or you're going to have a belly full of lead."

"One," Jack said.

A howl came from the other side.

"Two."

Sky had come down the ladder, and she held the pistol with both hands in front of her. The boy was scrambling down behind. Jack's attention was suddenly divided between what was happening at the door and the fear that Sky was placing herself closer to the danger. Jack did not know if there was one man outside, or more.

"You set one foot inside this lodge and I will slit your belly and eat your boudins while they yet steam," Jack said as he tried to get his shoulder more firmly against the door. "Before I am done, you will be crying out for your mother and your god, and neither will help you. If you be he or it that orphaned the boy at the wagon, I will savor your killing, and when I tell about it at rendezvous, they will pour my whiskey for free."

The growling turned into a curious howl that made the hair on Jack's arms stand up. The battering became even more fierce. Jack was uncertain what to do. If only he had a gun, he would shoot through the door, but there was only Sky's pistol, and it would be a blind shot through the door. Even if the ball was lucky enough to be sent in the right spot, chances are it wasn't powerful enough to pass through the door and do the damage that was needed.

"Three," Jack said, his mind beginning to cloud.

With his shoulder against the door, Jack couldn't reach any of the things that might be of benefit that were in the room: the iron rod used to stir the fire, the heavy cast-iron skillet, even one of the chairs at the table. Would it be better to abandon the door and use the few seconds before it came down to make a dash with Sky and the boy out a window into the dark, he wondered, or would they stand a better chance if he remained to fight? He had the unpleasant sensation that he was growing small and weak, and he desperately wished there were two of himself. Jack told Sky to get out the rear door, but she stood her ground. He cursed, but she refused.

"I will not be hunted," she said.

"Save the pistol until the last moment," Jack said.

"For myself?" she asked.

"No, for whatever . . . whatever is out there."

Then the hardest blow of all hit the door, and a forearm came through the planks. It was just a forearm with no hand on the end. The stub had been wrapped in some leather and bloody rags and it seeped blood. The intruder laughed insanely, then wrenched the stump away.

"Four," Jack said, then quickly backed away, the knife at the ready.

The next blow on the door broke the latch and sent it crashing inward. The intruder came with it, sprawling face-first on the floor. It was a man, but Jack thought he might as well have been a grizzly. He was large, three hundred pounds, and well over six feet. His clothes were rags that hung from him, revealing heavily muscled shoulders and arms. His head was mostly bald, with the hair bitten or pulled out in tufts, and there were many places where the scalp had been peeled back nearly to the bone. His eyes were far back in their dark sockets. His full brown beard was matted with filth.

"Damn you," Jack shouted.

The man laughed and put his left hand on the floor to push himself up, but Jack was already on top of him. Jack brought the point of the dirk down on the back of the intruder's hand, and he could feel the knife slide between bone and bite into the floor beneath.

The man howled like an animal and tried to jerk his hand away, but could not. With Jack pressing the intruder's head against the floor, he could not gain the leverage needed to raise his shoulder and bring into play the bloody stump at the end of his forearm.

The man growled and spit and struggled to free himself.

Jack put his foot on his neck and pressed his head to the floor.

"Be still," Jack said.

The man howled in rage.

"Are there more of you?"

His eyes burned with murder.

"At the wagon," Jack said. "There were three of you?"

He worked the fingers of his right hand and grimaced at the pain. Blood spread on the floor beneath the hand.

"Where are the others?"

The man was panting like a wolf caught in a trap.

"I saw your hand in the mouth of a wolf in the high

meadow," Jack said. "I shot the wolf and burned both it and your hand up. It was a damned unlucky sign and we have had nothing but trouble since, so you had better tell me what I need to know."

The man turned his head and bared his teeth, which were surprisingly white and strong. It was clear he would bite Jack if he could.

"Tell me," Jack said, putting more weight on his foot.

Despite the pressure, the man managed to turn his head away. Jack could feel the muscles and tendons in the intruder's thick neck working against the bottom of his foot, and it gave him a sick feeling in the well of his stomach.

"He cannot tell you," Sky said. "He is much too mad to even speak."

The man jerked his hand against the knife, deepening the gash. Jack put more weight on the foot pressing the head down. Sky had sat down on the floor, the pistol in her lap. She could see the man's face, his mad glistening eyes reflecting the dying firelight.

"Throw me some rope," Jack said. "That means you, boy. There's a coil on the wall, yonder."

Sky pointed. Hawk retrieved the rope.

"Can you make a knot?" Jack asked.

"He still can't understand you," Sky said.

"It's the goddamned Tower of Babel here," Jack said.

"I will do so," Sky said.

"No." This, more firmly than Sky had ever heard Jack speak to her. "Make the boy understand."

Sky made the motion of tying a knot and then patted

her ankles. The boy understood immediately. As the boy approached the intruder's feet, he began to kick out.

"Hold him well," Sky said.

"I'm doing my best," Jack said. "He is twice my size and crazy."

"Let me put a ball between his eyes," Sky said, pointing the pistol.

"Save it," Jack said. "It's our last bit of powder."

The boy looped the rope around one thick ankle and managed a square knot. Then he scrambled over, the line in his hands, and reached for the other ankle just as the man kicked out. The heel of the heavy boot struck Hawk's jaw. It sent him reeling backward to bounce from the wall of the cabin, bringing down a shelf overhead that held tin cups of various sizes. The cups clattered to the floor around the boy, who did not move.

"Get up," Jack said. "That was a helluva kick, but it didn't kill you. So get up."

"He can't understand you," Sky scolded.

"He can understand my tone," Jack said calmly. "Come on boy, get up and finish the job. We need you to do this."

The boy stirred.

"That's right, Hawk," Jack coaxed.

The boy got unsteadily to his feet. He put his hand to his mouth, and his fingertips came back smeared with blood.

"You're going to have a helluva goose egg," Jack said. "Might even have loosened some teeth. So watch those boots."

Hawk spat blood on the floor, then his eyes hardened and he walked over to the intruder. He thought for a moment, then straddled the man's thighs as if he were easing himself into the saddle of a horse. The man kicked furiously with both feet, but Hawk caught the rope, waited for the right moment, then threw a coil around the free ankle. He tied a hitch and pulled on the rope, bringing the ankles together and cinching them tight.

"Good job," Jack said, looking behind him.

The boy handed the end of the rope to Jack.

"Now get clear," Jack said.

Sky motioned for the boy to come to her. He walked calmly over and sat down.

Jack caught the flailing arm with the bloody stub, and cinched the rope around the elbow. Then he passed the rope beneath the intruder's neck, and put his back into pulling the elbow awkwardly to the man's chest, then made another loop around his neck. Jack pulled on the free end of the rope.

"Don't struggle," Jack said. "You'll just strangle yourself."

Jack pulled the rope tighter, making the man's ankles pull against the line that went around his neck. His hand was still pinned to the floor by the knife.

"One last time," Jack said. "Say your name?"

The man shrieked his rage.

"Take the boy upstairs," Jack said.

"He should watch," Sky said.

She took her belt knife and gave it to the boy. His look was a question.

"For protection," she said. "Do not be afraid to use it."

"Neither of you should watch," Jack said. "I can stand no more lessons tonight."

But Sky and the boy remained.

Jack took the hammer from the bag of things from the wagon. Then he rummaged in the bottom of the sack until he found the longest of the square-headed nails he had gathered. Holding the hammer in one hand and the nail in the other, Jack walked behind the intruder and put his left foot in the center of his back. The man kicked, but his feet could find nothing except the broken door.

"Have you remembered your name?"

The intruder was crying tears of . . . of what, Jack asked himself? Was it rage or was it sorrow?

"So be it," Jack said.

Jack knelt on the man's back, forcing his face forward into the floor, and brought the point of the nail in his left hand to the back of the man's skull. The man felt the cold point against his skin and snarled oaths.

"Jack," Sky said. "Not that way."

"How then?"

Suddenly the doorbreaker jerked his right hand free by pulling it through the blade of the knife, cleaving his hand in two between the index and forefinger. He reached back and hooked a finger around Jack's belt, the hand a geyser of blood, and threw him off.

Jack rolled into a corner, losing the hammer.

The intruder bellowed and reached behind him with his ruined hand, grasped the head of the nail between his thumb and finger, and tried vainly to pull out the nail. Then he tried reaching the rope, but even though his fingers closed on it, he could only pull on it, making the knots tighter. Then he saw the hammer on the floor and reached for it. Jack was on his feet now, and he managed to kick the hammer out of the intruder's reach.

Jack pulled the Damascus from where it was stuck in the floor.

"Damn you," Jack said.

He stepped forward, putting his foot on the intruder's shoulder, still struggling to keep him still. At that moment Sky flew forward, snatched one of the obsidian fleshing knives from a wooden box near the stove, and in one motion drew the blade deeply under the doorbreaker's jaw, below the right ear, severing the carotid artery. The cut was so clean that at first it seemed not to have cut. Then blood welled up in a line where Sky had drawn the obsidian blade, and then the line became a cascade.

The intruder continued to struggle for a moment, blood spurting like a firehouse from the wound, and then slowly the tension eased from his body. Jack crouched down, the Damascus in hand, ready for the intruder to rally one last time. But all the fight was gone. The dark eyes darted about the room and finally fixed on Jack's face.

"He is dead," Sky said. "He just doesn't know it yet."

With his breath rattling in his chest, he tried to form a word.

"Your name," Jack said.

The man's mouth and tongue worked to form the sound, but there was no breath behind it. Then he died, his forehead on the floor of the cabin, his eyes still open, and his mouth open, oozing blood and spit and bile.

Jack stumbled to a chair at the table. He sat down heavily, regarding the blood on the blade of the Damascus.

Both the blade and the blood gleamed in the firelight. His hands were shaking, and he could not remember feeling more tired. But there was much yet to do, because the body would have to be carefully disposed of and the cabin floor thoroughly scrubbed.

"How's the boy?" Jack asked.

Sky was kneeling beside Hawk, examining him.

"As you said. His jaw is unbroken but it will ache for some time."

"He showed courage."

"He did," Sky said. "As did you."

"It wasn't courage," Jack said. "I felt something strange. When he was on the other side of the door, and it was not yet clear what manner of danger we faced, I was torn between keeping my mind on the coming fight and my worry for you, the baby, the boy. I felt diminished and unequal to the task. My mind fogged and my fear bloomed. It is not a feeling I am accustomed to or wish to ever have again."

"You had the bad fortune of not being able to talk yourself to an advantage, because the thing could neither speak nor reason," Sky said. "Your fear was common enough among those who place the welfare of others before themselves, and it is something you must deal with after the baby comes. You must not allow the fear to numb your mind, because then you lose the advantage of detachment and boldness. You will serve us better as yourself, Jack."

"Perhaps," he said.

"You have often spoken of when you gambled," Sky said. "You have described to me hands of cards or throws of dice upon which your future depended. But you acted with detachment, and your understanding of the numbers—"

"—the odds," Jack said.

"—yes, the odds. Your advantage was coolness and knowledge. And it has continued to be so, along with your skill. So in desperate moments, you must put me out of your mind to keep me in the world. What lovers fear most is the loss of the other, and that fear is crippling, like looking down from a great height. Your fear contributes to the fall."

"There was a time when I was unafraid to fall."

"There was a time when we were both young and selfish," Sky said. "The winters have made our hearts tender and our actions cautious. We must defy the years."

Jack gestured to the dead man.

"At least the mystery of the hand is solved," Jack said.

Sky shook her head.

"Nothing has been solved," she said. "This creature is missing its left. The hand the wolf carried was the opposite. It was a right hand, Jack."

"You are sure?"

Her face said she was.

"Damn, I cannot recall."

"Did the thing bite you?" she asked.

"No."

"Be wary of the knife," Sky said. "There is blood all over it."

"It's the clear stuff we have to worry most about," Jack said. "His spit. His tears."

"And what of his body?"

"I will drag it behind 'Clipse to the smoking sinkhole on the other side of the ridge," Jack said. "Then I will roll it into the hole. It will be convenient for the devil, because the intruder will land on hell's front porch."

Sky smiled.

"Have you smudged the lodge yet?"

She said she had not.

"Do it tomorrow, please," Jack said. "Let us be through with this run of bad luck."

9 *The Soldiers*

A week later, three soldiers rode up to the lodge. Jack
was sitting on a stump next to the new front door, which
was green because Jack had built it from good lumber
taken from the sides of the wagon. He was almost finished carving a latch for the door. He had already fit it
in place several times, marking with a nail the portions
that needed to be trimmed, and he sat with the Damascus
in his hand, working carefully. The boy was sitting beside
him, watching as Jack worked.

Jack kept his eyes on the notch he was carving, even
as the soldiers neared.

Hawk tugged at Jack's sleeve.

"I saw 'em," Jack said, then blew some wood chips
from the notch.

There was one officer and two enlisted men. The soldiers were young, about twenty, and one had wild wisps
of red hair that escaped his cap. Their uniforms were
plain compared to that of the officer, who wore a leather-
brimmed hat and a blue wool jacket with a double row
of brass buttons. A dark blue stripe ran down the sides

of his sky-blue trousers. On his shoulders were gaudy epaulets that seemed to be made of tin. His belt was buckled over a red sash, and a saber and scabbard on his left side. A carbine hung from a saddle sling.

The officer waited uncomfortably atop the horse while Jack continued to work.

Sky came to the open doorway and stood just inside, her arms folded and her hip resting against the green door.

"Hallo," the officer said.

He had a crooked smile beneath a shaggy brown mustache.

Jack looked up and stared at the uniforms, which seemed familiar and yet different than he remembered.

"Hello yourself," Jack said.

It had been so long since he'd spoken to a human being other than Sky in actual conversation that his own voice seemed unnatural. There was a long pause before Jack put down his work.

"Who is president?" Jack asked.

"Andrew Jackson."

"Ah," Jack said. "News is a long time coming to this elevation."

"Sir," the man said. "I am Lieutenant Miles Maguire."

"What army do you belong to?" he asked.

"First Dragoons, Jefferson Barracks."

Jack frowned.

"St. Louis," Jack said.

"Near it, yes."

The officer shifted in the saddle. Jack was staring at the carbine.

"What's your business?" Jack asked.

"We saw smoke from your chimney," Maguire said. "Reckoned it for chimney smoke from your cabin, if you be Mountain Jack Picaro. Everybody seems to know of you along the Yellowstone—and the Missouri and her tributaries—and that you call your cabin Hell's Gate, but practically nobody knows where you actually live."

"Now there are at least three of you who do," Jack said.

"So you are Picaro."

"I am," Jack said easily, becoming more accustomed to the sound of his voice with others.

"At your service, Master Picaro."

"Are you?" Jack said. "I'm not even sure we're in United States territory. The Oregon Country is to the north, and that's American, and so is the land to the east, all the way to the Missouri line. But this particular region might belong to Mexico, best I can figure. But things change."

"If we are not in Mexican territory," Maguire said, "we are damned close to it."

The lieutenant looked at the bruise on the boy's jaw.

"What happened to him?"

"He got kicked," Jack said. "Could I see that rifle hanging from your saddle?"

"It would be irregular to hand my weapon over to a civilian."

"I'm interested only in its method of ignition," Jack said. "Spend the load into the clouds if you fear violence from me, but indulge my curiosity."

"Do not allow him to fire the gun, not even into the

air." Sky spoke quickly in French. "It would betray us to the handless ones who mean us harm. I do not like the uniform this man wears. And I do not trust this man."

"What did she say?" Maguire asked.

Jack smiled.

"Your squaw?" Maguire asked.

"My wife," Jack said. "Her name is Sky and she speaks damned fine English when she's in the mood."

"I said don't shoot that gun," Sky said in English. "It's not safe. It will signal others."

The private soldiers gave each other worried glances.

"What others?" Maguire asked.

"Others," Sky said. "There are always others."

"Begging your pardon," Maguire said, tugging at his cap. "Of course, you are correct, there may be hostiles about."

"Why don't the three of you climb down," Jack said. "I'd rather talk at eye level."

"Much appreciated," Maguire said, and nodded to his men. They all dismounted.

Maguire unlatched the rifle from the ring.

"It won't be necessary to discharge the carbine," Maguire said. "Observe."

Maguire pushed a lever and the forward end of the block popped up from the breech, revealing a lead ball that was about as big around as the tip of Jack's fore-finger. He pocketed the ball, turned the rifle upside down, and shook the gunpowder onto the ground. Jack shook his head at the waste of powder.

Maguire handed the carbine to Jack.

"Caliber?" Jack asked.

"Fifty-eight."

Jack pushed the breech back down until it locked into place. Then he inspected the hammer that rose from the thick, tulip-shaped breech. Beneath the hammer was a bright copper cap, like a miniature thimble, on a stubby nipple.

"Percussion ignition," Jack said.

"Aye, it is."

"I heard of this, years ago," Jack said, shouldering the weapon and sighting a passing cloud.

"It is a clumsy design, requiring the sights to be off-center," Jack said, lowering the rifle.

"It will put a ball in a man two out of three times at a hundred yards."

Jack snorted, remembering the rifle he once made that could shatter a dinner plate every time at five hundred yards. That rifle was now lost. The last time Jack saw it was in the hold of a burning keelboat that sank in the Missouri River, more than ten years before.

"The powder comes from a paper cartridge," Maguire said. "The ball is merely placed on top, and the breech locks tight when closed. There is no need to put the butt on the ground and ram the ball home with a rod. The rate of fire is two to three times that of other rifles."

"One round at a time?" Jack asked.

"Yes, of course," Maguire said.

Jack handed the carbine back.

"Why are you here?" Jack asked.

"I've traveled quite a distance," Maguire said. "Is there someplace we could take our ease and parley?"

"State your business now."

Maguire cleared his throat.

"Very well," he said. "I am with an expedition led by Captain Bonneville. We have toured the Oregon Country and we are on our return to the states, and a detachment of our men have suffered some difficulty."

"What difficulty?" Sky asked.

"They are missing," the lieutenant said.

Jack reached out and mussed the boy's hair. The boy smiled.

"All right," Jack said. "Come and sit at my table. I hope you can stomach sumac tea."

Maguire muttered his thanks and handed the reins of his horse to his men.

"You'll find grass for the horses in the back of the lodge," Jack said. "Our horses are staked there. Take care around the black one. He likes to kick."

Sky stood aside as Jack and Maguire entered the cabin. The boy started to follow them, but she held him back.

"Go play," she said, motioning with her hand.

Then she followed the men inside.

"Lost?" Jack asked when they both had cups of tea before them.

"Most likely. They are long overdue."

"They would not be the first soldiers to desert while on expedition," Jack said. "Not the first to find winter wives, or indulge in the Roman circus that is the rendezvous, or be captured by the Spanish as spies."

"No," Maguire said. "But these are reliable men."

"They would not be the first to die in the west."

"They would not," Maguire said. "But if that were the case, it seems unlikely all would perish and no word reach Fort Nonsense."

"Fort Nonsense?"

"That is the name the men have given to Fort Bonne-ville," Maguire said. "The snows were rather deeper in winter than expected."

Jack laughed.

"Captain Bonneville relocated his winter quarters to the Salmon River, but had to leave a small contingent at the fort, our outpost on the Green River, because that is where the various detachments he sent out were expecting to rendezvous for the return home. We've had detachments venture as far west as California, and all have returned except this group. Bonneville may have already returned east, but I cannot leave without the missing men."

"Just where were these missing men detached to?" Jack asked.

"They were assigned to scout between the Yellowstone and the Musselshell."

"That hardly seems a military objective."

"The expedition is under military command," Maguire said. "But it has been financed by John Jacob Astor, and we are to report on the territories controlled by the various competing fur trading companies, and to find new regions to trap where possible."

"Ah, now it is beginning to make some sense," Jack said, and gave a tight smile. "Surely you have enough men at this camp of yours to send out in search of your lost detachment. You do not need me."

"We are not many," Maguire said. "Most are involved in making the camp ready for winter, in storing up supplies and reinforcing the stockade. There were several hundred trappers and traders who came to the rendezvous on the Green River, which only broke up in recent weeks.

Frankly, sir, all of the free trappers have told us that nobody knows the area where the men disappeared better than you."

"And none of those men were interested in your assignment?"

"They were rather busy pursuing sin," Maguire said. "Many linger still along the Green River. The wagons bring many supplies to the rendezvous now."

"Ah, wagons," Jack said. "The world has changed since I last heard news of it."

"Captain Bonneville established a wagon road over South Pass," Maguire said. "There are now two fur-trading posts there, Fort William and Fort Platte. The first emigrants are now using the pass on their way to California and the Oregon Country."

"The wagons also supply Fort Nonsense?"

"Yes," Maguire said. "I could not help but notice your door."

"It came from a wagon, but not one of yours," Jack said.

"And the floor?" Maguire asked. "It's difficult to remove the blood once it seeps in."

Jack smiled.

"More bother?" Maguire asked.

"A bear," Jack said. "It smelled something it desired. Reduced the door to splinters and I had to kill it there."

"The grizzlies are fearsome," Maguire said. "It must have been a large one. I would rather like to see the hide."

"We disposed of it," Jack said. "Sky felt it was bad medicine to keep any part of it, for it was a doorbreaker.

She feared it had killed many times before, and she did not want its spirit to linger."

"Ah," Maguire said. "The natives are a superstitious peoples."

"She is Catholic," Jack said. "It is a faith that forbids the burial of suicides, mothers who died in childbirth, and unbaptized children in consecrated ground. Superstition, lieutenant, is other people's religion."

"You border on sacrilege, sir."

"I crossed that frontier long ago."

"Where'd you scavenge pieces from a wagon for repair?"

"We stumbled upon a pair of dead pilgrims and their wagon in the week just passed. They were dead when we found them and their wagon looted and burned. All we could do was bury them, and take in the boy."

"Do you know their names?"

Jack told him, and said they were bound for Flathead country. Maguire asked if there was any clue who killed the Yosts, and Jack shook his head.

"The boy cannot tell us," Jack said. "He speaks only Dutch and Flathead. Are you or your men conversant in either?"

"No," Maguire said.

"The mystery will remain, then," Jack said.

"Many endure," Maguire agreed.

"Dead missionaries," Jack said. "Churches cannot be far behind."

"We had a preacher at rendezvous," Maguire said. "A man named Parker. He gave a fine sermon about how all the Indians are descendants of one of the lost tribes of Israel or another. He had everybody's attention until some buffalo appeared in the valley and the men broke for their guns and horses."

"Wise," Jack said.

"Can you help us, Mister Picaro?"

"How many in this lost detachment of yours?"

"Seven."

"They are likely dead in the snow with Crow or Black-feet arrows sprouting from their backs."

"The arrows would not be in their backs," Sky said.

"But what if they are not?" Maguire asked. "Should we leave them to freeze and starve? These are white men we are talking about, Christian men. For the love of all that is good, Picaro, where is your compassion?"

Jack smiled.

"Left miles and years behind," he said. "At least compassion for good Christian men. I had quite my fill of them at St. Louis. There is but one law in the mountains, Lieutenant Maguire, and that law is enforced without regard to one's station or religious bent: The stupid, the weak, and the unlucky shall perish."

"You describe the society of beasts," Maguire said. "Is it not our duty to bring the love of Christ?"

"It is not," Jack said. "I have never encountered a beast that lied to me about its intentions, be they murderous or not. No, my uniformed friend, it takes a human being to lie and cheat and murder, and a human society to reward such behavior. More people have been slaughtered in the name of Christ than were ever eaten by beasts in the wild—or in the Coliseum, for that matter."

"You have been in the mountains too long," Maguire said.

"Perhaps," Jack said. "But I reserve my humanity for those deserving of it."

"Consider your help an act of charity."

"Such charity is good business," Sky said. "Better business to send one man who is not among your company than risk more of your own who might not come back."

Maguire smiled.

"We do not want to start a war with the Crows or the Blackfeet or any of the other hostiles," Maguire said. "Sending another detachment would risk that. We simply want to find our men, and Jack Picaro offers our best hope."

"It is foolish," Jack said.

"We will pay in silver."

"What use do I have for silver?" Jack asked. "I am already the richest man in the world, for I do what I please."

"Surely you need other supplies," Maguire said. "Whiskey? Or gunpowder."

"Do not listen to him," Sky said in French. She smiled to hide her meaning.

"Your woman," Maguire said. "She is heavy with child. Surely there are some things that Captain Bonneville could provide that would lighten your burden over the long winter. Food, robes, trinkets."

"I have no need of trinkets," Sky said dismissively.

Jack sighed.

"Whatever you ask for would be provided upon your returning the men to camp."

"No," Jack said. "What I ask for will be provided before I venture out."

Sky shook her head.

"There is no need," she said. "You said yourself we have all we need. And some trapper will come along sooner or later with the things we want. They always do."

"It is too late in the season," Jack said, his tooth throbbing. "I will be gone a month, no more. When the baby comes, I will be with you."

"Do not speak of things you do not know," Sky said.

Maguire drank the last of his tea.

"The weather turns ever colder," the soldier said. "And I am tired. If we are to strike a bargain, let it be soon."

"Have you a map?"

"Yes," Maguire said. He reached inside his jacket and pulled out a tightly folded sheet of paper. He handed the paper to Jack. It was hand-drawn, accompanied by notes on points of interest.

"Can you read?"

"Do you like your teeth where they are?"

"It was no insult," Maguire said. "Many of the trappers we deal with cannot."

"I am no longer a trapper," Jack said, unfolding the paper. "Astor is rich enough without my efforts."

"Astor's fortune is beginning to soften."

"How so?"

"Beaver hats are not as popular now as they once were," Maguire said, then leaned close to the map. "Fort Bonneville is clearly marked, as is the route the detachment was given to follow."

"Your map is wrong," Jack said. "If the men followed this

route, they would not be reconnoitering the Yellowstone, but instead the Madison. If they continued in the direction indicated, it would lead them to the Musselshell. Along the Musselshell the Blackfeet hunt buffalo and dry meat for the winter on its banks. And here is the heart of the Crow nation. Neither would welcome interlopers."

Maguire cleared his throat nervously.

"All of this area was trapped out long ago," Jack said, sweeping his hand over the area between the Yellowstone and the Madison. "The last good trapping is in the broad plateau leading up to Beartooth Peak, but it's a dangerous place for a white man."

"The detachment was instructed to establish an out-post there," Maguire said, placing his finger on the Madison. "A small encampment with a palisade, to be used as a base of operations and suitable for improve-ment should the trapping in the region prove superior."

"The trapping would," Jack said, "until the Crows lifted their scalps."

Maguire paused.

"They were also instructed to scout a pass," he said.

"Where?"

"Over the Beartooth and north toward the Mussel-shell," the lieutenant said.

"Then Bonneville has sent them to their graves," Jack said. "The Beartooth Mountains are sacred to the Mountain Crows, the largest of the three bands. What is of such interest there?"

"There were reports," Maguire said.

"There are no beavers at such an altitude," Jack said. "They would have passed through the best and last country for trapping in the Rocky Mountains. What were these reports of?"

Maguire glanced out the open door and saw his men lounging on the ground beneath a tree. Then he looked over at Sky, who was pretending not to listen. He leaned forward and whispered a single word.

"Gold."

Jack laughed.

"Bonneville must be quite the idiot."

"The reports were reliable," Maguire said.

"Just because somebody says it doesn't make it so."

"My concern is for my men, not for . . . profit."

"There is only one thing that will bring men together in a common enterprise," Jack said. "And that is profit. You may indeed be concerned for the welfare of these men, but if that were your chief concern you should have stayed home."

"Do not be impertinent."

"Do not treat me as one of your men."

Maguire cleared his throat.

"Would there be," he began, his voice raspy. "Would there be places where you might expect to find them? If they had not been killed by the hostiles, of course. Caves, perhaps, or dugouts where they might be holed up?"

"It is impossible to say. There's hundreds of square miles to search."

"But surely there are logical places to look?"

Jack paused.

"There is indeed a pass," he said. "Few know it."

"You have been there?"

"I am probably the only white man who has," Jack said. "And lived."

"Then that would be your objective."

"The pass is clear for only a few more weeks. Winter comes early there, and they may already be dead in the snow."

"Will you search for them?"

"It would be foolish."

"You would be rewarded whether you find them or not," Maguire said.

Jack fixed Maguire with a stare that promised he would exact satisfaction if betrayed.

"Non," Sky said softly. *"Non dans le monde, Jacques."*

Jack felt the blood pulse in his neck and his ears burn. He stared at the map and then at Maguire. He finally looked at Sky and felt necessity tugging in the pit of his stomach. His eyes softened, a plea for understanding.

"We have needs," he said in French. "There will soon be three of us."

Sky made a small sound in her throat, as if she suddenly could not breathe.

"Have you a pencil?" Jack asked. He did not want to fetch his own, because it would mean revealing the location of his ledger with the drawings. "Write the names of the men, and their particulars, on the obverse of the map."

Maguire nodded, and held out his right hand. Jack shook it.

"I will cross off their names if I find their bodies. You will deliver the supplies first?"

"Aye," Maguire said. "Give me three days."

"Then we will make a list of our needs. Do you have flour?"

"And gunpowder and other things that you require. But not whiskey."

"You have no whiskey in your camp?"

"There is whiskey," Maguire said. "But you will receive the spirits upon making your report to me at Fort Bonneville at the conclusion of your assignment, and not before. We have found that the men we associated with in these mountains cannot ration their whiskey once received."

Jack's tooth ached even more sharply now.

"As you will," Jack said.

Maguire removed a pencil from an inside pocket of his uniform and wrote the names of the men in a neat hand on the back. Then he took a blank paper and handed it to Jack, who began making a list of the necessary items.

"Have you molasses?"

"None to spare," Maguire said.

"Pity," Jack said.

It took him a minute or so more to finish the list. Then he handed the pencil and the list back to Maguire.

"You will stay here at Hell's Gate," Jack said. "But your men will return to your camp now with the list and send the supplies immediately. One of them will leave his rifle behind, with a supply of powder and ball."

"It's United States property," Maguire said.

"I am under contract to the United States for the duration of this assignment," Jack said. "And I find myself impossibly short of arms and ammunition. You can see the rifle in the corner is in need of repairs that I cannot spare the time to make."

"What happened?"

"Some bother with a mad wolf," Jack said.

"There were three nights of wolf attacks during the rendezvous this summer," Maguire said. "Several men were bitten and one died, as rabid as the wolf that mauled him. This was on Green River, a few miles below Fort Bonneville. Perhaps you heard of these attacks?"

"I have not," Jack said. "Rendezvous disagrees with me."

"Men spend their entire wages for the year on a week's worth of pleasure," Maguire said. "With your reputation as a gunsmith, some of those wages could just as easily have been in your pocket."

"Money does not disagree with me," Jack said. "Men do."

"Forgive me, but I was expecting you to carry a rather finer piece."

"It was taken from a trapper who no longer had need of it," Jack said. "I found him dead along the Bighorn River, his face hanging from his chin. A grizzly bear, I think. It was a fine rifle before the bother with the wolf."

"I have heard you possessed a special rifle of your own design, brought with you upriver years ago," Maguire said. "That its accuracy approaches the supernatural, that it rings like a bell when fired, and that the Indians call it the Ghost Rifle."

"Many are the tales told in the mountains," Jack said. "But I did have such a rifle. It has been at the bottom of the Missouri River for these ten years and more."

"If you are need of a rifle, why not take my carbine?"

"No," Jack said. "The lock is clumsy, the rifle is poorly balanced, and I do not trust the ignition. Your men carry the 1803 common rifle made at the Harper's Ferry arsenal. They are good and reliable flint guns. Short barreled and sturdy."

"As you wish," Maguire said.

Jack stood.

"You haven't finished your tea," Sky said.

"There is business at hand," Jack said, then stepped out the doorway.

Maguire followed. The two soldiers were lounging, and came to their feet when they saw the lieutenant. He ordered the soldiers to hand over first one gun and then the other. Jack examined the square brass patch boxes in the stocks, tested the fit of the barrels against the tang, peered at the rifling inside the barrels, and inspected the lock mechanisms.

"I will take this one," Jack said, shouldering the gun. "It has been cared for rather better than the other."

"Thank you, sir," the red-headed soldier said.

Jack lowered the rifle.

"How much powder and ball do you carry?"

"Enough for forty rounds," the soldier said.

"That will do," Jack said. "From each of you."

"You must not leave the men without powder and ball," Maguire said.

"It is but a few days from Fort Nonsense, but I may be gone weeks or months."

"You may have thirty from each," Maguire said.

Jack agreed.

The red-headed soldier unslung the black leather box that held the powder and patches and balls. He added ammunition the other soldier handed over. Jack took the box and slung it over his own shoulder. He cradled the 1803 rifle in the crook of his left arm.

Maguire gave the red-headed soldier the list of supplies.

"You can find this place again?"

Both nodded.

"Tell me," Maguire said.

"Ride west until you hit the Stinking Water," the red-headed soldier said. "Then turn south and follow the river to the place where it enters a narrow notch between the cliffs. Pass beyond the notch, and on the sunset side of the river look for a golden stand of aspens on the side of the mountain. The cabin is below."

He told the soldiers to saddle up and start for the fort immediately, collect the supplies, and be back no later than the evening of the third day.

"Understand?" Maguire asked.

The red-headed soldier nodded.

"Then get on with it."

The soldiers saluted and went for their horses. In ten minutes, they appeared around the corner of the cabin, saluted the lieutenant, and were off down the trail.

"Think we'll see them again?" Sky asked from the doorway.

"I won't," Jack said. "At least not soon. I am bound for the Musselshell."

"Wait for the supplies," she said.

"The sooner I find the remains of these men, the sooner I will be on my way back to you. And should by some miracle they be alive, a matter of three days would be a help in keeping them so. Soon they would freeze."

"But you aren't provisioned."

"The hills are full of meat," Jack said. "Keep the supplies safe for us, especially the flour. The dough starter in the root cellar is hungry for it. As am I."

"Don't go," she said.

"The good lieutenant and his magic carbine will provide you protection," Jack said. "He will stay here until the provisions arrive. There will be powder and shot. You know how to use the pistol. Keep it at hand until I return."

Sky looked away so Jack would not see her angry eyes.

Maguire cleared his throat and said he had the need to venture behind the cabin. When he was gone, Jack put down the rifle and the ammunition.

"Look at me," Jack said.

She reluctantly turned.

"This is necessary," Jack said. "There are things we need. Think of this as just a bit of business, as if I were going off to clerk in a store for a time. We're only losing a bit of time away from each other."

"You are such a fool," Sky said. "I've never seen a proper store, only the shabby goods in the barrels and boxes at one outpost or another, where the people of the nations trade their dignity and their honor for a swallow of cheap whiskey. Adventure is your cheap whiskey, though you've hungered for it these ten winters. But all that is lost after less than an hour after meeting with strangers at our door. You were speaking the truth when you said your hungers are dangerous."

She wiped a tear away with the back of her hand.

"Time, you say. All we are losing is time."

She shook her head.

"But time is all anybody ever has. Our lives are made of time and nothing else."

"You told me to put my feelings aside," Jack said quietly.

"You idiot," Sky said. "Only when we are in peril. The only danger here is your hunger."

Jack began to speak.

"No," she said. "You have made your bargain. Go quickly now and saddle 'Clipse and go. Pay the debt. Return if you can, and if you care to."

She reached out her hand. Jack grasped it tightly.

"The number of the thing from my nightmare," she said. "I heard you ask the question, although I pretended not. I was afraid to say the answer, although I don't know why it scares me so."

Jack loved the feel of her palm against his, the strength of her fingers, the grace of her wrist and forearm. He studied the curve of her shoulder and softness of her neck and the way her dark hair brushed against the antelope skin dress. He looked into her brown eyes, glistening with tears, and it seemed as if he could see all the way back to their first day together. He loved every inch of her, right down to her chipped front tooth.

Then she released his hand.

"Jack," she said. "The number is three."

10 *Something Pleasant*

"What is it?"

The thirteen-year-old girl sat on a weathered plank, her legs drawn up to keep her bare toes out of the mud. She was so thin that her elbows and knees seemed freakishly sharp. Her light cotton dress was riffled by a breeze that carried a touch of fall, and she gave an involuntary shiver. She had straight brown hair and pale skin. Her blue eyes were fixed on the curious smudge of light that had appeared in the night sky about a week before, and which had been the subject of much discussion and Bible-thumping by the couple who owned the farm.

"Don't know."

The boy was sitting atop a rail fence, his left foot hooked beneath the bottom rail, his right knee drawn up so that he could rest his chin on it. He was the same age as the girl, and his features were similar, for they were twins.

He wasn't looking at the sky because whatever the smudge was didn't interest him. He wore a dirty red shirt that was much too big for him, and with holes beneath the armpits, and a pair of overalls that were worn thin in the butt and the knees. He was wearing a ragged wool cap, with a stiff brim. His eyes were staring at the farmhouse across the lot, its windows glowing with yellow lamplight, and he was imagining what the family might have had for supper. Pork chops, perhaps. Or chicken. Corn and biscuits and molasses. It made his gut hurt just thinking of it.

"Hungry," he said.

"Don't think about it, Brother," the girl said. "It makes it worse. Think about the star."

"I can't help it," the boy said. "They work us like mules and feed us scraps. I don't care a whit for the star or whatever it is."

On the far side of the fence, they could hear the hogs rooting and grunting in the scraps and slop from the Granger kitchen. The girl did not like the sounds the hogs made. She was frightened of them.

"Some people say it's a sign," the girl said. "It's in the newspapers. End of the world, maybe."

"Good," the boy said. "I hope they all burn in hell."

"Don't talk so, Brother."

"But I do hope it. Cross my heart and hope to die."

"That's wicked," the girl said.

"Old man Granger is wicked," the boy said. "He stares at you funny."

"Don't talk about it."

She did not want to be reminded of Granger. He stank of sweat and chewing tobacco and cheap whiskey. He had tried several times to touch her in her private places, when he managed to catch her alone in the barn or out in the fields, and so far she had slipped away. He always laughed afterward, as if it were a game, but she knew that one day soon she would be unable to get away from him.

"He does," the boy said. "And someday I'm going to give him a tarring for it."

"You are like a twig next to Granger," the girl said. "He would snap you in half."

"I won't always be this small."

"Let's talk of something pleasant," the girl said. "It's a nice night. The air is just right, not too hot and not too cold. They say this is our birthday month."

The boy snorted.

"We do not even know the day we were born. So what's a birthday matter?"

"It matters," the girl said. "We'll know, eventually."

"How?" the boy asked. "I heard the old woman tell one of her church friends that they bought us as babies from an old French couple south of St. Louis for seventy-five dollars each, just as you would buy slaves. I reckon we were cheaper. She said the old couple had gotten us from a convent. We don't even have real names. They call us Sally and Silas just like we were—"

"We have real names," the girl said. "And parents, somewhere."

"I won't call you Sally," the boy said. "Not any longer, now that I know."

"You're Brother, and I am Sister. That's enough for now."

The boy brushed his blond hair from his eyes.

"We could run off," he said.

"Where would we go, Brother?"

"Anywhere," he said. "St. Louis."

"Which direction is it?"

The boy frowned.

"It's downriver," he said. "I know the river is to the east, where the sun rises."

"All right," the girl said. "What happens after we get to St. Louis?"

"We find work," the boy said.

"You can't even read," the girl said.

"But you can," the boy said. "You steal every newspaper or weekly you can get your hands on and hide them up here, in the hay. The old man said he's going to tar you for it if you don't stop, because girls should only read the Bible."

"He's a fool. Where else can I learn about the Piasa bird?" she asked. "There's an old Indian carving of it on a cliff on the Illinois side of the Mississippi. It is a fearsome thing, with wings and horns, the newspapers say, and when old Marquette saw it, it liked to have scared him to death."

The boy said the newspapers sounded as if they were full of lies.

"I would steal books if I could." She sighed. "But they are too expensive. They'd have me before the magistrate. But someday I'm going to teach you to read."

"Don't need to read," the boy said. "I can do numbers."

The girl scratched an elbow.

"Together we make a whole person," she said.

"Then we will always stick together. You mustn't marry."

The girl smiled wanly.

"I won't," she said.

"If we could get our hands on Granger's scattergun . . ."

"No," the girl said. "That's not the way. The time isn't right."

"You don't know, Sister."

"Yes, I do," she said. "Girls grow up a mite quicker than boys. But it won't be long before you catch up to me here," she said, pointing to her head. "And one day, I will tell you it is time, and when I do you must act quickly and ask no questions. That is the time we must fly."

11 *Baptiste*

On the seventh morning away from the lodge Jack rode
'Clipse across a shallow and unnamed stream toward a
silent and half-burned outpost. Jack had watched for
any sign of movement from within or without the walls
and, seeing none, felt confident enough to inspect more
closely. 'Clipse's hooves made holes in a crust of ice on
the stream, creating an eerie cracking sound with each
step. Jack had slipped the 1803 from the leather scabbard
and carried it in his right hand, the butt resting against
his thigh, while holding the reins in his left. It began to
snow before he made the gate, the flakes swirling down
from a pewter sky.

He found the first body by the open gate.

The soldier had been dead for weeks. His uniform and
boots had been stripped away, leaving only his flannel
underwear. His skin and sometimes his bones showed
through tears in the underwear, rents that had doubtless
been made by animals. A bit of sandy hair clung to the
top of the skull. Eyeless sockets stared upward at Jack,
seemingly in horror.

"Who are you?"

Jack took the map from his pocket and looked at the list of names and descriptions on the back.

"Your hair says you cannot be Butler, Henley, Reed, or Smith," Jack said. "So are you Anderson or Fry or Perry? Ah, I will just mark you down as one of seven."

Jack rode into the middle of the yard.

The outpost was square, with walls forty feet apart, with a pair of lean-tos against the wall opposite the gate. There was another body, facedown, in the middle of the yard, and this one retained its blue coat but not its trousers or boots. A pair of arrows with metal trade points were sticking up out of the back of the corpse and possibly had made removing the coat difficult.

Jack swung down from the saddle. He scratched 'Clipse behind the ear and told him to stay close. Then, rifle in hand, he knelt beside the corpse, then reached out with one hand and turned the body over.

"A private," Jack said, noting the single row of buttons. "Dark hair. Again, many choices. I have to say, my friend, that time and nature have not been kind to you. What's in your pockets?"

Jack found a few coins, a needle and a bit of thread on a card, a clay pipe with a broken stem. Then in the breast pocket he found a slip of paper from the garrison quartermaster that was a tally of clothing issued. On the back of the paper was a penciled note in a hurried hand.

If you find my body in the mountains & are able to read this kindly inform my parents Mr & Mrs Glendon Perry of Rocheport Missouri by means most convenient & express my regret at having

*run off and joined the army at Jefferson Barracks
for eight dollars per monthly instead of staying
and clerking as my father had wished & tell my
sister Abigail that at the end I placed my trust in
Christ the Lord & was only a little afraid of the
pagan Crow & I hope that I did not suffer over
much & acquitted myself as a soldier should.*

—*Jonathan Perry*

"I'll try, lad," Jack said, putting the note in his own pocket with the map.

Then Jack had the feeling he was being watched. Perhaps it was the way the birds flying over the unnamed creek chattered and suddenly flared, or perhaps it was something on the wind that he could smell just below the level of conscious perception, but it was as if a shadow had descended.

Jack stood, holding the 1803 loosely in his right hand, and looked through the open gate of the outpost. There didn't appear to be anything moving beyond, but he could see only a small rectangle of what was outside. He walked over and took hold of 'Clipse's halter and led him over to the far wall of the outpost and tied him to a tree beside one of the lean-tos.

Then Jack slung the rifle across his back and climbed the tree to the roof of the lean-to and stepped onto the narrow plank, four feet or so below the top, then ran the inside perimeter of the palisade. Hunching down so he could not be seen, Jack made his way around toward the gate. He stopped a few yards shy of the gate and dared a look over the top.

He saw nothing but the stream, the valley, and the snow-marbled mountains beyond.

"Wagh!" A voice like thunder came from below. "I could not tell from a distance if you be a white man or one of the red devils that committed this depredation. Either way, I saw you was robbing the dead and it did not sit well with this child, it did not."

"Show yourself," Jack said.

"Why don't you come down here and introduce yourself proper to Old Gabrielle Baptiste, the rightful master of all the territory from the Green River to the Bighorns and across the womanly Tetons. Ha! There ain't a beaver I cain't trap, a maid I ain't kissed, or a jug of Taos Lightning that I haven't drunk."

Jack leaned out cautiously to get a better angle and saw a man on a blue horse, with a loaded mule behind, waiting in the open gate. The man had a floppy hat with a rattlesnake band and a bushy brown beard that flowed down his chest. Across his saddle he carried a rifle and shotgun double, with percussion ignition.

"I'm coming down," Jack hollered.

"I ain't going anywhere," Baptiste replied.

Jack climbed down to within jumping distance, then landed heavily on the ground ten feet away from Baptiste. He stumbled and nearly fell because of a pain in his right hip that he had not felt before.

"Careful," Baptiste said. "Men our age shouldn't be hopping down so. The rheumatism will remind us not to."

"It's not that," Jack said, rubbing his hip with his free hand. "At least, I don't think so."

"You have a strange accent, friend," Baptiste said. "I should know, because I've heard just about all of 'em in my day. Kind of Old World, a bit of French, a dash of something else . . ."

"Basque," Jack said.

"I'll be skinned. You're Mountain Jack Picaro."

Jack shrugged.

"Some say you're dead," Baptiste said. "You've been scarce these many years. There are others who say they hear that famous rifle of yours, the one that rings like a bell, in the far corners of the territory."

"The rifle is lost," Jack said. "But I'm alive enough."

"I can see that," Baptiste said.

"Do you know this camp?" Jack asked.

"I did, when living creatures inhabited it. These men were killed three, maybe four weeks ago."

"Why?"

"The Crows don't need a reason," Baptiste said. "Especially not Greasy Guts of the Mountain band. This is his work. You can tell by the markings on the arrows. That dash of blue on the shaft is his signature."

"Where's his camp?"

"Beyond the Beartooth," Baptiste said. "But you'd want to steer clear of his lodge. I know Chief Greasy Guts and he is a good host with a pair of plump sisters for wives but is a fierce warrior who removes the private parts of his enemies to deny them their manhood in the other world. This poor devil seems to be walking sunlit fields as a eunuch."

"Do you recognize him?" Jack asked, motioning to the corpse.

"Can't say I do. But much of him is missing."

"You've been here before?"

"You ask a lot of questions, Jack Picaro. You are a seeker, a pilgrim, a palmer. What is it you're looking of?"

"To find the five others. Or their bodies."

"Scouting for the army?"

"It's temporary," Jack said.

"Ah," Baptiste said. "That is the common refrain. But I have the feeling that what you really seek cannot be found on the trail of some flatland soldiers who climbed too high in these, my Rocky Mountains. No, palmer, I'd say what you really seek is beyond, far beyond the blue horizon."

"You can tell that much, can you?" Jack asked, his lips curling into a mirthless smile. "Why, you seem to know more about me than I do myself. I can't say I ever harbored an ambition to glimpse beyond this mortal veil."

"You are special," Baptiste said. "Oh, you're not special in the way you fancy you are, but you have something that will transcend your mortal being. Trust me, for I come from a long line of Swedenborgians and we have the inner sight."

"Enough of this nonsense," Jack said. He was impatient, and the presence of the skeletal remains nearby reminded him keenly of his own mortality. "Can you help me?"

"I could."

"Then *will* you?"

Baptiste grunted, then reached into a pocket for a clay pipe. He carefully filled the bowl with tobacco from a well-worn pouch, then returned the pouch to his coat.

"I reckon I'd better smoke on it," Baptiste said. "Get your horse. Let's quit this place and find a good spot under a tall tree. We'll palaver and see what's what. But do it all easy and natural like because there's three Crow warriors been following me since yesterday."

"Kind of you to tell me."

"Oh, don't be like that. If they'd wanted me or you dead, we'd both be gone beaver by now. It's kind of like a game to them, to see what the crazy old man will do next. Now, I need a flame. Will you be good enough to oblige?"

Jack nodded.

He walked back to the back wall, untied 'Clipse from the lean-to, and slipped the 1803 into the saddle scabbard. Then he took his fire makings from his possibles bag and knelt next to some dry grass at the base of the lean-to and used a flint and the firesteel to throw sparks on a square of charred linen. The blackened cloth ignited immediately and, when the breeze came up, burned even more fiercely. The dry grass caught fire and soon flames were licking up the wall of the lean-to.

Jack led 'Clipse across the yard to the gate. There, he repeated the fire-starting operation, and soon the palisade was ablaze. Jack held a stick in the fire and then walked it over to Baptiste, who leaned down and lit his clay pipe from the fluttering flame.

"It is a nasty habit," Baptiste said, smoke trailing from the corner of his mouth. "But I love all the wicked things of life."

Jack put his moccasin in the left stirrup and swung up into the saddle of 'Clipse, whose nostrils were flaring because of the smoke. The horse began to shuffle nervously.

"Lead on," Jack told Baptiste.

12   *Rough Country*

Five miles away, on the bank of the unnamed stream, they staked the horses and spread tarps beneath a rock overhang. The sky had grown dark, even though it was the middle of the day, and Jack could smell the coming snow. In the north, the Beartooths appeared as a line of white cliffs and crags, with the peaks lost in the clouds.

"Keep an eye on the animals," Baptiste said, reclining on the canvas. "The Crows won't kill us, but the horses are a terrible temptation. They are notorious thieves."

"To them, it's not theft," Jack said. "It's warfare."

"I reckon so," Baptiste said.

"You speak their language?"

"Understand much," he said. "Can speak a little."

Jack nodded.

"You aiming to palaver with old Greasy Guts?"

"Yes," Jack said.

Baptiste laughed.

"You're a confident devil, I'll give you that. Now explain why you're hunting for these other five soldiers."

Jack did, but left out what Maguire had said about the gold.

"The sooner I find out what happened to them, the sooner I'm back home," Jack said. "So that's my story. What's yours? I see no bundles of plews on that mule."

"Ah, I lost my heart for trapping the little critters some years back," Baptiste said. "I went back to the flatland, but it didn't seem I fit in anymore. So I came back to the mountains to live as I like."

"You have tobacco and beans," Jack said. "That truck isn't free."

"I make a dollar or two when my belly's empty by hunting for the fur companies," Baptiste said. "I've gathered meat for Sublette and Campbell, Bent and St. Vrain, the American Fur Company. Even did some work for the Russians, deep in the Oregon Country. Now I'm just looking for someplace to pass the winter that isn't so high that I freeze to death and not so low that I have to put up with neighbors."

Jack said he understood.

"I have a family down in the flatlands," Baptiste said. "A wife, if she lives still, and children. Two boys. But they would be men now. I have not spoken to them in ten years."

Baptiste paused and smoothed his beard.

"I don't know why," he said. "There were no words, no unpleasantness, just an emptiness I could not fill. I cannot say that I have found anything in the mountains to plug that hole in my heart, but the landscape does ease the pain."

Jack was unconsciously rubbing his jaw.

"And you?" Baptiste asked. "What did you leave behind?"

"Trouble," Jack said.

"How long that tooth been aching?"

"A spell," Jack said, moving his hand away.

"Bad teeth have killed more men in these mountains than the entire Crow nation," Baptiste said. "It ain't a pleasant death. I can jerk it out with my worm ball puller. I did it on my own self, two years ago, in the Wind River Range. There might be some bleeding involved."

Jack winced at the thought of it.

"It will pass," Jack said.

"If you say so, palmer."

"Do you have whiskey?"

"Don't touch the stuff," Baptiste said. "It disagrees with my faculties."

"I thought you said you loved all wicked things."

"I said it disagrees with me," Baptiste said. "Not that I don't love it."

Baptiste pulled his tobacco pouch out of his pocket and handed it to Jack.

"Put a pinch of this stuff against the tooth," Baptiste said. "It will ease the pain some, and might make you sick if you've never developed a habit for tobacco."

"It won't make me sick," Jack said.

He plucked some tobacco from the pouch. He opened his mouth wide and pressed the tobacco against the tooth and the inside of his upper right cheek. Touching the tooth and its swollen gum with his fingertips gave him a jolt, and he cursed unintelligibly. The tobacco was dry and bitter and foreign in his cheek, and he could taste the poison from the bad tooth running down the back of his throat.

"Ha!" Baptiste said. "You're going to lose your breakfast."

Jack shook his head.

"I had no breakfast," he mumbled, leaning forward to rest his spinning head on the ground.

"If I were a Crow warrior," Baptiste said, "I would consider that a mighty inviting pose, considering how much neck you're offering me."

"But you ain't," Jack said.

"That's true," Baptiste said, taking off his hat and placing it upside down on the canvas. He was bald, and his scalp was a mottled pink and white. Seeing Jack staring, he ran a hand over his head.

"Lost my hair after a Blackfeet war party had me and my partner Solomon cornered in a bend of the Bighorn," he said. "We'd been trapping for nigh onto a month and had gathered a mighty pretty bundle of pelts. But our success made us reckless, and we ventured a little too boldly down the river. Solomon was a proud man and he defied the Blackfeet in word and ball. They shot him full of arrows and I can still remember one of those iron trade points jutting out of his neck below his chin, and him looking at it afore he fell down and died at my feet."

Baptiste fiddled with his pipe.

"I had never been so scared in my life, before or since," he said. "All the fight went right out of me, and I dropped my rifle and fell to my knees in the sticks and the mud and threw out my hands, beseeching the Almighty for a little help. I started belting out 'New Jerusalem,' a hymn I admired as a child. The Blackfeet must've thought I was singing my death song, and it spooked 'em. The whole party just turned and rode off."

Baptiste scratched the top of his head.

"That was twenty years ago. I haven't grown a single hair on the top of my head since. And I think about poor old Solomon with the trade point jutting out of his neck every day."

"This is rough country," Jack said. "We who make it our home must have rough ways."

"You'll get no arguments from me on that score."

Baptiste rummaged in a pack that he had beside him and removed a cap. It was made of the fur of a red fox. He blew on the fur, admiring the quality, and then threw it to Jack.

"You'll need this," he said.

"So, will you help me?"

Baptiste allowed that he might.

"Lead me to the camp of Greasy Guts."

"That's not help," Baptiste said. "It's suicide."

"What?" Jack said. "You want to live forever?"

"I reckon not," Baptiste said. "To the camp, then. I will translate some and do what I can to help you find your lost soldiers, but I will not fight unless cornered. Greasy Guts believes in a twilight world between this one and the next, where the ghosts of the fighting dead linger in perpetual combat. Says he saw it in a vision. I've made enough enemies in this life, and I will not store up more to fight in purgatory."

13 *Beartooth Pass*

With triangular Beartooth Peak looming over them, Jack and Baptiste rode across a treeless granite landscape that had the feel of a massive medieval fortress. Their path was one of alternating rock and snow, with the drifts sometimes coming to the shoulders of the horses and to the neck of Baptiste's mule. The wind howled constantly and the cold numbed their fingers and slowed their minds.

On a flat granite stretch, Baptiste drew close to Jack and leaned toward him in the saddle.

"We are lucky," he shouted. "The weather is yet mild for this time of year. We are only one decent storm away from the pass being closed until next summer."

Baptiste's whiskers around his mouth were caked in ice, which he tried to brush away with a gloved hand.

"I have never crossed it this late," Jack said, clasping the collar of his jacket to his throat. His fox fur cap was pulled down to his eyes and his hands were wrapped in scraps he had torn from his wool blanket. "I do not remember it being this cold."

"They say the air gets thin at this altitude," Baptiste

said. "It doesn't take as long to boil coffee, but it cools quicker. I don't know what the Almighty was thinking when he made this high and loathsome place, but He damn sure didn't make it for man. The Book says there were giants in the earth in the days before the flood, and I reckon this must have been where some of those horny old bastards lived."

"This view," Jack said, "makes me almost believe it."

"How high do you reckon we are?"

Jack shrugged.

"Not the highest range in the Rockies," Baptiste said, "but high enough. We lost the trees around two thousand feet below, so I'm guessing twelve thousand. If we had a mercury, we could boil some water and get a damned fine estimate from the temperature."

Jack held up his hand.

"What?" Baptiste asked.

"Look," Jack shouted.

Reclining against a boulder thirty yards away were two soldiers in blue uniforms. A snow drift covered them up to their elbows. Their heads were touching and they appeared to be in some kind of private conversation. If their faces had not been a marbled blue, they could have been mistaken for a pair of friends taking their ease.

Jack handed the reins of 'Clipse over to Baptiste and slid clumsily down from the saddle.

"Don't be long," Baptiste shouted. "We'll be as dead as those two if we linger."

Jack brushed the snow away from the bodies and could see that their uniforms were intact, with no signs of violence. Their rifles were upright beside them. They were both young, so Jack took them as private soldiers.

One was somewhat bigger than the other and had curly black hair and the other brown, and both their lips were shrunken back, exposing their teeth, as if they were laughing at some secret joke.

"Froze to death," Jack shouted over his shoulder. "Reed and Smith, from the description."

"Sometimes you get so tired up here that it seems a good idea to sit down and rest," Baptiste said. "And you never get up. Or maybe they misjudged distance and dark caught 'em. How many you have left now to find?"

"Three," Jack said.

He tried unbuttoning the coat of the bigger soldier, thinking he could use an extra layer of wool, but the garment was laden with ice and plank-like. The pair were also frozen to each other, and disturbing one also shook the other.

Jack cursed.

He dug in the snow and found a cartridge box, still slung over the shoulder of the dark-haired solider. Jack managed to wrench the box free from the body, but the straps were impossibly frozen. He drew the Damascus from his belt and used it to pry open the box, then he gathered handfuls of powder in paper cartridges, and shot and caps, and stuffed them into his own pockets.

"Give the rifles a try," Baptiste called.

Jack sheathed the knife and grabbed one of the rifles by the barrel and, after some effort, managed to pry it away. Then he did the same with the other rifle, except when he pulled it from the snow drift he saw that the hand of the brown-haired soldier had snapped off at the wrist, still attached to the stock. Jack pried the frozen fingers from the rifle and tossed the hand back to its owner.

"Good," Baptiste said. "Two less rifles that will be in Crow hands."

Jack trudged over to the mule and clumsily secured the rifles beneath the straps of one of the packs.

"You still cold?" Baptiste asked.

"What?" Jack asked, taking 'Clipse's reins.

"I asked, are you cold?"

"Yeah," Jack mumbled. "Not much, maybe."

"That ain't encouraging, palmer," Baptiste said. "Get up in the saddle and get moving. It's downhill from here, and you'll be miserable enough again when we shed some height."

14 *Night Bird*

"How would you like to play this?" Baptiste asked.

It was three days after they had descended from the pass and they were in the saddle looking, from two hundred yards away, at a Crow camp of a score of lodges that occupied a bend in the Crazy Owl River.

"Easy," Jack said. "I'd like to play it easy."

"I could ride in first and remind the old bastard we're friends," Baptiste offered. "Then, when things are all cozy and kinlike, I could make an introduction to my cousin Jack."

"Best if we ride in together," Jack said. "Otherwise, it looks like we're scared."

"I am scared, palmer."

"Why the hell do you keep calling me palmer?" Jack asked.

"I call everybody palmer," Baptiste said. "We're all pilgrims hoping to return with a palm frond from the Holy Land."

"No desire," Jack said.

"Well, I don't mean it literal," Baptiste said.

"You are a strange creature," Jack said. "What does your inner sight tell you about our situation now?"

"To be careful," Baptiste said.

"Let's get on with it," Jack said, urging 'Clipse forward.

They rode into the circle of lodges without challenge or welcome, but Jack knew that all of the camp—the women cooking meals and fleshing hides, the children fighting in the dirt, the men who took their ease on robes positioned by their lodge doors—were watching.

"Don't look left or right," Jack said. "Just keep on riding."

"I'll be sad if I didn't see that arrow what will kill me."

Baptiste drew to a stop in front of a painted lodge. Black and yellow ribbons fluttered from the tips of the lodge poles, forty feet above the ground. Smoke curled from the smoke hole. The slightly tilted cone of buffalo hide was decorated with stars and lightning bolts and rows of blue stripes. Seven arrows were pointed skyward, and one arrow had a splash of blue near the fletching.

"What does all that mean?" Jack asked, drawing alongside Baptiste. "I've seen painted lodges before, but not like this."

"It's old Greasy Gut's bona fides. His battles, his visions, his dreams. He is some powerful, Jack, so just imagine this is a monument like the statue of a general on horseback. Difference is, there's no boast here. He wouldn't think twice about gutting you and having the village historian paint a picture of it in your own blood."

"Ain't nobody dying today," Jack said.

"I hope you're right," Baptiste said.

Then he stood in stirrups and called to the lodge.

"Chief," he called. "It's your old friend, Gabriel Xavier

Baptiste, seeking the hospitality of your lodge." After a pause, he repeated the greeting, in the Crow language.

Nothing stirred. Far across the camp, a dog began to howl, and then was joined by another.

"Now what?" Jack asked.

"We wait," Baptiste said. "It shows respect."

Five minutes later, the hide door moved aside and a Crow warrior emerged into the autumn sunlight. He was neither young nor old, but of some middle age that conferred the benefits of both; his eyes shone with intelligence, but his arms rippled with muscle. He wore a porcupine quill vest, a breechclout, deerskin leggings, and moccasins. Even though his breath came out in clouds in the air, he did not seem to mind the cold.

Baptiste and the warrior spoke to each other in short sentences, sometimes punctuated by hand movements. Jack sat easy in the saddle, his hands crossed over the horn, trying to look unconcerned.

"What's he saying?" Jack asked.

"I've told him that he is looking well," Baptiste said. "He told me I grow fatter every year, so I must be prospering. I have told him you are my cousin, because kin is important to these people."

"Cousins?"

"That's right," Baptiste said, smiling broadly. "Welcome to the family."

"He seems suspicious."

"He said we don't look alike," Baptiste said. "I told him my aunt was a homely woman and married poorly."

"Bastard."

"In fact, I am," Baptiste said. "Now, old Greasy Guts

is going to invite us into his lodge and we're going to eat some and smoke the medicine pipe. Behave yourself."

"Tell him the truth."

"What?"

"Tell him we are not cousins," Jack said. "Explain who I am."

Baptiste hesitated.

"I'll ride away," Jack said.

"That would be an insult. We'd both be dead right quick."

"Then best tell him."

Baptiste smiled and took off his cap, revealing his bald head. He was talking slow and careful, and occasionally motioned to Jack, and then to himself. When he was done, he sat silently in the saddle.

"Was it the truth?"

"Yes, damn you," Baptiste said. "I explained that we was cousins in the dream world, that you had considerable medicine, and that you walked between worlds so often that I was confused."

The chief reflected on what Baptiste had said, then nodded. He spoke a few sentences to Baptiste, then made a motion as if slashing his knife across his chest.

Baptiste laughed.

"What did he say?"

"That your reputation precedes you," Baptiste said. "Old Greasy Guts knows it was Jack Picaro who had a terrific fight with Standing Wolf. His people call it the Day of Dreams Fighting. He says there are still lodge skins with that fight painted on the side. Was that you, Jack?"

"It was thirteen years ago."

"Ho boy," Baptiste said. "You are some kind of royalty to these people. Old Greasy Guts has some fun in store for you."

"Revenge?"

"No," he said. "He's inviting you to join him in the dream world."

"What, with whiskey? Smoke? Something else?"

"No time to talk about it," Baptiste said.

The chief was motioning for them to join him inside the painted lodge. A young warrior appeared and reached for 'Clipse's halter. Jack drew the reins back, and the horse shuffled awkwardly.

"Hand him over," Baptiste said.

"It don't feel right."

"If we end up dead they'll have the horses anyway."

"No matter what happens," Jack said, "'Clipse is likely to kick one or two of them into the other world."

Jack released the reins to the young man and swung down from the saddle, leaving the 1803 in the scabbard.

"Now, palmer, I want you to behave yourself."

"I've been in many lodges before."

"The rules are different than most other tribes," Baptiste said. "Especially with the Mountain Band. These are a fierce and amorous people who practice wife hospitality with those they like, so mind that you do not offend them."

Jack and Baptiste passed through the *ozan,* the inner lining of the lodge, and took a pair of reed chairs, near where the chief sat. They were facing the lodge fire, and around the pit there were a half-dozen men, all senior warriors of the chief's band. A few women came and went, some with bowls of meat or boiled squash.

"Eat," Baptiste said.

Jack avoided the dog meat but ate some of the buffalo and the squash.

Then a Crow woman of about twenty came into the lodge. She wore an elk skin cape over a dun-colored muslin dress and her long black hair was in braids, with red ribbons. Around her neck was a Jefferson Peace Medal. She stood perfectly still, her shoulders back, her hands clasped in front of her.

The chief spoke at some length, and Baptiste translated.

"This girl is named Night Bird," he said. "Old Greasy Guts sent for her. He says she's the daughter of that Crow warrior you fought long ago. The girl's father is dead these three years, he says, taken by a fever. She is married to one of Guts' warriors. Night Bird has long heard stories of you and wanted to see you for herself."

Jack felt a chill take him, as if the past had washed over him in waves.

"Please tell Night Bird that I am sorry to hear that her father is dead," Jack said. "Tell her . . . tell her that my fight with Standing Wolf was the fiercest of my life. He was a fine warrior."

Baptiste had just started to translate when the girl smiled, showing fine white teeth and sharp chin that reminded Jack of an animal.

"You have told me yourself," the girl said.

"You speak English well," Jack said.

"As did my father," she said. "Your accent is unknown to me. It is strange. What is your native tongue?"

"Euskara," Jack said. "I am Basque."

"I know not your nation."

"It is of the Old World," Jack said. "Across the ocean."

"Ah," the girl said. "You are far from home."

"The journey has been long," Jack said. "I am sorry that my encounter with your father was brief and bloody."

"Our shame was great," the girl said. "Why did you let him live after the Day of Dreams Fighting? How much kinder it would have been for you to have killed him."

"I did not want him to die," Jack said. "I wanted him to live, just as I wanted to live."

The girl shook her head.

"You said something that troubled my father until the day he died," Night Bird said. "Do you remember? That to be an American is to be free to dream."

"Yes," Jack said.

"My father's dreams were fettered birds," she said. "'Only the whites,' he said, 'were free in their dreams, as only the willfully ignorant can be.' You were in his dreams, often. He was speaking of you, as if you were still fighting together in the snow, the night he died of the fever. Now he haunts my dreams, trapped in his shame."

"I am sorry," Jack said. "But I remember the day of the fight well. I also told him that we are free to choose our dreams."

Night Bird laughed.

"This reveals the depth of your ignorance," she said. "All wise men know that our dreams choose us."

The girl walked slowly around the circle of men, her hands still clasped in front of her, as solemnly as if she were in a funeral procession. Her head was high, and she walked with the confidence of knowing she was desired. She stopped when she came to Jack, then crouched, sitting on her feet.

"I have a question for you."

She leaned forward.

"What is it?" Jack asked.

She smelled of sage and woodsmoke.

"Tell me about my grandfather," she said.

"I do not know your grandfather."

She stared at Jack with eyes that reflected the fire and slowly shook her head. Her right hand came up and brushed her hair back behind her ear, as if to listen more carefully to Jack's words.

"All the whites know him," she said. "His name is Captain Clark."

"I know of only one Captain Clark," Jack said.

"William Clark," the girl said. "His friend was Lewis. They brought these up the river with them," she said, clutching the Jefferson Peace Medal on the silk ribbon around her neck.

"I recognize it," Jack said.

"Clark is my grandfather. You know him."

"Yes."

"Tell me of him."

"I have not seen him in many years," Jack said. "But when I did, he was a kind of chief—"

"—you do not have chiefs. Do not speak to me as you would a child."

"He was a governor," Jack said. "He was the most powerful man in St. Louis, and one of the most famous men in the country. I met him only once, and he was not a happy man. He was a smart man, and brave, but not happy. He feared his past. He feared your father."

"Why?"

"He believed him immortal."

"He was, once," Night Bird said. "As I am."

"That's the kind of nonsense Clark feared."

Night Bird smiled, a sly and crooked smile, full of wit but little mirth.

"Ah," she said. "So he turned coward in his old age?"

"No," Jack said. "He was afraid of things one cannot fight. Ghosts and phantoms."

"Do I look like him?"

"No."

"Good," Night Bird said. "That would be a terrible burden."

"Have no fear," Jack said. "You are a handsome young woman, and you bear no trace that I can find of Captain Clark."

"Do you truly think I am handsome?"

"Yes," Jack said.

"Then it is settled," Night Bird said, then spoke in low and quick tones to the chief. The chief listened, then nodded.

Baptiste laughed and slapped his knee.

"What?" Jack said.

"She's yours," Baptiste said.

"What do you mean, she's mine?"

"I belong to you," Night Bird said. "You may do with me as you please, my lord. It is necessary to restore my family's honor."

"But what about my honor?" Jack asked. "I am already married."

"So am I," Night Bird said. "But no longer."

"Just like that?"

"Yes, like that," Night Bird said.

"But why? You obviously hate me."

"There is a debt to be satisfied, and you like all men have a need for a full belly and a strange bed," she said. "I can provide both, my lord, for a few nights or many winters. It will lighten the burden of your other wife."

"Even if I found this bargain acceptable," Jack said, "I would get little sleep for fear of having my throat slit during the night."

"Oh, you will get little sleep," she said pridefully.

"Don't argue, palmer," Baptiste said. "There ain't a man in these mountains that wouldn't envy your position right now, but you're about to argue the point and get both of us killed. Besides, you might not even survive the dreaming to introduce the missus to your new cook and bedmate."

Jack asked what he meant by surviving the dreaming.

"Best it be a surprise," Baptiste said.

"Now look here," Jack said. "Tell old Greasy Guts this—this arrangement—just won't do."

Baptiste shushed Jack.

"That's just a name I used for him, between us," Baptiste said. "The last time I saw him he must have ate something that disagreed with him because he emanated a cloud of gas that was biblical in its power."

Night Bird shook her head.

"White men," she said. "Always more ignorant than I remember. The chief's name is Earthshaker. And your friend here has said you have already agreed to the dreaming, that you will find my father and ease his restless ghost."

"How am I to do that?"

"By giving him the fighting death he deserved," she said. "Once that is done, this medal will be surrendered and arrangements made for its return to my grandfather in St. Louis. Then, finally, my father can continue his journey to the west."

"I have fought your father once," Jack said. "I will not do so again, even in dreams."

Night Bird frowned.

"It is not up to you," she said. "The dream awaits and will not be denied, my lord."

"Stop calling me that," Jack said. "I am not your lord. I have no interest in a dalliance with a Crow witch, no matter how beautiful. Once my business here is done, you will never see me again."

She stood, turning her head dismissively away from Jack, and walked over to Earthshaker. She spoke rapidly to him.

"Now you've done it," Baptiste said in English to Jack. "She's told Greasy Guts that you ain't game, and the old bastard is not happy. He's saying that you must not want them three soldiers very damn bad."

Night Bird looked at Jack.

"I could always count on men being hogs," she said. "Until you."

She walked behind the chief and disappeared into the shadows at the back of the lodge.

"The soldiers?" Jack asked. "Where are they?"

"He didn't say," Baptiste said, smiling broadly. "And now is not the time to press him."

"Why not?" Jack asked.

"Because," Baptiste said, "it's good night for you."

Night Bird was standing behind Jack, and in her right hand she held a war club shaped like a gunstock. She swung the club decisively, clipping Jack behind the right ear. She uttered a cry of satisfaction as Jack slumped to the ground.

Baptiste held up his hands.

"Don't blame you a bit," he said. "I've wanted to do that to Jack Picaro since the day we met."

15 *Missouri Harmony*

It was a Sunday morning in late October and, because the weather was mild, Sister was in no hurry to return. She walked slowly with a reed basket hanging from one hand, following the creek bank through a deep stand of hard timber, sometimes stooping to gather mast for the hogs back at the farm. The oak trees were so massive that, walking beneath their skeletal canopies, Sister felt as if she had been transported to another land where she was the only living person. She enjoyed the feeling, and the warmth of the autumn sun on her skin, and the stillness and majesty of the woods. She did not know how far she had strayed, but it would be a simple matter to follow the creek back, so she kept walking, listening to the wind sigh in the branches overhead.

Sister eventually reached a spot where the timber gave way to wide, low fields, and for a moment she heard a sound that sent a shiver down her spine. At first, she thought the sound was caused by the wind, but it was more alien than that, the kind of sound she imagined that angels might use to announce their presence on earth.

She dropped the basket and turned away from the creek, toward the sound, and climbed up the bank to the field.

Far across the stubble-dotted field was a white frame church. The building shone brilliantly against the drab colors of late autumn. Wagons and buggies were parked in front and to the sides, and horses were hitched at rails. The sound that had captivated Sister was emanating from the church, and it was the sound of dozens of voices singing a powerful kind of harmony, which made the human voice an instrument of power, like the pealing of bells.

Sister stumbled across the field, and the closer she got, the clearer the music became, and she began picking out words and phrases. *Man is a pilgrim across scorching sands . . . a wandering sheep in a howling wilderness . . . seeking rivers of salvation and pleasant fields of paradise.* Tears sprang to her eyes, and she did not know if they were of joy or sorrow. She did not believe in God, but so many voices singing of death and devotion moved her darkly. As she neared the church, she could feel the power of the bass notes reverberate through her body, giving her a shameful thrill. She put her right hand out, and her fingertips grazed the whitewashed walls of the church, and for a moment her hand buzzed with the music. She followed the wall to the back of the church, where she sat, drew her knees close, and leaned against the church to better feel the power of the music. She closed her eyes tightly and cradled her head in her arms, concentrating only on the music.

Ten minutes or an hour later—Sister did not know which—she felt a hand touch her shoulder. She looked up. It was a woman in a dark dress and a white bonnet.

"Where's your people?" the woman asked.

Sister blinked against the sunlight.

"I'm sorry," she said. "I was just listening."

"Your clothes are filthy," the woman said. "Is this how you come to meeting? I would have a word with your mother."

"So would I," Sister said. "But she is dead as many years as I've lived."

The woman's face softened.

"How did you come here?"

"I came up the creek yonder."

"You live . . ."

"On a farm," Sister said.

"Which one?" the woman asked. "Is it the Stiles or the Granger place?"

"I've got to go."

"You look thin," the woman said. "Are you hungry?"

Sister was, but she did not see that it was any of this woman's business.

"We are laying out supper now," the woman said. "There is enough. We could wash you up and you could sit with my girls."

"No," Sister said. "I have chores undone. I should leave."

"Tell me the name of the family that owns your farm."

The girl shook her head.

"You're older than you appear, aren't you?" the woman said.

"I'm thirteen."

"What's your name?"

"They call me Sally," the girl said. "But that ain't my

name. I don't know what my mother called me, so I guess I don't have one."

"Everybody has a name," the woman said. "I'm Sarah Williams."

"Missus Williams."

"Yes."

"I had better go."

"Let me get you something to take with you," the woman said. "Some apples. Some cheese. A bite of bread."

The thought made Sister's mouth water.

"No, thank you kindly."

She stood and brushed her hair from her face.

"I think you should stay with me," the woman suggested quietly.

"Like I said, chores," Sister said. She took a step toward the creek, but paused and turned back to the woman. "Please, if you don't mind. What was the music?"

"The hymns?"

"The kind of music," Sister said. "I've never heard anything so beautiful or so frightening. What's it called?"

"Why, dear, that's sacred harp."

The girl waited for more.

"It's shape note singing," the woman said. "It's a system that teaches people how to sing. There are schools and traveling masters that teach it. The hymns are from a book called the Missouri Harmony."

"Shape note," Sister said. "Shape note."

"Yes."

"Someday I will sing, too."

"I'm sure you will," the woman said. "If you come again next Sunday, I will have a simple but clean dress for you. And you will stay and take supper with me and my girls. Will you come, dear?"

"I don't know . . . I have a powerful lot of chores."

"Tell me, Sally, do you know Jesus?"

The girl felt as if she had been struck mute.

"It is time for all to know Him," the woman said. "There is the black cholera in St. Louis and many are sick and dying. There are prayer meetings every day to fight the sickness. The disease is the work of the devil, and the only salvation is through Jesus—whether one recovers or dies."

The girl turned and ran on shaking legs toward the creek.

16 *Scourged*

When Jack Picaro woke, the world was upside down and slowly rotating.

"Baptiste!" he shouted.

Jack could feel the rope that bound his ankles. Looking down—or rather, up—he could see the taut rope leading to the apex of a tripod of lodge poles. Beyond, the sky was blue and cloudless. Letting his head drop, he could see Earthshaker and others watching from a distance.

"Baptiste!"

He struggled to free his hands, which were tied behind his back, and the motion made him twist a bit faster, with the chief and his council disappearing from view. He could hear the blood rushing in his ears, and his head throbbed with every beat of his heart. In addition to his toothache, he now had a dull pain behind his right ear.

Night Bird swung into view.

She was standing close, and her head was about at the level of Jack's. She was cradling the war club shaped like a gunstock.

"Your friend cannot help you," she said.

"Dead?" Jack asked.

"Drunk," Night Bird said.

"Get me down," Jack said.

"You are in no position to give orders," Night Bird said.

"Where are the soldiers?"

"It is also unwise of you to ask questions," she said.

"Are they alive?"

"Did you not hear me?"

Night Bird reached out with the war club and stopped Jack's rotation.

"I heard you," Jack said, staring into her eyes. "Show them to me or kill me now. If you wish me to help you, prove to me that the men are still alive."

She made a dismissive sound in her throat and pushed Jack with the club, which started him swinging like a pendulum. But she spoke in quick tones to Shine on Water, who nodded.

A pair of Crow warriors appeared two minutes later, pulling a trio of white soldiers by ropes. One had yellow hair and the other two, brown. The ropes were looped around the soldiers' necks, and they stumbled and fell trying to keep up.

Their elbows were tied in place behind them to staves, and their hands were black and swollen and their fingers jutted out at unnatural angles. Their sky-blue trousers were ragged and torn, and their bare feet were bloody. Their hair was covered in dirt and twigs, and their mouths were gagged by wads of blue wool that had been stripped from the sleeves of their jackets.

They were deposited on the ground next to Night Bird.

"There," she said. "See for yourself."

Jack caught glimpses of the men as he swung.

"Why are they treated so?" Jack asked.

"They are animals," Night Bird said. "They deserve no treatment better than that of animals. They are hogs, as far as the Crow nation is concerned, but worth even less, because if they were hogs, at least we could eat them."

"What was their offense?" Jack asked. He blinked hard, because he was beginning to see flashes of red.

"Desecration," Night Bird said. "They crossed our sacred land without our permission and scratched in the earth of our ancestors for your glittering yellow god. We have been lenient with them, thus far."

"Let them go," Jack said.

"More commands," Night Bird said. She drew back the war club and struck a sharp blow on the tip of Jack's left elbow. The arm immediately felt as if it had been struck by lightning, and then burst into flame. The sensation made Jack gasp, and Night Bird smiled in satisfaction.

"Is this the way you treated your last husband?" Jack asked.

She told the warriors to drag the soldiers away.

"Agree to go to the land of dreams," she told Jack, "and the soldiers will live. Fight my father. Then come back and live the rest of your life."

Jack was having difficulty speaking. His tongue was swollen, and his throat felt as if it were closing on his windpipe.

"You must do more than allow the soldiers to live,"

Jack said. "They cannot live as slaves. You must free them."

"Bargaining now?" Little Bird asked.

"Not bargaining," Jack said. "Condition."

She did not understand.

"Requirement," Jack said. "A must have."

"Ah," she said. "Very well. They shall be freed."

"Then let me down and let's get on with it," Jack said. "I'm damned dizzy and my head is about bursting with my blood. How do I cross over to the dreamland?"

"We will use this," Night Bird said, reaching inside the collar of her dress and bringing out a buckskin pouch. "It is the boiled meat of the redcap mushroom. This was taught to me by a woman of power long ago."

"We?" Jack asked.

"You don't think I'd let you go by yourself," she said. "I must witness your fight with my father. And you will require my guidance to return to the land of the living."

"The odds of us having the same drug-induced vision are slim," Jack said. "Now let me down."

"You must be purified first," she said.

Before Jack could ask what that meant, one of the warriors brought Night Bird a smoldering bundle of sage and sweetgrass, and she wreathed the smoke around Jack's head while chanting a prayer.

"Could be worse," Jack mused.

Then Night Bird struck Jack sharply across the back with the club, then moved past. Behind her was a warrior who locked his hands together and swung them against Jack's jaw, and behind him was a young man anxious to swing his sheep horn bow.

17   *The Night of Shadows*

Jack woke, flat on his back, staring up at a rough-hewn rectangle floating in a mist-shrouded sky. For a moment he thought he was dead, but decided that death likely did not come with the myriad of aches and pains he had accumulated on earth. He turned and raised himself on one tender elbow and looked about.

He was on a rocky and wind-swept hillock from which all the cardinal directions seemed to have receded. The rectangle above him was a wooden platform, a rickety affair supported by four weathered lodge poles. The wind rippled the feathers and fur at the edges of the platform, and through a wide crack in the bottom Jack could see a splayed human rib cage, yellow against the veined blue of the sky.

Jack was bare-chested, but covered by a pile of elk robes.

He shivered and clutched an elk robe and pulled it to his chin. A corner of the robe drew back to reveal a woman's naked thigh.

"Night Bird," he said.

"What is it?" she said groggily, flinging the robe away from her face.

"Where are we?"

"Sky burial," she said, then searched for an object hidden in the robes. She found it and placed it between them. It was a bone-white skull with a full set of teeth and deep and empty eye sockets. "My father awaits."

"Does he have to wait between us?"

"The skull fell months ago," she said. "It was the wind, or a buzzard, or perhaps another animal that knocked it from its sleep. Eventually gravity holds us all fast to the earth."

She picked up the skull and carefully placed it to the side, with the eye sockets pointing away.

"Was the scourging necessary?" Jack asked.

"Strictly, no," Night Bird said. "But it did beat some of your arrogance away."

Jack was too tired to argue.

Night Bird sat up, revealing her breasts. They were perfectly shaped, Jack thought, with hard dark nipples.

"Did we?"

"You have been unconscious for the better part of a day," she said. "I had to drag you here behind my horse on a travois. There was much blood and moaning and you would have made a poor partner."

"Good," Jack said.

"It is of no concern," she said with a shake of her head. "Your first wife is of the Mandan or Arikara peoples, no? And the hated French, I understand. She of all people would understand the ways of human coupling."

"She is not the bother," Jack said. "I am. There are bonds I will not break."

Night Bird made a phlegmy sound deep in her throat.

"You make me ill," she said. "Your queasiness makes me retch. Here we are about to look beyond the edge of the world, and you are living as if the *waisichu's* Sunday school god is looking over your shoulder, when it is you that are standing on his shoulder."

"I once talked as you do," Jack said. "But I grew wise."

"You grew old," she said.

"Thirteen winters separate us."

"It is not the winters," she said. "You became rooted to the earth. Tell me, is there a hearth you long for? A great stone thing in a wooden box hidden away somewhere where you sleep with cedar shingles between you and the night sky? Do you creep about in the mornings and go about the same business every day and bed down with this same woman at each setting of the sun? Of course, you do. This is not the Jack Picaro of the Day of Dreams Fighting. This is the Jack Picaro waiting for death to come stealing."

"Death comes to us all," Jack said.

"I hope to die while I yet live."

"You will get your wish."

Night Bird frowned.

"It is time to travel," she said. "We are lucky, you and I. Few people are allowed to journey to the land of the dreaming dead and return to tell of it."

"Odysseus," Jack said.

"Who?"

"An ancient hero," Jack said.

"How did he cross over?"

"Libations. Blood offerings. And the help of a comely witch."

Night Bird reached below the robes and retrieved the medicine pouch from inside her dress. She loosened the drawstring and dipped a forefinger inside.

"Here," she said, offering the mushroom paste on the tip of the finger. "It will ease the pain."

Jack hesitated.

"There is no other way?" he asked.

"No," she said. "Your path home is through the land of the dead."

Night Bird put the finger in her own mouth and sucked down the stuff.

"See?" she said. "We're going together."

Jack took the next scoop.

Night Bird smiled at the feeling of her finger in his mouth.

"There is water in the gourd beside you," she said. "You should drink some now. There are other things, with the horse. Most of your clothes, some food."

"Where is the horse?"

"Hidden," she said. "But not far. Horses are not allowed in this sacred space."

She scooped more of the stuff from the pouch, and they both ate.

"What will happen next?"

"Nothing," she said. "Everything."

Night Bird reclined and pulled the robes around her.

"Your stomach may turn inside out," she said. "If so, crawl a distance away to retch. I do not want to wallow in your filth. If you have to make water or do other business crawl far away as well. Do not defile any of the white rocks you see yonder."

"What are they?"

"They mark the medicine wheel," she said. "Do not enter the sacred hoop. It is not for you."

"What, then?"

"It is our church and our calendar," she said. "There are coming of age ceremonies for the young, healing dances for the sick. The two biggest cairns mark the shortest and longest days of the year. It marks the directions, tells us where we come from, and where we are bound."

Jack eased himself down into the robes.

"Hoops," Jack said. "Everything is a circle in the far world."

But Night Bird did not answer him.

It had seemed to Jack that only a few minutes had passed, but the sky had grown dark and the girl was asleep.

Jack was aware of a slight trembling in his limbs and, despite the cold of the night, he was sweating. Then his stomach began to heave and he remembered Night Bird's instruction and he crawled away from the robes, in the opposite direction of the medicine wheel. He vomited explosively, while on his hands and knees, and it seemed to him that the same few minutes when he was most sick were repeating endlessly. Time narrowed to the eternal now and there was no past or future, just the hard rocks cutting into his bare knees while he doubled over, holding his stomach, and then lurched forward and spread his hands wide on the ground while he emptied the contents of his stomach. The reflex was strong and each spasm contracted every muscle in his gut, and it felt like there was a cord that reached down into his groin and tried to jerk his testicles back into his body. When the eternal now finally slipped to the next moment, Jack's body was so wrenched by pain that he fell onto his side and clasped his knees to his chest, trying to calm himself.

That's when he noticed the shadows approaching.

Jack snatched a fist-sized rock and stumbled to his feet, ready to defend himself. He looked over to the robes where Night Bird lay, but she was no longer asleep. She was sitting cross-legged, dressed in a white elkskin dress with fancy beadwork, and floating above the robes. Her body shone with a pale blue light and, for the first time, Jack thought her face kind.

"Stay back," Jack shouted at the shadow.

"Why, Jack," a voice called. "It's me. Don't you recognize your old buddy?"

"State your name!"

A fear that seemed greenish-yellow gripped Jack.

"It's me, your old pal Johnston. Don't you remember I was spitted like a Christmas goose by an Arikara arrow during the attack on the keelboat? Why, you were just a greenhorn, but you did good. Look, I still have the hole in my belly."

The shade walked into the bluish circle of an unseen fire.

Jack turned his head away from the gruesome wound.

"I am ever so glad to see you, Jack," the ghost said. "I've been lonely, buried on the bank above the burned-out wreck of the keelboat, with nobody to keep me company except the other forgotten dead. Won't you remember your old pal and tell a story every once in a while about when you was young and I was yet living? Whango! But we had some shining times."

"Yes, we did," Jack said. "I will. I will tell our stories."

"That's all an old mate can ask."

Jack started to apologize for his nakedness, but when he looked down he saw his body was clothed in beaded elkskin leggings, moccasins, and a fine shirt.

"That rifle of yourn," Johnston said.

"Lost," Jack said. "Rusting these years at the bottom of the Missouri."

"It is not," the ghost said. "The mystery will be revealed, in time, if you listen hard enough."

"Explain," Jack said.

"Remember me," the ghost said, receding. "Remember."

Shadows began to crowd around the ring of light from the unseen fire.

"Who are these others?" Jack asked.

"All those who died by your hand," the ghost said, and began to dissolve. "The unhappy dead. Do not worry, they cannot hurt you. There are others you knew in life, but are now gone. But you may only palaver with those that you shared blood."

Then Johnston was gone.

A small figure in a blue robe stepped forward.

"My son, how did you come to this dark realm, you who are still alive?"

The figure spoke the Basque language.

"Mother?"

The figure brushed her hood back, revealing the face of a gray-haired woman in her fifties.

"You have grown old."

"I am neither old nor young," she said. "But I am eternally your mother. You have ventured far from your home, across the wine-dark sea that separates the Old World from the new, and deep into the wilderness of this new land. Never again will you cross the gulf of ocean, see Carcosa or the home your grandfather built. All must live now in memory alone."

"No," Jack said. "Say it isn't so."

He stepped toward the shade of his mother.

"There must be something to be done."

"There is nothing," she said. "Alas, my child, you are ill-fated above men."

Jack put his arms out to embrace her, but his hands clutched at empty air.

"Once we die, our sinew and bones are consumed by the fire below," his mother explained. "Our souls slip away as dreams. What you see is but a shadow of our former selves, a gossamer cloak, a rustling of the wind in dry grass. Return to the light, my son, and seek no more answers in this earthly abode. There is no joy here, only the sorrows of memories and desire."

Jack was vexed.

"But what of the new religion?" he asked. "Of Jesus Christo? And of Mari?"

His mother smiled.

"We unlucky dead know only of this realm," she said gently. "But there may be others. The goddess rules this domain, as she does all on earth and beneath, but she only intercedes on behalf of the living. If you are lost say her name three times loudly and she will appear to show you the way. Look for animals of the color red, and you will know she is with you. Of the Roman god I cannot speak, for the old ways are the true ones. His crucifixion is said to have redeemed humanity, but it seems to have only robbed believers of the necessity of seeking their own answers in the underworld."

His mother paused and held up a forefinger, in the way that Jack had seen some figures depicted in paintings and statuary in Christian churches.

"Mari is the mother of gods and is the intermediary between the old and the new, and many know her by a similar name. You will recognize her in this role because she will be clothed in blue. The old religions never disappear, my son, but are simply transformed into new ones, with new names. But the old ones endure."

"And what of love?" Jack asked.

"A mother's love is eternal."

"And the love of a maid?"

"You speak of the girl you knew," the shade said. "Abella."

"Yes," Jack said. "What of her?"

"You should not ask questions you do not want answered," the mother said. "Remember what I have told you. Seek the light. Dwell among the living. Find happiness."

As the shade of his mother dissolved into mist, another shadow came forward, and even before this new ghost lowered her hood, Jack recognized her from the set of her shoulders and the way she held her head.

"Abella," Jack said. "Is it you?"

Jack reached out, but the shade of the girl avoided his hand as easily as smoke.

"You cannot touch me, Jacques."

"No," Jack said, tears spilling onto his cheeks. "You are dead."

"You ruined me," she said. "And left me behind, discarded like an old . . ."

Jack fell to his knees before her ghost.

"My regret consumes me."

"Your regret was never great enough for you to return downriver," she said. "Your concern was always for yourself, never for others. The lives you ruined were just an inconvenience to you, obstacles in the way of your hungers. My family showed you nothing but kindness and you repaid us with betrayal."

"I have changed," Jack said.

"Oh? What woman are you with now? Have you betrayed her yet?"

"No." Jack choked on the word.

"You will," the ghost of Abella said. "Then she will join the joyless dead you have left behind."

"Please," Jack said. "Your brother—he must be here. He can tell you the truth of my feelings for you. And for him. I made many mistakes when full of whiskey and pride, but you were always in my heart."

"Farewell, Jacques," the shade said.

"Don't go," Jack pleaded.

Abella swirled away like dust thrown into the air.

"Jesus and the goddess Mari," Jack cried. "Please, no."

Jack remained on his knees, sobbing, for what seemed to him a long time. When he finally wiped the tears from his eyes, he was aware of a lone figure standing before him in the gloom.

It was Standing Wolf.

"I have waited for you lo these many years," the Crow warrior said. "Did you die well?"

"I don't know," Jack said. "I am a stranger in this land."

"You live?" Standing Wolf asked. He was dressed for war, as Jack had last seen him during the fight in the snow.

"I do," Jack said. "And must soon return to the light above."

"Why are you here?"

"I come at the bidding of your daughter."

"What message do you bring that Night Bird could not?"

Standing Wolf pointed beyond the pale blue firelight. Night Bird was standing at a distance, watching, holding her father's luminous skull, but too far away to hear their conversation.

"No message," Jack said. "We are to fight."

"Why?"

"I aim to give you an honorable death."

Standing Wolf laughed.

"My daughter has deceived you," he said. "You might as well attempt to fight the morning mist. Nothing we can do here can change what happened above. The Day of Dreams Fighting will remain forever as it was. My shame burns within me."

"There was no shame," Jack said.

Standing Wolf thumped his chest.

"You know nothing," he said. "You cannot take my shame from me."

"How are we to fight, then?" Jack asked. "I am flesh and you are mist."

Standing Wolf smiled.

"I will ask you three clever questions," he said.

"Ah, riddles," Jack said. "These are known to my people."

"You must answer all correctly to defeat me. If not, then you will be lost between the living and the dead. In the world above you will appear asleep, unable to wake, until your body finally wastes away and only your shade remains with me here—forever."

Jack looked around him. Night Bird had drawn closer, and she held her father's skull in both hands, over her stomach. Beyond the pale light, the unnamed shades shuffled aimlessly.

"You ask the riddles?" Jack asked.

"Yes."

"Who will judge?" Jack asked.

"My daughter," Standing Wolf said. "She can speak only truth while death dreaming."

"You have made clear the stakes for me," Jack said. "One wrong answer and I turn gradually to mist. But what is it that you are risking? There must be stakes or the game is not worth playing. If I answer all correctly, then your condition remains unchanged. You will still be the shameful dead."

"This is true," Night Bird said.

"Your path back to the world of the living passes through me," Standing Wolf said. "Refuse to accept the challenge and you pass no further, forever. Win and you regain light and life."

"Sweeten the pot," Jack said.

Standing Wolf shook his head.

"I had forgotten how much talk you make," he said.

"Let's raise the stakes," Jack said. "If all this is not just a dream, and the Roman god is powerless and Mari beyond hearing, then all of us are bound for this mirthless place in the end. What matter is a few more days or months or years of life compared to eternity?"

"The movement of the sun in the sky is all," Standing Wolf said. "That and what is beneath it. The smell of spring rain, the touch of a woman's hand, the final joy of a warrior's death."

"The rotting of teeth," Jack said. "Sickness and infirmity, the secret shames we carry like soiled clothes, our blind unimportance among the vastness of the universe. Watching those we love die. These are not things to which I am anxious to return."

Jack rubbed his jaw. It did not hurt, and he was suddenly frightened by his own logic.

"Your path lies beyond me," Standing Wolf said.

"Or it might end here with you," Jack said. "That's the thing about gambling: a square game is an uncertain one. You can do better. Give me something I want."

"My daughter does not please you?"

"She is not for me," Jack said.

"I am yours all the same," Night Bird said. "I know your wickedness. I am your dread angel and your nightmare wife. I cannot see the good, for your heart is denied me, but I know every hunger and each violent delight. Offer him the weapon, Father."

"What do you mean?" Jack asked.

"The rifle that rings like a bell when fired," she said.

"The ghost rifle," Standing Wolf said.

"You have it?" Jack asked.

"No," Standing Wolf said. "But if you win, events will allow you a chance to recover it. To seize the opportunity or not will be your choice. Your fate will be yours to control, for joy or sorrow."

"How will this opportunity be created?"

"The world keeps its balance," Night Bird said. "A great opportunity takes great sacrifice, but the sacrifice will not be yours. The bargain will be struck with secret words carried on the night wind. The debt will be paid by me, and by one or perhaps two others, but it is something we will never speak of again. If you are victorious, and you awake, you will have no memory of raising the stakes. Agreed?"

Jack did not hesitate.

"Agreed," he said.

Standing Wolf nodded his head.

"Very well," Jack said. "I'm ready."

Standing Wolf clapped his hands together.

"Here is the first puzzle," he said. "What is vanquished once you say its name?"

"Silence," Jack said.

"Correct," Night Bird said.

Standing Wolf thumped his chest in anger.

"Next one," Jack said. "Come now, be quick."

"What road branches forever away from home but which one may never walk?"

"You'll have to do better than that," Jack said, stalling for time. "These are puzzles you would ask children."

"What is your answer?" Night Bird asked.

Jack shook his head, as if in disbelief. Then the answer came to him.

"A river," he said.

Standing Wolf let out a cry as if he had been burned.

"This was best two out of three, right?" Jack asked.

"If only I could have the use of muscle and bone for only a moment," the warrior said. "Then I would beat the arrogance out of you and jerk your liver out through your mouth. I would bathe in your blood and use your skull as my drinking cup."

"Bold talk for a wisp of smoke."

Standing Wolf uttered a war cry, lunged forward, and wrapped his hands around Jack's neck. The hands did not pass through Jack, but they had no more force than that of a light breeze.

"Come on, let's finish it," Jack said. "Ask your last riddle."

Standing Wolf withdrew and began to pace.

"You must ask," Night Bird said.

"Let me think, Daughter."

"There is no time to think," she said. "Just as there is no time to answer. Ask now or forfeit."

"All right," Standing Wolf said, and then his face brightened. "I have it, a puzzle for men."

"Shut up and deal," Jack said.

"You are in a council lodge that is bigger than you have ever seen," Standing Wolf said, and such a lodge materialized around them, complete with a fire pit with dancing blue flames.

"How'd you do that?" Jack asked.

Night Bird shushed him.

"There are two exits to the lodge."

Two hide-covered doors appeared.

"A pair of fearsome warriors stand guard at each door."

The warriors materialized, in full paint and holding war clubs at the ready.

"One of the doors leads to the sunlight road," Standing Wolf said. "But beyond the other door is the black road, which leads to eternal torment. You may only choose one exit, and once chosen you must go through it. Do you understand?"

"Perfectly," Jack said. "What's the challenge?"

"One of the warriors belongs to a society that tells only the truth. He is incapable of lying. But the other warrior is a contrary and must always lie. His logic is backwards and he can never tell the truth."

"Go on," Jack said.

"You must ask only one question, and only to one warrior," Standing Wolf said. "Here is the challenge: What is it that you ask so you know which door leads to the sunlight?"

Jack fell silent. His head dropped, but behind his closed eyes he was thinking furiously about the possibilities. He imagined a deck of cards, and each warrior as a red or a black suit, and he spread them in various combinations that represented lines of logic of the green felt of the table in his mind.

"Do you have an answer," Night Bird asked.

"Yes," Jack said, while in his imagination he was scooping dead-end cards from the table until there was only one possibility remaining.

"Say it," she commanded.

"You ask one of the warriors what the other one would say if asked whether his door leads to the sunlight," Jack said. "It does not matter which of the warriors you ask."

"And?" Night Bird asked.

"The truth will be the opposite of whatever answer is given," Jack said. "It is a logical certainty."

Standing Wolf let out a sigh of relief.

"Thank you," he said.

"Why?" Jack asked. "I won."

"Yes, but the act of besting me has satisfied my honor," he said. "It was an honest contest with dire consequences. I remain dead, but at peace. Farewell. We shall not meet again."

Standing Wolf dissolved in a burst of blue flame.

Still holding the skull, Night Bird walked over to Jack and leaned close, so close that her dark hair brushed his cheek. Jack did not pull back.

"We will continue to dream for a time," she said softly. "That is the way of the redcap. We must now leave this place, but we will continue to float between worlds."

"Was this real?" Jack asked. "Or just a dream?"

"Who can say what is real, even when we are awake," Night Bird said. "Only the fullness of time will reveal. But for a little while longer we are travelers beyond the reach of pain, the demands of others, or the physical laws of the world. What we choose to do now is both fleeting and eternal."

She kissed him, and Jack could feel his longing for her grow.

"I am your shadow wife," she said.

As she leaned into him, he could feel the skull of Standing Wolf between them, pressing into his stomach. Then the skull shattered and fell in pieces at their feet.

18   *The Wind in the Corn*

Sister woke before dawn. She sat on her straw-filled pallet in the loft of the barn, her knees drawn up to her chin, while Brother slept nearby. It was cold and dark, but at least she had time to think. Overhead, she could hear the lonely honks of a flock of wild geese, and she wondered where they were headed. Someplace warmer, she hoped.

In another hour old Granger would come rambling into the barn, rubbing the stubble on his chin and fiddling with his stinking pipe and reaching a meaty hand down the front of his overalls to scratch his balls. He had a full head of dark hair, which was rarely combed, and perpetually bloodshot eyes and a way of talking at a person, instead of with them. Whenever he found Sister with a book, he would knock it out of her hands and curse and declare that girl children should not learn to read.

In the last year his rheumy eyes had begun to linger on her figure. When his old woman wasn't around, Granger would stand uncomfortably close to her and adjust his private parts and take delight when the hogs or the horses or the cows were in the act. He would be particularly crude when a mare was in season, making jokes about how hunger makes the best sauce. He had gotten increasingly bold when he could manage to find Sister alone in the fields, and it was those times that frightened her most, because she knew how strong he was. She also knew that he carried loose in the pocket of his overalls a razor he could open with the flick of a wrist. It was an old razor with a yellowed bone handle, but every day he took off his belt to strop the blade to an edge that shimmered like sunlight. He used it to cut the throats of the pigs that were hauled up by their hind feet to be bled after slaughter.

Sister knew he could use it just as easily on her throat.

That's why, one summer day after a rain, when Granger grasped the top of her head with his right hand, as if it were a melon, and he forced her onto her knees in the mud between rows of corn stalks, she did not fight. He used his free hand to unbutton one strap of his greasy overalls and then shook his shoulders, letting them fall to the ground at his feet. He stood there throbbing and proud before her, the fingers of his right hand still encircling her head, muttering words she did not understand.

"Go on, you little bitch," Granger had said, pressing himself against her closed lips. "This is what you've asked for all along. Take it." When she turned her head, Granger struck her with the back of his hand, knocking her onto her back. He grabbed her by the shoulder and turned her over, then she felt his unbearable weight on top of her. He put a hand on the back of her head and forced her chin into the mud. He shoved her skirt up to her waist and tore her underclothes.

She gave a muffled cry of pain.

Then her mind hovered somewhere above her body.

She became aware of the wind stirring the corn, the buzzing of a grasshopper flitting by, the sound of a dog baying in the distance. When he was done, he rolled to one side, his chest heaving, her bright blood smearing his private parts.

"Look at what you have made me do," he said, panting. "This is your fault. Not a word to anyone, you understand?"

Only later would she notice all of the bruises on her body, and the fine cuts on her arms and legs from the leaves of the corn stalks. Her insides bled for days and she was in pain for weeks, but whenever she thought of telling Brother or someone else what had happened, she imagined that old-bone handled razor and her mind would go again to the sound of the wind stirring in the corn.

She hated old Granger and she reckoned if she got a chance to kill him, she would do it. But he was so large, and she so small, the chance seemed remote. When it came right down to it, she thought, she didn't want to have to kill anybody. What she truly wanted was to fly away, like those wild geese, to someplace safe and warm.

But without wings, she would have to find another way to fly.

When she heard Granger rummaging in the stalls downstairs, she began to pull on as many layers of clothes as she owned. Her first chore would be to gather the ashes from the fireplaces in order to make soap. It was dull and dirty work but at least it would keep her away from the hogs for a time.

"Sally?" Granger called from below. "You up?"

"Yes, sir."

"And Andrew?"

"Brother is still asleep."

Granger muttered something about lazy children.

"Then kick his ass out of the straw," the man rumbled.

"I will," the girl said. "Then I'll be down to gather the ashes."

"Not today, girl," the man said. "The missus is sick. You come to the house to tend to her while I fetch the doctor."

Sister crept to the ladder and looked down. Granger was looking up, his watery eyes shining in the weak light of dawn, his hair sticking up from the top of his head like a rooster's comb.

"Sick?"

"That's what I said, ain't it?"

"What kind of sick?"

"Don't waste time asking questions."

"Yes, sir."

Brother was awake now, leaning on an elbow.

"What is it?" he asked.

"Don't come near the house today," she whispered.

Then she gathered her boots, slung them by the laces around her neck, and climbed down.

19 *Ostraca*

The sky was streaked with red when Jack woke and it took him many minutes to realize that it was dawn and not dusk. His tooth ached and his stomach cramped and he had a thirst that burned like fire.

Night Bird's head rested on his bare chest. Her eyes were closed, and she was breathing so lightly that at first Jack feared she was dead. He touched her shoulder and she came immediately awake, sitting up clear-eyed.

"Water," Jack said.

She flung away the elk robe and moved like silk across his body to reach the gourd. He took it from her, uncorked it, and took a deep drink, water dribbling from the corners of his mouth.

Then he stoppered the gourd and ran his forearm across his mouth.

"Ah," he said, feeling something sharp poking him in the thigh. "What is this?"

He pulled the robe aside and saw it was a shard of bone. He gave a cry and moved aside, and saw they had been sleeping amid a heap of teeth and potshard-like bone. It was the broken skull of Standing Wolf.

"Crushed," she said as casually as if she were describing a clay pipe. "During the night."

"Jesus and Mari," Jack muttered. "Did we make the beast with two backs on the bones of your father?"

Night Bird smiled slyly.

"No," she said. "Not in the waking world."

"It's the only one that matters," Jack said.

"What do you remember?"

"Very little," Jack said. "Shadows, mostly. I dreamed of my mother, who is long dead. A few others."

"Standing Wolf?"

Jack shrugged.

"Where did you go in your revery?" he asked.

"With you, of course."

"Then you tell me what happened."

Night Bird laughed.

"Expect no truth from me in the daylight world," she said. "Ah, do not look so surprised. You do remember but are afraid to say. Why deny the power of the dream world?"

"Because it was in my head all along," Jack said. "My dreams were woven into the story of Odysseus, a tale I have known since childhood. Drunk on the flesh of your redcap mushrooms, imagination and memory merged."

"Yes, you must be right," she said. "You always are. I should not attempt to trick you because you are too smart for that. I will keep my snares and my charms well clear of you now."

"Now you mock me."

"No, not at all," she said. "But someday you must tell me how you knew the answer to the final riddle."

Jack laughed.

"You have heard the old Greek tales, as well."

"Never," she said. "But what I know is that not one man in a thousand or more could have worked out the answer to the puzzle so quickly. Tell me, how did you know that asking one of the warriors what the other one would say was the key?"

Jack was silent.

"Yes, I know," Night Bird said. "A lucky guess, or I heard you talking in your dreams, or some other equally reasonable explanation. You will believe what you will, until the truth taps you on the shoulder."

Jack looked up at the burial scaffold.

"It will fall soon," he said. "It leans more than it did yesterday."

"We have been here for three days and nights," she said, slipping her dress over her head and then sweeping her hair from beneath the collar. "We must return. You have fulfilled the bargain. This I will say to Earthshaker, and you and your hog soldiers will be free to go."

"What am I to tell the chief?"

"Whatever you like," she said.

"How will I know that you won't betray me?"

Night Bird feigned offense.

"Why, Jack," she said. "After all we've been through these last three days?"

"You are a cunning little witch," he said.

"Look," she said, turning suddenly serious. She picked up a shard of the skull. "Here is the vessel that contained my father's spirit. Look at how fragile. It shattered like a broken jar." She turned it over to reveal the concave side. "And look, here, you can see the channels where his blood coursed like rivers inside his head. That same blood rushes inside my own skull. Long ago I realized that all the shaman and their sacred bundles were just mimicking the real magic that goes on inside our heads and is passed down from father to daughter, sacred bundles of thought and spirit, carried in these delicate jars perched atop our necks. The whole wide world floods our eyes and our ears, stings our nostrils, tastes bitter or sweet upon our tongues. Our moments are fleeting, but we pass the bundles on, we struggle and fight and come together in congress and sometimes we are dashed upon the rocks, spilling our dreams impotently into the open air. All the sacred and the profane exists in this jar, here."

She touched Jack's forehead.

"It would be filled by only two or three pints of water," she said, "and yet it holds all the world as we know it. The generations after us will carry worlds yet undreamed of, but our blood will rush in their ears."

She took Jack's right hand and brought his fingertips to her own forehead.

"This is my religion," she said. "It is not to be found in the sun or the sky, but only inside oneself. This is the source of all dreams and visions, all magic, all endeavor. On this sacred font I swear that I will not betray you."

She pressed the shard of her father's skull into the palm of his hand.

"Keep this," she said. "Remember the blood of my father and of me by it."

The wind stirred, rustling the fur and feathers and cloth atop the burial scaffold.

"And obey?" Jack asked. "You will obey my wishes?"

Night Bird laughed.

"You are confused," she said. "I have sworn never to betray you. I belong to you, if only in dreams. But I am not your servant."

20 *The Doctor*

Sister sat on a stool in the corner of the bedroom, watching the woman's chest rise and fall with each quick, ragged breath. Mrs. Granger—she did not know her first name—looked older than her forty years. Her skin was pale and strangely figured, and the skin on her arms had a peculiar mottled pattern that reminded Sister of a snake. Her eyes were deep in their sockets, the skin was tight over her cheekbones, and her gray hair spread like a wispy halo on the pillow.

The room stank of sweat and soiled bedclothes. A pot beside the bed was filled with something that resembled rice water but that smelled far worse and that issued from Mrs. Granger at distressingly irregular intervals. Sister knew she should empty the pot, but she could not bring herself to touch it again. It all made her feel unclean, and she longed to go to the spring house on the hillside far beyond the house and wash herself in the cold, clear water. She had never felt sorry for Mrs. Granger before, but she did now. Clearly, the woman was in misery.

There was a sponge in a shallow pan of water beside the bed, and every so often the girl would wet the woman's lips. Mrs. Granger did not like this and would shake her head and try to slap her hand away, calling her a name that Sister did not recognize.

In mid-afternoon, when the woman stopped speaking and moving, the girl became afraid. The woman was still breathing, but when the girl sponged her lips, she could feel the heat radiating from her head.

"Dear God," the girl muttered as she opened the window to let in the crisp November air. "Do not let this woman die while I am in the room with her."

A half an hour later, Sister heard the clatter of hooves and the rumbling of buggy wheels outside. A few minutes later, she heard the kitchen door open and Granger and the doctor enter the house and climb the stairs to the bedroom.

The doctor was a thin, tall man dressed in black, like a preacher, with a pair of spectacles balanced on his nose. He carried a valise in one hand.

"What are you doing, child?" the doctor asked, and rushed over and closed the window. He had a pronounced German accent. "This woman must be protected from poisonous miasmas."

"What's your name?" the girl asked sharply.

"That is a disrespectful tone," the doctor said, sitting on the edge of the bed and feeling the side of the patient's neck. "We are in luck. There is life yet in her."

"I just wanted to know how to call you," the girl said.

In a flash old Granger slapped her across the face with the back of his hand, knocking her to the floor and overturning the stool. For a few moments flashes of light spiraled in front of Sister's eyes.

"You will speak when spoken to," Granger said.

"You may call me Doktor Schwartz."

"Yes, sir," the girl said.

"Hand me my bag," the doctor said.

Schwartz took the bag from Granger and placed it on the bed.

"Is it . . ." Granger began.

"Yes, the cholera," Schwartz said. He opened the bag wide and rummaged inside. "It is caused by a number of things. Cold fruits, such as cucumbers and melons, and excessive emotion. Tell me, sir, is your wife given to excessive passion or rage?"

The farmer shuffled his feet nervously.

"She is quick to anger," he said.

"And melons?"

"Yes, we eat the watermelons we grow."

"Ah," the doctor said. "My treatment will be threefold. I will administer an emetic to purge her stomach, then a clyster to cleanse her bowels." He rummaged through some disturbing-looking implements from the bag.

The girl instinctively knew that it wasn't poison air or watermelons or a bad temper that had caused the illness, but filth and poor hygiene. She was so revolted by the thought of the woman lying in her own excrement that she knew this must be the cause, although she didn't know exactly how. The woman needed water. Instead, the doctor was going to induce vomiting and give her an enema to pass more of the rice water.

"But first thing first," Schwartz said.

He produced a scalpel from the bag, breathed on the blade, and wiped it on the sleeve of his shirt. The doctor loosened the woman's night shirt and rolled the right sleeve above her elbow. "Bring me a bowl, please." Granger nodded to the girl and she scrambled to the kitchen for one. When she returned, the doctor was probing the veins on the inner side of the woman's forearm.

Sister held out the bowl with her left hand.

"I've told you not to use that hand," Granger said, taking the bowl. "You must use the other, the right one. Next time I see you use your left hand like that I will slap the devil out of you."

"On the floor beneath," the doctor mumbled. The handle of the scalpel was between his teeth, and he was using both hands to inspect and thump the woman's arm. Granger slid the bowl beneath the limp hand.

"Ah," the doctor said, and took the scalpel from his mouth with his right hand. Then, holding the scalpel like a paint brush, made a deft cut across the inner forearm. Blood spilled down the arm to the hand like a crimson snake and dripped from the finger into the bowl and splattered next to it. Watching the flow of blood, the girl became suddenly light-headed.

"Get a rag," Granger said.

The girl did so, but she was so distracted by the sight of blood that she forget not to use her left hand to offer it to Granger. He struck her hard across the face with the back of his hand, sending her reeling against the bed.

"Satan is strong in her," Granger said.

"She's a child," Schwartz said.

"She is old enough to know how to beguile," Granger said. "I see her looking at me when we are alone. She mocks and tempts me. Whatever befalls her will be her own doing."

"I'm sorry." She offered the rag again, with her right hand.

"Don't give it to me," Granger said. "Clean up the mess on the floor."

The girl got down on her knees and began to mop up the blood from beside the bowl. She had to look to see what she was doing, and she again became woozy. She looked away but kept scrubbing.

"Watch what you're doing," Granger said. "You're moving the bowl."

"Sorry."

"Don't say that. Just mind your work."

The girl turned her head toward the floor, repositioned the bowl, and when the coppery scent of blood filled her nostrils, her vision narrowed and she suddenly could not resist the pull of gravity. She hit the wood floor, upsetting the bowl and splashing blood on herself and the toes of the doctor's boots.

"Dammit," Granger said, reaching down and jerking the girl upright by an upper arm. Her eyes fluttered but did not fully open.

"Don't," the doctor said, turning the woman's arm to achieve a better flow. "The child may be sick, as well."

Granger released the girl and she slumped to the floor.

"I will treat her when I am done with Mrs. Granger," Schwartz said.

"What?" the girl asked.

"You may require attention, as well," the doctor said.

"No," the girl said.

"What?" Granger asked.

"I mean no, sir, I'm feeling better."

The doctor looked at her, concerned.

"Still," he said. "It would be best to submit to an examination. A private word would also be in order."

The girl attempted a smile and struggled to her feet.

"You mind the doctor," Granger said. He had backed several steps away and was close to the bedroom's window.

"Yes, sir," the girl said. "I have to . . . I have to go to the privy. May I be excused?"

"Make it quick," Granger said.

The girl said she would and walked as calmly as she could for the door. Once outside the room, she closed her eyes and leaned against the wall for a few moments. She took a breath and continued on through the kitchen and to the door. She lifted the latch and swung the door open but stopped on the threshold and looked back.

"You're killing her," she shouted.

Then she ran toward the woods.

21 *Sing the Story*

"I'll be damned," Baptiste said, rising from the antelope-skin backrest in Earthshaker's lodge. "If it ain't Jack Picaro returned from the dead, with his comely witch in tow. Tell me, Mountain Jack, what you saw in hell."

Jack had paused at the door of the lodge, his feet planted wide, with Night Bird behind his shoulder, waiting for Earthshaker's permission to enter. The chief was sitting next to Baptiste, and they had been rolling dice on a plank situated between them. The chief stared at Jack for a full minute without speaking or gesturing.

"It is ourselves," Night Bird said, finally. "We are not ghosts."

The chief looked skeptical.

"Look," she said, and drew the Arkansas toothpick from Jack's belt. She closed her left hand around the blade and drew the knife sharply down. Then she held the hand up, showing the blood trickling down her palm. "Ghosts do not bleed."

The chief told them to come in.

Jack took his knife and replaced it in its scabbard.

"Do not do that again," he warned her.

"Then don't be dull," she said.

They walked into the lodge and stood by the fire, warming themselves. On either side of Earthshaker and Baptiste were the band's subchiefs. Behind the lesser men were their women, mostly wives and the sisters of wives.

"Free the soldiers," Jack said, feeling the fire warm the palms of his hands.

"The bargain is complete," Night Bird said. "He returns from the land of the dead."

"First you must come and sit close to me and tell me of the dreaming," Earthshaker said, and Baptiste translated. "Sing to me the story of this man who has been driven far from home on a fool's errand, with many twists and turns. Tell me, immortal daughter of Standing Wolf, of the deeds of this traveler in strange lands. Has the bargain been kept?"

"It has," she said.

Then she took Jack by the sleeve and led him around the council fire to stand before Earthshaker. "I am happy to sing for you, my chief, but it would be better if Picaro told the tale himself. His wisdom and courage exceed my powers of description."

Jack looked at her questioningly.

"This hero in your ancient tale," she said. "Does he lead?"

"Yes," Jack said.

"Then lead."

Night Bird walked to the rear of the lodge, behind Earthshaker, and sat cross-legged.

Jack looked around at the waiting faces. He drew himself to his full height, put his hands on his hips, and allowed the silence to build. Then he spread his arms wide and began to speak in a rumbling voice that seemed to come from the bottom of his stomach.

"Lo," he said. "Listen! We have been three days in the underworld. I have spoken to the ghosts of those long dead—"

Earthshaker held up a hand.

"Do not say their names," Baptiste cautioned. "It is bad luck."

Jack nodded.

"I have spoken to the ghosts of the unnamed dead," he continued. "These shades were well known to you in life. One of them I battled many winters ago. Our business is now resolved."

Earthshaker leaned over and spoke to Baptiste.

"The chief here wants to know how you settled things."

"There was a contest," Jack said.

"He would like to know the details," Baptiste said. "As would I. How exactly do you fight a ghost?"

Jack smiled.

"If you do not believe me," he said, "Night Bird can bear witness."

"No, Jack," Baptiste said. "Old Greasy Guts wants to hear it from you. Oh, don't worry, I'll translate accurate enough."

Jack paused.

"In the land of the dead all is shadow," he said. "Imagine a clear but moonless night where all things are rendered mist by starlight. So too are the weapons there, shadow blades and arrows and clubs, and we fought with them all. For three days and nights we battled, each inflicting grievous wounds on the other, our black blood flowing. With knives and arrow points we gouged at each other's flesh, with clubs we battered bones, and at last we fought with our hands and our feet and our teeth."

Jack paused to allow Baptiste's translation to catch up.

"Eventually we became exhausted and we fell to the ground, crying out for water," he said. "We were bloody and bruised and our flesh hung in strips like ragged pieces of cloth. We were missing teeth and chunks of our hair and one of my eyeballs was loosened from its socket and dangled on my cheek, always looking down. The floor of the underworld was stinking and slick with our gore. But from where we fell, weak and panting, we could hear the sound of running water."

Baptiste translated. Night Bird was leaning forward, her chin on her hand.

"What of the water?" Baptiste asked. "It's the chief what wants to know."

"It was the whisper of the river Lethe," Jack said. "There are five rivers that flow through the Underworld, and each of them have a special power. To drink from the river Lethe is to forget, and the dead must drink deeply to forget and leave their lives on earth behind."

Night Bird turned her head, as if to ask Jack where this was going.

"We both of us dragged ourselves on hands and knees to the river's edge, driven nearly mad by thirst, and we were about to cup our hands in it and drink our fill."

Then Jack pointed at Night Bird.

"It was then that this one saved us."

"Saved you?" Baptiste asked. "How?"

"With her knowledge," Jack said. "Being neither fully

human or fully immortal, she lives between worlds, and her knowledge of the geography of hell is unmatched. She told us not to scoop our hands in and drink too much, because then we would forget all—our families, our loves, the roles we played in either. Instead, she said, we should simply dip a hand in the river and allow the drops from our fingers to touch our tongues."

Night Bird raised her eyebrows.

"Oh, how we pleaded with her," Jack said. "Our thirst was like fire, and all we could think of was quenching it with great handfuls from the Lethe. But Night Bird insisted and so we each just dipped a hand into the water and dribbled a trace into our mouths."

Jack smiled.

"Our thirst faded and we became drowsy," Jack said. "We slept, and when we awoke our bodies had mended. My eye was back in its socket. All of our teeth were firm in our mouths. We knew almost everything about the past, but we could not remember what had brought us to fight. The shame of the ghost who cannot be named was washed away, as was my own murderous intent. We rose from the floor of the underworld as brothers. Our business concluded, we embraced and swore a pact of peace. Then we bid farewell. The unnamed crossed over into the next realm of the underworld. I followed Night Bird back to the daylight. That is the song of our three days in the underworld."

Baptiste finished the translation.

Then he shook his head.

"Well, palmer, you've outdone yourself now."

Earthshaker sat for a moment, unmoving, turning the

story over in his mind. Then he called for the medicine pipe and the wild tobacco bundle.

"You're going to smoke on it," Baptiste said. "Come sit."

Earthshaker carefully prepared the pipe and used a twig from the fire to suck life into it. When smoke was curling from the pipestone bowl, the chief lifted the pipe to the four corners of the world, saying a prayer each time. Then he handed the pipe to Jack, who puffed vigorously, the bitter tobacco stinging his throat. He passed the pipe on to Baptiste, who would then pass it to the subchiefs and other men in the lodge.

The chief looked Jack in the eyes and spoke gravely.

"Old Greasy Guts wants you to stay with the band," Baptiste said. "Winter is here and Beartooth Pass is snowed under. He says he'll give you a fat wife for company, since you don't fancy bedding Night Bird."

"Ask him about the soldiers."

"It ain't a bad offer, Jack. Take it."

"It's not what I'm here for."

"I'm not going to ask about the soldiers and spoil his mood," Baptiste said. "For some reason you seem determined to get both of our scalps lifted when there ain't no need. Bide your time and we'll see about the soldiers in the morning."

Night Bird walked over and sat next to Jack.

"Who is the hero of this tale?" she asked.

"Which tale?"

"Our tale," Night Bird said. "It has always been me, but in your telling you've cast yourself as the hero. This is an obvious weakness of character on your part."

Jack laughed.

"It is an old story and the sailor is the hero," he said.

"The witch beguiles him. She gets him drunk and turns men into hogs and lures the sailor to her bed, keeping him from returning home."

Night Bird snorted.

"All she did was reveal the true nature of men," she said. "Some would say it is a blessing to be a beast instead of a thinking being. Intoxication can be enlightening. No man ever needed tempting to climb into the bed of a beautiful woman and delay a return home. And she was the one with the power and the wisdom, no?"

"That's right."

"As I thought," Night Bird said. "But you told a pretty story."

Jack shook his head.

Night Bird leaned close in, nearly resting her chin on his shoulder.

"Before the soldiers are released," she said, "there's something you should know." She drew a small leather pouch from inside her dress and put it in Jack's hand.

It was heavy.

"Lead?" he asked. "I have plenty of rounds."

"It's not lead," she said. "It came from the soldier with hair like the sun."

She teased open the pouch and poured a bit of the contents into her palm. It was gold, gleaming warm and yellow in the firelight.

22   A Conclave of Serpents

The girl ran with the winter wind whispering in the bare trees above, an insistent voice that urged speed. Her boots kicked up dry leaves and twigs behind her. She scrambled over a log across the creek she knew, the one that led to the church downstream, and continued deeper into the woods. The trees were bigger here, and there were brambles and poison oak and other obstacles to avoid. She jumped over or darted around these, sometimes snagging the hem of her dress on a thorn and leaving behind a bit of torn blue fabric. She could feel the sweat on her hot face, despite the chill of the afternoon air, and she sucked down great gulps of air into her heaving chest in an attempt to keep her body moving. She kept moving, and soon glimpsed a river ahead, much wider than the creek she knew, glimpses of brown water flashing through the trees.

She did not know how long she had run when she hooked the toe of the left boot beneath a root. She put her hands palm-out in front of her to break the fall, but her momentum was such that she tumbled heels-over-head for several yards. She came to a stop facedown with her shoulder against a gnarled old cedar tree and her head spinning. When she tried to get to her feet, her left ankle buckled and she fell back against the cedar tree.

"Son of a bitch," she yowled, holding the ankle in both hands, her face tight with pain and rage. "Son of a fucking bitch!" Her shout echoed satisfyingly in the stark woods and somehow eased the pain.

Part of the root she had tripped on seemed to be stuck in the laces of her left boot, and she leaned over to knock it away with her hand. When she did, the root stirred and struck at her hand, but missed.

It was a copperhead.

The girl screamed and rolled away.

The snake raised its lumpy reddish head, flicking its tongue from the side of its mouth. Its body was pinkish tan with darker, chestnut-colored bands that looked like hourglasses. The tip of its tail was vibrating, which caused a rustling in the leaves.

Pushing against the ground with her right boot and using the heels of her hands, the girl clawed her way backward. Then her right hand touched something dry and scaley. She had backed into a ball of copperheads, males knotted in mating around a female. The girl shrieked and snatched back her hand, but not before three of the snakes lashed out almost quicker than she could see and plunged their fangs into the back of her hand.

She rose on her one good foot and hopped about, two of the snakes still hanging from her hand. She screamed and whipped her arm back and forth, flinging the snakes away. Then she looked down in horror and realized the ground was covered in copperheads. There were dozens if not hundreds of them, all spread around the cedar tree, with some hanging from the low branches. The girl stumbled away. But before she had made it twenty yards her head felt numb and sparkles floated where she looked.

"No," she muttered, dragging her left ankle. "Please God, don't let me die among snakes."

When she finally fell, another thirty yards on, it was as if someone had thrown a black curtain over the world. She could not see, but she could hear the sound of the wind above. She also could hear the voices of men approaching, speaking in low voices.

When she woke, she was in a rope bed with a heavy quilt spread over her. It was morning because she could hear cocks crowing in the distance. The bed was in a rough-hewn cabin chinked with mud and clay. On the table beside the bed was a white china pitcher of water and a mug.

She tried to sit up, but could not.

She tried to move her right arm, but could not. The arm was covered by a plaid cloth.

"Where am I?" she asked.

"You must be thirsty."

A black woman came and poured the chipped cup full of water and placed it in the girl's left hand. The woman was dressed in a worn but clean white blouse, a dark skirt, and her hair was bound in a strip of red cloth. The girl drank one, and then another cup of water. The black woman replaced the cup on the side table.

"Thank you," the girl said. "Now, tell me where I am."

"You're at Eury's cabin," the woman said.

"Are you Eury?"

"Who else would I be, child?" the woman asked. "Some men brought you here last night. They were afraid you would die, but I knew you would not. Copperhead bites will make you mighty sick, but even three are not enough to kill."

Eury picked up something from the table and held it up. It was a fang.

"This was still hanging in your arm," she said.

"Can I look at my hand?"

"If you wish."

The woman removed the cloth.

The girl's right hand was purple and swollen to the size of three hands. Smeared over it was a poultice of yellow clay and ferns the girl didn't recognize.

"Sonuvabitch."

"No more of that," Eury said.

"I can't feel my hand. Am I going to lose it?"

"You might," Eury said.

The girl's eyes went wide.

"Would you rather me lie to you?"

"No," she said.

"We'll know in time," Eury said. "A few days or a few weeks. It's hard to reckon yet what kind of price the serpents will exact. You might keep the hand, and even regain full use of it, but there could be other maladies."

"Such as?"

"It could leave you with some type of nervous tick," Eury said. "Or you might be barren."

"You talk about the copperheads as if they were vengeful."

"They are among the most vengeful of creatures," Eury said. "You stumbled into their conclave. That cedar tree is the throne at the center of their kingdom. It has been that way for years, and when so many gather together they delay hibernation because their business is done. You interrupted that business. I think they were talking about the comet."

"How do you know this?"

"They have been using that tree for years. Always best to avoid it this time of year."

"That's not what I meant."

Eury paused.

"I'm a power doctor," she said. "I heal the sick the old-time way."

"Magic."

"Some call it that."

"There was a river just beyond. What was it?"

"The Salt," Eury said. "We're just outside town."

"Which town?"

"Ashburn."

"How far are we from the Mississippi?"

"You ask a powerful lot of questions for a sick white girl."

"I want to know where I am in the world."

"The Salt empties into the 'Sip, about five miles yonder."

The girl closed her eyes, resolving to remember these details.

"Is the Mississippi really as big as they say?"

"Miles across in places," Eury said.

The girl tried to imagine it.

"I've read stories of a great bird that hunts the Mississippi, looking to devour men," the girl said. "Or at least it used to. A painting of two of them was found on the side of a cliff at Alton, Illinois, down near St. Louis. The Indians said they were the Piasa birds. They have antlers like a deer, red eyes, a face like a man's, a body that's covered in scales, and a long tail that ends in fins like a fish."

"Such stories are nonsense," Eury said.

"But it captures the imagination, doesn't it?"

"It captures something," Eury said. "Now it's time for you to tell me your name."

"Don't have one."

"Everybody has a name."

"Well, I have one but I don't know what," the girl said. "The folks I live with call me something but it ain't true."

"You're an orphan."

"Yes."

"What's the name of the people you live with?"

The girl shook her head.

"Tell me," Eury said. "I'll find out anyway."

"Granger."

"You are twenty miles from home."

"I wish it was twenty thousand," the girl said. "But I have to go back. If I don't, the old man will take it out on my brother something fierce. It's better if he takes it out on me."

"It will be a spell before you can go back. Tell me how the old man takes it out on you."

The girl was silent.

"Do you know how it is with women and men?"

Eury looked at her with kindness.

"At least tell me what they call you, even if it's wrong."

"No, I hate it," the girl said. "Who were those men what found me in the woods?"

"Never you mind," Eury said. "You don't tell anybody about them. We're going to tell folks that I found you."

"But you didn't."

"We're going to play act like I did. It's important."

"All right," the girl said.

"No," Eury said. "You must swear."

"I swear to God."

Eury stared at her as if she were examining her soul.

"I'm satisfied," she said. "We are going to have a few nights together, you and me. By and by I'll send word to the Granger place for somebody to fetch you, but you need to rest up."

"Thank you."

"I'll be gone during daylight," Eury said, "but I'll ask my cousin to come keep you company. When the sun goes down, we'll have time to talk. I want to know more about your life at the Granger place. And we'll talk about some things it's time you learned."

The girl slept late into the next morning, and when she woke there was a large black woman of about forty sitting next to the bed, humming to herself. She had soft eyes and strong hands and she seemed protective of the child.

"Good morning," the woman said.

Sleepily, the girl tried to stretch, forgetting about her hand until pain knifed all the way to the shoulder.

"It will hurt like that for a few more days," the woman said. "Then the swelling will go down and eventually the black will turn to purple and then to blue and then we will see what there is to see."

"Where's Eury?"

"Working," the woman said.

"Who are you?" the girl asked, a bit sharply.

"I'm Eury's cousin," she said. "My name is Portia."

"Thirsty," the girl said.

The woman poured her some water in the cup and the girl drank half of it down.

"You're staring at me like you know me," the girl said, struggling to get a better grip on the cup with just one hand.

"I do know you," Portia said.

"I've never seen you in my life."

"That's not true," Portia said. "You and your brother saw me on the day you were born. We haven't seen each other since you were babies, and I was your wet nurse, but I know you."

"That's ignorant," the girl said, taking another sip of water.

"You're rude," Portia said. "I've told my cousin Eury the story of your birth many times, and she remembered it. Because of your age and you mentioned a brother, she thought she knew who you were. But sent for me to make sure. Now that I see you, I see your mother."

The girl dropped the cup and it rolled from the side of the bed and shattered on the floor.

"Tell me about my mother."

"You look like her, child. Same dark hair, those blue eyes, the pale skin. Delicate nose and high cheekbones. She was a proud and good woman who loved you very much."

"What was her name?"

Portia began to answer, but the girl stopped her with another question.

"No," she said. "Tell me my name first. Do you know it?"

"April."

"April!" the girl said, and a thrill ran through her like the time she had put her back against the wall of the whitewashed church and listened to the sacred harp singing. "April. Now that I know my name, it feels strange on my tongue."

"It suits you," Portia said.

"April," the girl said again. "April!"

"Yes."

"And my brother?"

"Augustus," the woman said.

"What strange names."

"Your name is for the ship that carried your father to America," Portia said. "Your brother's name is for the month of your birth."

"You knew my father?"

"No, but he had a reputation. I knew that."

"It was a good reputation?"

"It was a reputation," Portia said.

"My mother's name. Tell me."

"Abella Rapaille."

"Spell it."

She did.

"French," the girl said.

"Yes. She died giving birth to you."

"And my father?"

"Jacques."

"Jacques Rapaille."

"No," Portia said. "Your mother and your father were not married. His last name was Aguirre."

The girl frowned.

"Spell it."

"I cannot," she said.

"Spanish?"

"I don't know, child," Portia said. "Nobody seemed to know for certain. He came from the Old World, but not a country that many seemed to know."

"And his reputation?"

"He was brilliant," she said. "A gun maker. But also a gambler and rooster."

"Was my mother ashamed?"

"She was not ashamed of you or your brother. Her dying wish was for me to tell you that, and now the Lord has arranged it so that I could, thirteen years on. But you had to fall into the serpents at the base of the Tree of the Knowledge of Good and Evil. The Lord has tested you as surely as He tested Job."

"I don't think it was that tree," April said. "Where is my father now?"

"Gone."

"Dead?"

"Could be," Portia said. "He ran off before you were born."

"Because my mother was with child?"

"I don't think he knew, child," Portia said. "It seems

your mother did not tell him. No, he ran because of some other trouble. Remember when I said he was from the Old World? Well, he was indentured in the old way to your mother's family."

"Indentured?"

"He had sold his freedom for a period of years for passage to America."

"He was a slave."

"No," Portia said. "It was his choice, and his indenture would have ended in time. But he grew impatient. The guns he made were the best in St. Louis and maybe the whole wide world. He wanted to be known for them—and to profit from them."

April felt dizzy. She closed her eyes.

"Do not send word to old Granger," she said. "I do not want him to know where I am. He has treated me badly."

"What kind of bad?" Portia asked.

"Bad," April said. "In the way that men do."

"Not all men, honey," Portia said.

"The bad ones," April said drowsily. "They are all bad, just some are worse."

"Tell me, child, do you have your monthlies?"

"What?"

"Do you bleed?"

"Sometimes," she said. "After."

"No," the woman said. "Does your body follow the moon's cycles?"

"Oh, that," she said. "No, never."

"This Granger is a wicked man," she said. "But at least . . ."

"What?"

"Never you mind," Portia said. "Rest some now."

"I will," April said. "But just one more question, please."

"Ask, child."

"If our mother had family, why didn't they take us in?"

Portia clasped the girl's hand.

"The family was ashamed," she said. "They did not want you. And they sold you, in the old way, as babies."

23 Hate from Afar

Jack used the Damascus toothpick to cut the ropes binding the hands of the yellow-haired soldier. The soldier stretched his fingers while he looked about apprehensively with eyes that were bloodshot from the wind and snow.

"It's all right," Jack said. "They won't hurt you now."

The soldier said he didn't believe him.

"You must be Fry," Jack said. "And the other two, Butler and Henley?"

Jack had already freed the pair of dark-haired soldiers, and they had taken refuge from the snow by crouching beneath a ratty lodgeskin that had been thrown over a rail to make a lean-to. They were eating corn and squash that Night Bird had carried from Earthshaker's lodge.

"That's right," Fry said, the big flakes clinging to his hair. "Who might you be?"

"I might be Jack Picaro."

"Mountain Jack?" Fry asked. "Everybody thought you was dead."

"Well, they thought wrong," Jack said. "Tell me about this."

Jack showed him the pouch that contained the gold.

"You know what it is?"

"Yes."

"Then talk," Jack said.

"A creek," Fry said. "About five miles west of here. We panned it from the black sand along the creek bank."

"All three of you?"

"Just me," Fry said. "The others were across the next ridge."

"You didn't tell the others, did you?"

"Why wouldn't I?"

"A man alone finds a year's worth of soldier's wages in gold in the ground," Jack said. "It's what you were sent to find. But it's a year's worth of wages. It was easy just to slip it in your pocket and not tell the others. Maybe later, years after the army, you can come back to the creek and make your fortune. Is that about it?"

"That's about it," Fry said.

"But you have a problem," Jack said.

"What's that?"

"You won't be able to find the creek again five years or even five months from now," he said. "The mountains are a puzzle that don't stay solved. We're just five miles away, and your memory is fresh. But the more time and distance you put between yourself and this place, the slimmer your odds become."

The soldier scratched his neck.

"I ain't giving it up to you," he said. "I'll tell Maguire about it first."

"You tell the army what you found and you'll start a

war," Jack said. "Come spring, troops will pour into these mountains and hell will follow, because Earthshaker won't let anybody budge him off his land. And your share of any gold that is clawed out of the ground is going to be just about zero."

"I have to eat something," Fry said, starting for the lean-to. "I'm so hungry I can't think."

Jack grabbed him by the arm.

"No," he said. "We settle this now, before you talk to the others."

"What do you want?"

"We're going to leave here tomorrow bound for Fort Nonsense," Jack said. "On the way I want you and me to take a little detour. Show me the creek and the place you found the gold. Then I never want you to speak of it again. You get back to Nonsense, and you tell Maguire and Bonneville and whoever else that asks that you found nothing."

"Why should I help you?"

"The Crows won't hurt you, but I will," Jack said. "Show me where it is, and I will come back when it's safe, without starting a war."

"What's stopping me from coming back my own self and beat you to it?"

"Nothing," Jack said, "except the entire Crow nation."

Fry strode off to the lean-to.

Night Bird came up to Jack.

"Will there be war?" she asked.

"No," Jack said. "Not now."

"Pity," Night Bird said. "Now that my father has gone, I'm bored."

"War would not be kind to your people."

She smiled.

"You are naive," she said. "Comparatively few are killed by bullets and arrows. Many more die of sickness, of starvation, of decisions made far away. Better for the Crows to fight when our numbers are still strong, while there is still a chance to win. Better to die with honor in battle than to fade away. Don't you feel the same?"

"I have felt the same, yes."

"You are leaving in the morning?"

"There are some things to take care of," Jack said. "I will have to trade the pair of rifles taken from the dead soldiers at the pass to Earthshaker for horses for these men. We will need food and robes and other things. With the pass closed, it will take weeks to return home."

"If you return at all," Night Bird said. "Winter makes for rough travel."

"It's fair enough now, but if the weather doesn't hold, we'll find a Mandan village to spend the worst of it," Jack said. "I'm sure that would delight Baptiste."

"Don't spend the winter in a muddy Mandan lodge," Night Bird said. "They burrow into the earth like moles. Stay here, with me, beneath warm robes in a proper lodge of poles and bison skin."

"You are too fierce for me," Jack said. "Your people are too fierce. How long before your old husband or a would-be lover decides to split my skull with a trade axe?"

"This is not a worry," she said. "You would kill him."

"Like I said, fierce. You already haunt my nights. Is that not enough?"

"This is not the reason," Night Bird said. "It is the woman who waits along the Stinking Water River. She must be a beauty with strong magic. I hate her from afar."

"Home," Jack said. "I long for home."

"Let us say farewell," Night Bird said, "for I will not watch you ride away in the morning like some lovesick cow. I will remain here, and take many lovers for a winter or two, and then before I have grown too old, I will go to the wide river and follow its course down to the heart of your country. There I will seek my grandfather Clark and my life's journey will be complete."

24   *Stealing Fire*

About midnight at the cabin there was a rapping at the door and Eury extinguished the candle on the table by licking her fingers and snuffing out the flame. Then she went to the door and a white man slipped inside. Eury leaned out of the doorway and made sure nobody was stirring, then she ducked back into the cabin and set the door latch.

"Was you followed?" Eury said.

"No," the man said.

It was April's third night at the cabin. Eury had allowed her to stay in the only bed in the cabin while the woman slept on the floor, but this night April was feeling well enough to sit at the table where the candle curled smoke upward from a still-glowing wick. But there was enough moonlight coming in through the windows that April could study the man's features.

The man was twenty-five or thirty, April reckoned, with sandy hair that was a bit too long and a pair of spectacles with lenses that seemed the size of dinner plates. His nose was hawk-like, and his lips thin and blue-looking in the moonlight. He wore a dark suit, like a preacher, and in his right hand he clutched a pocket Bible.

"How's the girl?" the man asked.

"Mending," Eury said.

"Can she be trusted?"

"You can trust me. My name's April. Did you find me in the woods?"

"Yes, and brought you here."

"Thank you," April said. "What's your name?"

"I cannot tell you," he said. "I'm sorry."

"Because what you're doing is criminal."

"That's enough," Eury said.

"Are you robbers?"

"Some people think so."

"Stop it, April."

"No, it's all right," the man said. "God put her in our path for a reason. She is one of us now. When I asked if you could be trusted, April, what I meant was can you keep a secret?"

"All I have are secrets."

"Then keep ours," he said.

"Tell me your name, then."

"Briggs," the man said. "I teach at the Mission Institute at Quincy, on the other side of the river. We steal slaves. We are abolitionists."

April blinked.

"You mean like William Lloyd Garrison."

"Yes, I suppose," the man said. "How do you know of him?"

"He is the most hated man in America," April said. "At least that's what the cartoons in the St. Louis papers say. I'm not sure I agree with them."

"How is this girl reading newspapers?"

"The people I live with collect old newspapers from their neighbors and bundle them for the privy," April said. "I take my time to read them first, and some I'll save if I want to read them again. I steal books when I can. When I was little, I was sent to a subscription school down the road to learn my letters so I could read Bible verses aloud. I can say now I favor the newspapers over that book in your hand."

"You may change your mind as you get older," the man said.

"Are you alone?"

"Two friends are waiting in the woods," he said.

"Where do you take the slaves?"

"Canada," Briggs said. "Slavery is outlawed there."

"But I've read Illinois is a free state."

"It is in name only," Briggs said. "The Black Act of 1819 continues forms of slavery and indentured servitude, and runaways are returned to their masters in other states."

April remembered what Portia had said about her father's indenture.

"You are against indentured servitude, as well?"

"Yes, it is inhumane, as well."

"How many slaves have you sent to Canada?"

"None, yet," Briggs said. "Finding you in a distressed state in the woods disrupted our plan. But we will try again, during the next new moon. The Mission Institute is consecrated to fight this stain on our land."

"You're risking everything," April said.

"It is dangerous work," Briggs said. "If we are caught, we will be imprisoned or worse. But, as the book says,

He who observes the wind will not sow, and he who regards the clouds will not reap. We will reap the seeds of goodness."

April wished that she was brave enough herself not to observe the wind or regard the clouds. As she was thinking this, the fingers of her left hand twitched.

"Where does courage come from?" she asked.

"From God," Briggs said.

Eury laughed.

"For a few," she said. "For the lucky few. For the rest of us, child, it comes from desperation."

25   *A New Moon*

Under the new moon the girl slipped into the barn and felt her way up the ladder to the loft. Her right hand had returned to its normal size, but still ached and was mottled purple. She crossed to where her brother slept, the boards creaking beneath her boots. He stirred, and she shushed his cry.

"Whisper," she said.

"You're alive," he said. "Everybody thought you was dead."

"Well, I ain't," April said. "Now, remember what I told you about when it's time, you must do what I say and not ask questions?"

"Yes."

"It's time," she said. "Get dressed."

"Why?"

"That's a question," April said.

The boy mumbled he was sorry.

"We're leaving here," she said. "Grab a burlap sack and put a few things to eat in it. Pick some things from the smokehouse. Get some vegetables. But not too full, because we have to travel light."

"Where are we going?"

"What did I say?"

"I don't know why I have to take orders from—"

She slapped him across the mouth.

"That's why," she said. "That's all I have time to explain. Your choice is to stay here or go with me. Which is it?"

"Go with you," the boy said through stinging lips.

"Good," she said. "Now, give me your cap."

He looked at her.

"Do as I say."

"Yes, Sister."

"You must call me April from now on."

The boy clamped his jaw tight to keep from asking a question.

"And from now on I will call you Augustus—no, Gus. The time for us to be known only as Sister and Brother is over."

His eyes were wide, as if he were looking at a lunatic.

"I'll explain it later," she said. "It will make sense then."

He nodded.

"After filling the burlap sack, come back to the barn," she said. "I want you to free all of the horses and mules. Make sure they all get clear of the barn, and open the paddock gate. You'll probably have to swat Charley to get him to leave." Charley was the oldest and most stubborn mule. "We're not stealing them, just . . . making it seem like somebody tried to steal them."

Gus nodded.

"I'll be up at the house while you're doing this," April said. "I'll have to deal with the old woman first—"

"Mrs. Granger is dead. They buried her yesterday morning out back of the house. It was the black cholera."

"It wasn't the cholera, it was that damn fool doctor," April said. "You didn't go inside the house before she died, did you?"

"No."

"I suppose old Granger still draws breath?"

"Yes."

"Not even sick?"

"No."

"Of course not," April said. "All right, that makes it simpler. I'll be up to the house for a spell. Not more than a quarter of an hour. You do all the things I told you, then you wait at the edge of the field and watch the house. When you see a light, you run back behind to the creek. I'll meet you there."

"You're scaring me," Gus said.

"There's no time to be scared," April said. "Now, go on, find a sack."

The boy finished pulling on his boots and climbed down the ladder.

April walked over to the hay door and swung it open so she could have a view of the house. Smoke trailed from the chimney. Every window was dark. Far above the roof peak, the comet glowed faintly in the sky.

Using both hands, she gathered her hair on top of her head and put on her brother's cap. It was a black wool cap, worn, with a short brim, the kind a deckhand on a steamboat would wear. She brushed some stray hairs beneath the cap and pulled it firmly down, nearly to her ears. She smoothed her skirt and knelt down and made sure the laces of her boots were fast. Then she turned, found the ladder by feel in the dark, and climbed quickly down. On her way out of the barn she took a canvas seed sack hanging from a post and slung it across her shoulders.

April put her left hand to the kitchen door but found it was securely latched from inside. She had expected as much, but it would have been convenient if old Granger had left it open.

There was a maple tree close by the kitchen, and she climbed up and stepped gently over onto the roof of the kitchen. Then she crept across to the upstairs window that overlooked the rear of the house. She could see nothing through the glass. She put her hands on the window jamb and felt with her fingertips for leverage, but she was shaking so hard she had to stop. It was cold out, not far above freezing, but she felt as if she were burning up. She put a hand to her forehead and it seemed as if she was touching an iron. Suddenly she was aware of how dry her lips were, and how salty, and desperately wanted a drink of water.

Wind and clouds, she told herself silently. *Is that what it is to be for the rest of my life? If not, stop shaking and get on with it.*

She put her hands to the window again, palms up, spread her fingers wide against the rail, and gently pushed. It remained firm for a few seconds and then gave with a sharp sound like the snapping of a twig. April waited for anything to stir inside, but there was nothing. She raised the window more, enough to allow her to duck inside, and then she eased herself down to the floor.

There was just one room upstairs.

At the end opposite were the stairs, and April walked toward them. Granger's bedroom was downstairs. As she approached the stairs, she heard his snoring, from the bed downstairs where she had watched the doctor bleed the old woman.

She tested each tread with her foot before putting her full weight on it, fearing that a creak would betray her. It was slow going, one stairstep at a time, and by the time she reached the bottom her calves were quivering. She rubbed them to get the blood flowing again, and then went down the hall. The fireplace in the room at the front of the house was well-banked and emitted only a little orange glow.

The door to the bedroom was ajar.

Granger was still snoring.

April slowly pushed the door, fearing the hinges would protest. She opened it just far enough to slip inside. The room was dark, but she remembered where the furniture and the bed were. Now that she was so close to him, she found that her courage had grown. She walked across the room to the chair she knew would be beside the bed. She found Granger's overalls where he had thrown them, across the back of the chair. She rifled through the pockets until she found the bone-handled razor.

From the way Granger was snoring, she knew he was in bed opposite of how someone would normally sleep in it. The head of the bed was against the wall. But his head was at the foot.

Then she made her way around until she stood directly behind him.

It was still too dark to make out much. It was all just

shadows, but she stared so hard into the darkness that flashes of light floated in front of her eyes. This distracted her, so she closed her eyes and concentrated on the sound of the snoring, aligning herself with it, imagining the position of his head. She couldn't be more than a few inches away.

She opened the razor with both hands, then got a good grip on it with her left hand. She contemplated for a moment the best angle to strike. Then she planted her feet as if she were about to swing a bat. She carefully leaned forward, her arm encircling Granger's head, until she could feel his hot breath on the heel of her left hand. Then she knew exactly where his throat was.

Then the snoring stopped.

April drew the blade toward her and felt it bite into flesh. For an instant her mind went to the cornfield, to the wind sighing between the stalks, but she forced herself back into the moment. She reached out with her right hand and gathered a fistful of Granger's hair and jerked his head backward, drawing the razor cleanly across his throat. He bucked and struggled and would have soon been out of her grasp had it not been for the freshly sharpened and stropped razor, which effortlessly opened his throat. It was both easier and harder than she had imagined.

She jumped back, still clutching the razor.

There was a terrible gurgling sound and she heard Granger trying to form words, but only air came out. He rolled off the bed and crashed to the floor, kicking, and knocked over the chair. The rungs crashed into April's shins, and she yelped, more from surprise than pain, and dropped the razor.

The worst was over, but there was still quick work to do.

She ran from the room, took a candle from the mantel, and stirred the fire with a poker. Tongues of flame shot up from the ashes, and she lit the candle. Then she went back to the bedroom door, chasing darkness as she went, and pushed the door open wide.

Granger was on the floor beside the bed, his body twisted. He was naked, and she was revolted by the amount of dark hair on his chest and his upper arms and from his belly to his genitals.

His balls hung against his thigh, like a pair of eggs in wet cheesecloth, and his penis was purple and soft, like a dog's. His genitals were a source of both revulsion and fascination for April, and she wished she could have made a more elaborate plan, one that would have involved castration and humiliation before death. But that would have been beyond both her ability and her strength, and likely would have meant her end instead. Still, the quick death for Granger seemed all too kind.

Granger's right arm was stretched out, fingers reaching for something leaning against the wall, near the overturned chair. It was the butt of his double-barreled shotgun. April realized that was what he had been trying for when he rolled from the bed to the floor.

Then Granger's right index finger quivered, as if he were about to spring up and seize the shotgun. April snatched the gun from the wall, holding it by the barrel. It was cold and heavy in her hand. She did not like the feel and did not think she ever could.

Holding the shotgun, she waited. But there was no more movement.

Granger's head was flung back in death, his open eyes already turned milky. Beneath his mouth there looked to be another mouth, one that ran from his right ear and went down toward his left collarbone, red and wet with flecks of yellow fat. Blood seeped across the floor.

April bent over and spat in his dead face.

Then she flung the shotgun onto the bed.

Then she took off her brother's cap, letting her hair spill to her shoulders. She turned the cap inside out, then leaned down and, wearing the hat like a glove, soaked up as much blood and gore as it would hold. Then she shoved the sticky mess into the seed sack.

There was no point in looking for silver in the house, because old Granger wouldn't have much. Everything worth stealing April already had. She snatched a coal oil lamp from a side table, flung away the chimney, unscrewed the burner, and pour the contents over Granger and the bed. She found another lamp and did the same, and then she tossed the candle onto the bed. A blue flame raced across the bed, down to the floor, and danced over Granger's body.

April went to the bedroom door. The fire was growing, so bright now that she could not look into the middle of it. Granger's hair was burning, and the smell was sickening. The bed was also on fire. One barrel of the shotgun discharged from the heat, the buckshot blowing a hedge apple–sized hole in the bedroom wall. The recoil knocked the gun from the bed, and it hit the floor and came to rest across Granger's body. When the second barrel went, the buckshot tore a chunk of flesh from the dead man's upper thigh, spraying blood and bone across the floor.

April winced.

Then she walked back into the bedroom and found the razor on the floor. The fire had not yet reached it, but when she stopped to pick it up she could feel the heat washing in waves over her face, and it was suddenly hard to breathe. She buried her face in the crook of her right arm and ran to the hall. There, she closed the razor, slipped it into the pocket of her dress, and allowed herself a smile.

April went to the kitchen, opened the cupboards, and pulled everything down. Soon the floor was filthy with flour and cornmeal, prickly with broken crockery, and sticky with molasses. When she reckoned she had done enough to make it look like robbers she wiped her hands on a towel and then threw that into the mess.

Then she left the house, leaving the back door open.

She walked calmly across the yard and down to the barn. She looked inside and saw all the horses were gone. She took a hay hook from among the tools hanging overhead and walked outside. She reached inside the seed bag, took out the bloody cap, and smeared the point of the hook with blood. Then she swung the hay hook as hard as she could and drove it into the barn door, at about the height of her own head. She took the cap and pushed it up against the door, staining the wood with gore, then turned the cap right side out again and tossed it on the ground.

She looked back at the house.

The downstairs windows were aglow with flame.

She retraced her steps across the mud lot until her boots touched grass, then she turned for the woods. Even in the dark she could go quickly, because she knew the path well. When she reached the creek, she put some stones in the feed sack and threw it in the water.

"What have you done?" Gus asked.

He was standing beside a tree, lost in the shadows.

"What I had to do," April said. "Now, we've got some walking to do. There's some men with a boat tonight. We're going to give them a hand, and they're going to carry us over to the Illinois side."

26 *Honor*

Jack was impatient. He was standing at the edge of the creek, cradling the 1803 rifle, keeping watch as Fry walked back and forth on the bank, the pebbles crunching beneath his feet. He held a tin dinner plate.

"Are you sure this is the place?" Jack asked.

"Yes," Fry said.

"You said that about the last three places," Jack said. "It's getting late. The others will have expected us to have returned by now. I told Baptiste that if we weren't back by mid-afternoon, they were to reckon us for dead and go on without us. Besides, I can't shake the feeling of eyes on us."

"I recognize that boulder across the river," Fry said. "The one that looks like George Washington in profile."

"I don't see the resemblance," Jack said. "Looks more like Benjamin Franklin to me."

The soldier walked back and forth along the bank, hopping over driftwood, sometimes digging a boot heel into the sand. He walked to the water's edge and used his hands to scoop sand and gravel into the pan, then began to shake it to separate out the larger material. He picked these bits out and tossed them aside, and then began to shake the pan more. Again, he removed material. After doing this a dozen times, he walked out into the water a few feet, crouched down, and submerged the pan in the cold, clear flowing water.

"You'll regret that when those boots freeze to your feet tonight," Jack said.

"I'll dry 'em," Fry said.

The water washed over the pan's contents as Fry rocked the pan from side to side. Every so often he would use the side of his hand to brush more material away, and then continue rocking. Then he stopped and plucked something the size of a gooseberry from the pan. Holding it between his thumb and forefinger, he brought it close to his face.

It was a piece of quartz, shot through with gold.

"This is the place," Fry said.

Jack walked over.

"Let me see," he said.

Fry reluctantly handed the piece over.

"You're right," Jack said. "It is gold."

"There's more bits in the pan," Fry said.

"Leave it," Jack said.

"Are you mad?" Fry asked. "We're probably standing on a fortune, right here under our boots. In an hour we could be set for the rest of our lives."

"If we stay, an hour might be all the life we have left," Jack said. "If the Crows find us here, they're going to have our livers for breakfast. We've found the spot, across from old Ben."

Jack handed the quartz nugget back to Fry.

"Smooth the hole out," he said. "It's time to get on the horses and get the hell out of here. For all we know, Earthshaker's men are already watching us. We'd never know until they decided to ventilate us with arrows."

"It ain't going to hurt to spend just a little more time," Fry said, turning back to the hole he had scooped out. "It's worth the risk."

"How long did you spend trussed up like a Christmas goose and starved and beaten by the Crows?" Jack said. "That wasn't enough for you? You'd still be there, either miserable or dead, if I hadn't come along. You're in debt to me, and I say we move."

Fry was motionless.

"I can't leave you here," Jack said. "You'll tell Earth-shaker everything you know once they start pulling your fingernails out, and then they'll come after the rest of us."

"Go to hell," Fry said over his shoulder.

"This is tiring," Jack said.

"What are you going to do, shoot me?" Fry asked.

Jack walked over and kicked the pan out of his hand.

"All right," Fry said. "You win."

"We can return in seasons to come," Jack said. "Either or both of us, as agreed."

Fry picked up the pan and smoothed out the hole with his feet. Then he followed Jack to the horses, which were tied to some trees at the edge of the forest, thirty yards away. Jack slid the rifle into the scabbard hanging from 'Clipse's saddle. He touched the horse affectionately on the muzzle, then reached to untie the rope from the trunk of the tree. There was a male cardinal in the tree, hopping from branch to branch. Jack could not help but stare at it for a moment. When he turned back, the rope in his hand, Fry was pointing a rifle at his head. The hammer was cocked and Fry's forefinger was in the trigger guard.

"I've heard of your reputation," he said, "but I ain't seen nothing that says you deserve it. It seems what you do best is talk. I haven't seen you do a damn thing except talk. And I'm hell and tired of your conversation."

"Take it easy," Jack said coolly. "Don't pull that trigger."

"I kill you and I get to stay and load my pockets up," Fry said. "And with you dead, nobody knows this place but me. I get to come back without worry that you've beaten me to it."

"I'm asking you polite to lower the rifle."

"Ah, now you're pleading for your life."

"Nope," Jack said. "It's just that if you blow my brains out, the Crows are likely to hear the shot and you'll be dead, too. Or it might not be the Crows. The Blackfeet nation could have a war party here, and they'd oblige to kill you, as well, although I hear they take their time doing it."

"You're just trying to put a scare into me."

"No," Jack said. "I'm trying to put some sense into you."

"Are you calling me a fool?"

"Put down the rifle and we'll forget about this," Jack said. "You probably are not your right self, considering what you've been through. Privation can do peculiar things to a man, make him do things he ordinarily wouldn't do. I reckon that whoever you are now, it isn't who you want to be."

"Rich, you mean?" Fry asked.

"Crazy," Jack said.

Fry took three steps forward, the end of the barrel wavering just a few inches from Jack's nose.

"Didn't the army teach you not to do that?"

"Do what?"

The cardinal in the tree suddenly took flight, a streak of red passing close by. Fry's eyes darted in the bird's direction.

"This," Jack said.

Jack swept his left arm upward and knocked the barrel away while reaching for the lock with his right hand. His goal was to jam his finger between the flint and frizzen to keep the rifle from firing, but he was a bit too late. The hammer fell and sparked the pan. The rifle fired into the air, followed by a cloud of blue smoke drifting with the breeze. 'Clipse flung his head and moved ten yards away, trailing his reins.

"Damn you," Jack said, jerking the rifle out of Fry's hands. "That could just be the death of us."

He tossed the rifle in disgust on the creek bank.

"You'll wish you had kept that as a club," Fry said.

Fry drew a knife from his belt and stepped between Jack and 'Clipse, where the 1803 rested in the scabbard. Jack put his hand on the hilt of the Damascus at his waist and turned to face Fry, but he kept his feet planted.

"Come on," Jack said, urging Fry to approach. "Make your move."

Fry stepped awkwardly forward and made a pair of slashing motions with the blade. Jack easily ducked and stepped out of the way. Then he drew the Damascus and held it casually in his right hand.

"The army apparently doesn't teach you knife fighting, either," Jack said. "The trick is to drop your shoulders and relax. It gives you a little more accuracy and a lot more speed."

Jack took two steps forward, a motion that seemed as if he were gliding, and flicked the tip of the Damascus across Fry's ear, separating the earlobe. The soldier slapped his hand against the wound, blood pouring from his fingers.

"Drop the knife," Jack said.

"Only when you're dead."

The soldier lunged at Jack, making wide sweeping motions with his knife. Jack stepped back, just out of reach of the blade each time. Then he stepped forward, planted a boot on top of the soldier's foot so he couldn't get away, and brought the Damascus down decisively on Fry's wrist, severing the tendons. Fry's knife dropped to the ground.

Jack released the weight on the foot, brought the Damascus back, and drove its hilt into the bridge of Fry's nose. The soldier staggered backward, streams of blood running from his nostrils, his eyes squeezed tight against the pain.

"Give up?" Jack asked.

"No!"

"Then I'm going to have to kill you," Jack said.

Jack drove the Damascus into a spot just below the soldier's solar plexus. The knife parted the soldier's uniform as if it were paper. The knife went in all the way to the hilt.

Fry looked down at the knife and then back at Jack.

"I'll be damned," he said.

"That's a fair bet," Jack said.

Jack put a hand on Fry's chest and pushed him off the blade.

The soldier stumbled backward, then gained his footing. Blood stained the front of his uniform and dribbled down his trousers toward the ground. He placed a hand over the wound and took a few uncertain steps toward the horses. Then his legs folded beneath him, and he hit the ground hard and rolled over to one side, his head resting on the ground and his eyes open.

"I'm cold," he said.

"It'll pass," Jack said.

In the time it took for Jack to walk over and kneel beside him, Fry was dead.

Jack took the quartz nugget out of Fry's pocket and clasped it in the palm of his hand. It was cold and heavy. Jack opened his fingers and stared at it, wondering how much food it would buy for Hell's Gate. But he could not shake the feeling that he was robbing a dead man. Jack walked over to the edge of the creek and threw the nugget in the water.

"I'll be back," he said. "Someday, maybe."

Jack picked up Fry's rifle and knife from the ground and walked over to the horses. He secured the rifle to the saddle of Fry's horse, slipped the knife in a saddlebag, then untied the horse from the tree and held the lead in his hand. 'Clipse had moved back in close now, and Jack put his left foot in the stirrup and climbed up to the saddle. Leading the other horse, he rode past Fry's body.

"Sorry," he said. "No time for buryin' today. But the critters here will clean you up right quick."

He was twenty yards past Fry's body when the Blackfeet warrior appeared in front of him. He might have come from the edge of the woods, or from behind a boulder, but if so Jack hadn't seen it.

The warrior was young and his face was painted blue with white dots. He wore an elaborately beaded buckskin shirt. The beadwork was all variations on a theme of circles and stars, in red and blue. He had a trio of eagle feathers in his hair, and in one hand he carried a shield. The other grasped the shaft of a six-foot lance with an old-fashioned point of flaked flint at the end.

"You could do some damage with that," Jack said, crossing his hands over the pommel to show he wasn't reaching for a weapon. "I reckon you saw all that business back there. Did you wait to see who would win before deciding to come out of your hiding place? We must have solved a problem for you by making the odds even."

The warrior crouched down, sweeping the lance low over the ground.

"We don't speak any common language, do we?"

Jack watched the tip of the lance as it made an arc that was fourteen feet across. Then the point came up, the warrior twirled the lance overhead, and brought it down with the blunt end pointing at Jack.

"I know you want to count coup on me," Jack said, "but the idea kind of leaves a bad taste in my mouth. Even if I let you slap me upside the head with the backwards end of that thing, it doesn't mean you'll let me pass without a fight."

The warrior advanced and brought the end of the lance toward Jack's head. Jack caught the shaft in his left hand. It was what the warrior wanted, because he jerked hard on the lance, nearly pulling Jack out of the saddle before he released it.

"That's rude," Jack said.

The warrior began a song and stamped his feet as if he were wading in water. He turned the lance around and advanced again, crouching low, and Jack feared the warrior was going to try to pierce 'Clipse's belly.

Jack pulled the 1803 from his scabbard and slid down from the saddle. He dropped the reins on the ground and touched 'Clipse on the flank, urging him to move away. Both horses retreated a few dozen yards down the creek bank.

The warrior took on a fighting stance, shield up and the spear at the ready.

"I don't want to fight you," Jack said. But he held the rifle at the ready and pulled the hammer to full cock with his thumb. "Put down that spear. Let's talk about trading for that surplus horse back there. That's what you really want, isn't it?"

The warrior shouted something in his own language.

"All right," Jack said. "You want both horses, then. No deal."

Jack was tired. His hand stung from having caught the lance and stopping the warrior from counting coup, and his tooth ached fiercely. The cocked and loaded rifle in his hands seemed to weigh more than he could ever remember.

"You're out for honor," Jack said. "Part of a war party, or maybe by yourself, but you're on foot. That means you're poor in possessions and reputation. And here I am, the enemy, with just everything you need to gain respect—if only you can count coup, take my weapon from me, and steal my horses."

Jack hooked his thumb over the hammer of the 1803, depressed the trigger, and gently uncocked the weapon. He did this slowly, so the young man could see. Then he put the rifle on the ground. He followed this with his belt, which held the Damascus.

"You follow?" Jack asked.

The warrior looked confused.

Jack shed his coat and pulled his shirt off over his head. He tossed the clothes in a pile next to the rifle. He was bare chested except for the medicine bundle hanging from a piece of leather.

"How about now?" Jack asked, his hands up, his empty palms turned to the warrior.

The warrior put his lance on the ground.

"That's right," Jack said, nodding. "Now the shield."

Soon the warrior had removed his shirt and placed it carefully on top of his shield. His chest was deep and his arms were heavily muscled. He, too, had a medicine bundle around his neck.

"Fair enough?" Jack asked. "You've got twelve or so years on me, but I've had more fights. So, lay on."

The warrior put his hands up, but did not close his fists. Jack took a boxing stance, leading with his left foot and hand. They circled each other for a moment and then the warrior stepped forward and swung his knuckles back-handed at Jack's face.

Jack dodged the blow and stepped in.

The warrior was expecting one of the fists, but Jack

swept the warrior's legs from beneath him with the side of his left foot. The warrior went down, a surprised look on his face.

"Guess that's coup for me," Jack said.

Jack withdrew a few steps and motioned for the warrior to get up.

The warrior did, with a new look of determination on his face. Both he and Jack advanced, and as Jack threw a couple of left punches and missed, the warrior kicked Jack in the stomach with a right foot.

Jack staggered back, unable for a moment to breathe, but he did not go down. The warrior did not wait for Jack to catch his breath, but instead pressed forward, turned, and whipped an elbow toward his rib cage. Jack moved just enough to turn it into a glancing, if painful, blow, instead of one that would have broken ribs.

After the elbow strike, the warrior was turned-three quarters away, and Jack saw his opportunity. Even as he was fighting to regain his wind, he drove his right fist into the back of the young man's neck, and the blow sent him to his knees. Jack followed with a right heel between the shoulder blades. The young man sprawled face-first into the rocks and pebbles and remained motionless.

"Whango," Jack said.

Jack cautiously circled the warrior, then crouched down in front of him, looking at the blood that trickled from an ear. He could not tell if the warrior was breathing or not, so he moved a little closer. The warrior came up with a pear-sized rock in his right hand and drove it against the left side of Jack's face, setting him back on his heels.

Jack was stunned and outraged that the young man had broken the rules.

"What don't you understand about no weapons?" Jack mumbled. The blow had knocked a tooth loose, a molar in his upper left jaw. He spat the tooth out, blood trickling from the corner of his mouth.

Jack cursed, spluttering blood, and snatched up a bigger rock from the creek bed.

The warrior was on his feet but was still unsteady from the blow to the back of his head. Jack had the rock poised behind his head, as if he were throwing a ball, ready to bring it down with killing force. The young man saw the rock in Jack's hand and crossed his forearms over his head to protect himself, his eyes closed.

"Fight, dammit," Jack said.

The young man did not move.

Jack lowered the rock.

"All right then," Jack said, his chest heaving and glistening with sweat and streaked with blood. "I guess you've learned a thing or two from an old man."

He loosened his fingers and allowed the rock to fall to the ground. Then he walked over to the lance and used his foot to snap the shaft closed to where the flint point was attached with sinew. He flung the flint into the creek, followed by the shield, which sailed in an arc and then skipped on the water three times before floating away.

"I'm gathering my things and the horses," Jack said. "If you get in my way, I'll make you as dead as ignorant Fry there. I don't know if you're more or less dangerous because you've been disgraced, or what kind of story you'll tell your mates, but I'm not going to stick around long enough to find out."

The warrior looked up.

Jack spat blood.

"Just my luck," Jack said, rubbing his right jaw. "You knocked a perfectly good tooth out of my head and left the bad one. Now both sides hurt like the devil."

27 *The Piasa Bird*

April stood at the end of a ramshackle dock on the levee below Quincy and stared out at the Mississippi, the wind whipping her hair across her face. It was just after dawn. She brushed her bangs aside and gestured at the water.

"Look, Gus," she said. "Did you think we would ever see it? Now here we are, on the other side of the river, looking back at from where we came."

Gus was unimpressed.

The city, which was situated on a bluff overlooking the river, was a neat and proper place, with freshly painted houses and clean streets. It seemed alien and cold to Gus, who had only known rustic surroundings. It was their third morning in Quincy, of sleeping in the cold and begging food, of being the subject of contemptuous and sometimes ravenous looks from the townspeople.

"What will we eat? Where will we sleep?"

"I don't know," April said.

"Those men the other night," Gus said. "Where were they taking the three darkies?"

"Canada. They are members of the Underground Railroad. But we mustn't talk about that. Illinois is a free state, but it's against the law to aid fugitives. Those men could be sent to prison if the sheriff found out."

"Are we fugitives?"

"Yes."

Gus frowned.

"Are we going to prison?"

"Not if we don't talk about it," April said. "And if we don't get caught."

Even though the sun was barely above the horizon, the levee was already filled with people, mostly working men. April had never seen so many people, all with some task to complete. A steamboat was coming down the river, preparing to dock. It was a side-wheeler, with black smoke belching from the stacks, its decks piled high with cargo. On its sides in ornate letters was the boat's name: *Comet*.

"Ain't she grand?" April asked. "Could you have ever imagined anything better?"

"No," Gus said. "It scares me a little."

"Don't be."

"The people here are all so different."

"Why, they're just the same as us," April said. "They just have more money."

Gus looked doubtful.

"How do we get money?"

"In the time-honored way of the world," April said. "We are conspicuous here on the dock. I see the men glancing our way, looking at our modest clothes, and soon they will come and tell us to move on. We would be just as out of place in town, I think, and likely to end up in some kind of institution fortified by brick—the jail, the courthouse, an orphanage."

"To hell with this town," Gus said.

"Yes, to hell with it," April agreed. "I rather like the look of that steamboat that is just coming in to dock. Its name is a good omen. I say we sneak aboard and hide ourselves among all the truck stacked on the decks. We can catch a ride downriver, and there is nary a brick wall to block the sun."

"And when we're caught?"

"The worst they do with stowaways is to put us ashore at the next town," April said. "They have schedules to keep. They won't waste their time on us."

A man hurrying to the end of the dock to meet the steamboat brushed by, his shoulder nearly knocking April in the water. As she recovered her footing, the man looked over his shoulder and said, "Mind where you're standing."

"Mind where you're walking," April shot back.

The man stopped. He considered for a moment what to do, and then turned on his heel and walked back to the pier. He had slicked-back dark hair and a three-days' growth of beard. He was dressed in fine clothes, including a tall beaver hat and a wool coat with bright brass buttons. He right hand grasped a cane.

"Were you speaking to me?" he asked.

"Nobody else damned near knocked me in the river, did they?"

The man smiled.

"You wouldn't have fallen in," he said. "The rope would have prevented it. And I hardly touched you."

"If that's what you call hardly, I feel sorry for your wife."

"I am unmarried," the man said.

"Now, there's a surprise."

The man kept the forced smile.

"Let me explain myself," he said. "My name is Hollister Hamlin, and I have urgent business on the *Comet,* as soon as it docks. There is a gentleman who owes me a sum of money that I simply must meet at the gangplank or allow him to slip me forever. But, I will pause for a moment and risk losing my investment if only to teach a lesson. Are you game for a lesson?"

"Always."

"Let us now turn to the both of you."

"Oh, let's," April said.

Hamlin put a finger to the side of his face in mock concentration.

"Sixteen years old," he said. "Your companion, somewhat younger."

"My brother."

But she did not correct his error about her age.

"From your clothes you come from the hinterlands, perhaps across the river. Your clothes have seen many seasons and were bought when you were not, let us say, so ripe. You look like your womanly figure is about to burst through in places. There is a natural health to you, your cheeks are rouged with youth, and your blue eyes are bright with health. But your hair belies a casual indifference to the way you appear to others, which is a pity, because there is some beauty hiding there. Normally I would take an interest, but you are too rough even for me. Can you even read?"

"It never interested me," April said. "What good has books ever done anybody?"

"Exactly so," Hamlin said. "Your brother there wears

a homespun jacket, but no particular care was taken making it. His eyes are dull, indicating a lack of intelligence, and his weak chin signals a failure of initiative."

Gus began to speak, but April put a hand on his arm to silence him.

"That's incredible," April said. "You must be the smartest man in Illinois."

"Hardly," the man said, but could not suppress a smile. "So the next time you see one of your betters approaching—"

"We will move out of the way right quick," April said. "We should have taken you for the quality right away."

"I'll hold you to your word," Hamlin said, tugging the brim of his hat.

"Thank you," April said. "We're just poor country folk and we are lost in the city."

Hamlin turned to go.

"Sir?" April asked. "Might could we take another moment of your time?"

"I said I had pressing business."

Hamlin stepped away.

"I'm sorry," April called. "We'll find someone else to show our Piasa bird."

The lie, with its embedded snare, came so naturally to April that it surprised her. When she would think of it later, she knew that hunger and desperation were the parents of the lie, but she could not deny a certain natural skill.

Hamlin stopped again.

"Really?" he said.

"Oh, it's just a small one," April said. "A chick. It probably ain't worth much."

Hamlin walked back, shaking his cane at April.

"They are mythical creatures," he said.

"Ain't nothin' mythical about 'em. We live on the yonder side of the river, below Ashburn," April said. "We see 'em all the time. They live in a cave and come out at night to eat cattle and hogs. But all that stuff about them eating people, that's hokum."

April paused.

"We figured maybe the bird would be worth a few dollars as a curiosity, perhaps to display in a tavern or other public place," she said. "We figured people might could pay money to see the critter."

"You're saying it's alive?" Hamlin asked.

"Come on, Tom," April said. "We'd better go down and check on the chick. We ain't fed him a cat in a couple of hours and he'll be peckish. Maybe we should let it go if it's ain't worth nothin'."

April took Gus by the upper arm and practically shoved him down the dock. He started to ask a question, but she hissed at him to stay quiet. They had reached the end of the dock when Hamlin came running, the tails of his coat flapping behind.

"Could you show me the animal?"

"We've taken up enough of your time," April said. "We wouldn't feel right about it. Would we, Tom?"

"Um, no," Gus said.

"You'll have to forgive him," April said. "He is a bit slow. Goodbye."

"No, wait," Hamlin said. "Take me to the animal. How far is it?"

"Why, it's in a box on our boat," she said. "We're tied up downriver, not far past the bottom of the levee."

Hamlin glanced back at the *Comet*. It was approaching the dock, deckhands at the ready with coils of rope in their hands.

"Wait here," Hamlin said. "My business will only take ten minutes."

"Oh, Pa would skin us for sure," April said. "He's expecting us back."

"Just ten minutes," Hamlin said. "You see, the debt I must collect is a considerable amount, in cash. I will give you a few coins for your time."

"I reckon that would sit okay with Pa," April said. "But don't be long."

"Good," Hamlin said. "Good. I'll be back directly."

He hurried down the dock.

When Hamlin was out of earshot, April turned to Gus. He was about to ask a question.

"Listen, don't talk," she said. "There's a string of rowboats tied up down below the levee. Find one that doesn't have an owner nearby, climb in, and wait. I will be along with the damned fool shortly, and you are to wave to us from the boat you've found."

"What then?" Gus asked.

"You're talking," she said. "Now, go."

"All right," Gus said. "They'll feed us in jail, right?"

"Go!" April shouted.

He did so.

Passengers from the *Comet* were now trickling down the dock, and April stepped aside to let them pass. Finally, she spied Hamlin, pushing something into an inside pocket, carrying his cane.

"All right," he said. "Show me."

April led the way. They left the dock and threaded their way through the passengers and workers and slaves to a path at the bottom of the levee. The path led through a tight patch of woods to a broad eddy where a collection of small boats was either pulled up on the bank or tied to trees. This was the place where they had landed with the abolitionists in the middle of the night.

Gus whistled and waved from the biggest of the boats. It had a high bow and stern and at one time had been painted green, but now only carried the memory of the paint.

"Where's Pa?" April asked.

Gus made the motion of tipping a jug.

Gus was standing on the middle seat, the one nearest the oarlocks. The weathered oars were shipped beneath the seats. Below Gus in the bottom of the boat was a beaten old trunk, its humped wooden lid closed.

"Here we are," April said, walking out on a log and then stepping into the boat. It rocked badly, but Hamlin put a foot on the gunwale.

"This made it across the river?"

"She's stronger than she looks."

April put out her hand and Hamlin grasped it.

He stepped lightly into the boat, making it rock hardly at all.

"Tom," April said. "Clear back and give us some room."

Gus moved to the bow.

"Come on," April said, standing over the trunk. "Open it up and take a gander. It can't fly yet."

"All right," Hamlin said, and stepped up to the trunk.

He turned around and sat on the seat, but held his feet wide on either side of the trunk, to keep them out of the half-inch of water that had collected in the bottom.

April moved around behind him, leaning close. She noted the cane was out of his hands, resting against the seat.

"Go ahead," she whispered in his ear. "This here's the fun part."

April slid her left hand into the pocket of her dress and grasped the razor.

Hamlin undid the latch and swung open the lid, revealing an empty and water-soaked trunk. As this was happening, April produced the razor, opened it with a flick of her wrist, and laid the gleaming blade against Hamlin's throat.

"Now," she said. "I'll have that payday in your pocket."

"I'm afraid not," Hamlin said.

April felt something nudging her side. She looked down to a stubby, single-shot flintlock pistol pressed against her ribs, held in Hamlin's left hand. Her own left hand began to tremble.

"Lower the razor," Hamlin said.

"You'll shoot me," April said.

Gus moved toward one of the oars, but Hamlin told him not to move.

"I am not in the mood to kill children today," Hamlin said. "But I make a poor guardian, so I will if I have to. Lower the razor, girl, and I will pocket the cannon."

April lowered the razor, closed it, and put it back in her pocket.

The single-shot disappeared into Hamlin's coat.

"Sit down," he told April. "And you, boy, move to where I can see you better."

Gus did.

"Are we going to jail now?"

The man pushed the hat back on his head.

"You will, if you don't practice," Hamlin said. "You made a series of mistakes, not the least of which was failing to recognize a superior practitioner. I have spent years honing my art, first in my hometown of Cincinnati and then at Memphis and Natchez Under the Hill."

"So you knew from the start."

"Your presentation was rough," Hamlin said. "Inspired, but rough. The Piasa bird is a trick worth refining. Did you come up with that on your own?"

"Yes," April said.

"The trunk was a nice touch, but too last-minute," Hamlin said. "It should shake and thump as if there were really something alive in it. And no, you can't open the lid yet because the thing can indeed fly."

"Ah," April said.

"This Piasa is good, but you're thinking too small," Hamlin said. "What you attempted was armed robbery, with the tale used being the means to get the mark somewhere private."

"The mark?" April asked.

"The one you intend to relieve of his money," Hamlin said. "The goal is to get the mark to willingly hand his money over, and either be so confused or embarrassed afterward that there's not much fuss. But cut his throat, or threaten to, and there will be much fuss of the most unpleasant kind. Violence is a last resort, a pistol in a pocket for when everything goes wrong and the mob comes to tar and feather you. Besides, I don't think you could have carried out the threat. You don't strike me as a murderess."

"You would be wrong," April said.

"Your appearance and station in life are also wrong for the Piasa."

"It's all we have," she said. "Our clothes reflect our station."

"That's where your thinking has betrayed you," Hamlin said. "Do not be yourself. Be whoever or whatever is needed to sell the story to the mark. In this case, you need to be the daughter of a wealthy and eccentric old professor who has caught one of these things. If your appearance suggests you need money, or you betray hunger or some other infirmity, the purse strings will close tight. People detest giving money to those who truly need it. But act and dress as if you have no thought for money and people will trip over themselves to hand you their fortunes."

April knew instinctively that what he said was true.

"Why did you bump into me?"

"I wanted to see how you'd respond," Hamlin said. "You were out of place and desperate. Giving you that shove gave me more information than if I'd stopped and asked for your life history. There was resentment and anger, which I expected, but talent, which I did not."

"But why?"

"Because having a bespoke niece and nephew would suit my trade," Hamlin said. "And because I felt sorry for you. You are a few days away from earning your crust of bread on your back."

"No," April said.

"There's no arguing with the dull compulsion of need," Hamlin said. "If you don't throw in with me, you will end up in a crib on some floating brothel downriver. Is this really your brother or someone else? Ah, that would be hard for him to take."

"I wouldn't let that happen," Gus said.

"Boy, you need to grow a bit before making such claims," Hamlin said. "What are your real names?"

She told him.

"Now, don't get me wrong, April," Hamlin said. "I have a soft spot in my heart for the Cyprians of the river. Some of them make a good purse. But the way to avoid the cribs is not to sell just the act itself, but the story that goes along with it. Be a girl to fall in love with, someone to fight over, a woman whose rate is a hundred dollars a night, if you're lucky enough to get her nod, and worth it."

April put her chin in her hands.

"What if I'm not a virgin?"

Hamlin laughed.

"You can be whatever you need to be," Hamlin said, "or want to be."

"I want to be someone who owns lots of books."

"A reasonable ambition," Hamlin said.

"Gus goes where I go," April said.

"Of course," Hamlin said. "We will be a family."

"I will not lay with you."

"Nor would I have it," Hamlin said. "If you are to be convincing as my niece, and I as your uncle, the tells would be too great to overcome. The secret to being somebody else is to believe it. So, what say you to an apprenticeship of two years? You and Gus will share in the proceeds, but I will take the lion's share. But I will teach you as much as I can in that time."

"And when the two years are over?"

"You are free to practice for yourselves," Hamlin said.

April bit her left thumbnail, pondering the matter.

"I have only a few rules," Hamlin said. "We don't hold out or lie to each other. If one of us winds up in jail, we keep our mouths shut about the others. I always eat first and get the best bed. And you must never pull that razor on me again."

"Gus," April called. "What do you think?"

"If it means we eat soon," he said, "I'm for it."

"Deal, then," April said.

"Spit on it," Hamlin said.

They each spit in their palms and shook hands.

"You are now my protege," he said. "Our first task is to get you and your brother some appropriate clothes. I will pay for them and—no, I will also choose them. You wouldn't know what to buy, would you? Don't worry, we'll make everything just so. And when the *Comet* pulls away from the levee tonight, we will be aboard. Professor Ashburn and his wards, April and Augustus. And thus the tuition will begin."

28   *Fox Teeth*

"Where's Fry?" Baptiste asked.

"Dead," Jack said.

"Ain't surprised," Baptiste said. He was reclining near a small fire, leisurely smoking his pipe. Suspended over the fire was a rabbit on a spit. Overhead was a canopy of midnight stars. "Was it redskins or was it you?"

"It was me," Jack said from the saddle. "It was necessary." He leaned over and patted 'Clipse's neck, not wanting to converse further on the matter.

"I'll wager it was," Baptiste said slowly.

"I told you not to wait for me," Jack said.

"Never been one to take orders," Baptiste said.

"What have you over the fire?" Jack asked. "It is so small it might be a rat."

"Oh, so you don't want any of my rabbit?"

"I didn't say that," Jack said, swinging down from the saddle. When his feet touched the ground, his legs became weak and he nearly fell. With his body aching, he led 'Clipse over to the line where Baptiste's horse and mule were tied. He looped the stirrups up on the saddle horn and began to uncinch.

"You'd better come eat before you fall down," Baptiste said.

"After I tend to my horse," Jack said.

Once he had the saddle and blanket and tack in a neat pile, and whispered a few gentle words to 'Clipse, he took the 1803 and walked over to the fire. He leaned the rifle against a log and sat down.

"We make good targets on a night like this," Jack said.

"How else were you going to find me in the dark?" Baptiste asked, taking the rabbit from the fire. He declared it was done and handed it over to Jack. "We can douse the fire now."

"Obliged," Jack said, picking at the meat with his fingers.

"Don't burn yourself, palmer."

Baptiste kicked a few scoops of dirt onto the fire.

"Any trouble?" Jack asked, chewing carefully. His tooth still raged.

"Only the regular kind," Baptiste said. "A gristly bear. A Blackfeet war party. We managed to avoid both."

"Ah," Jack said. "How far ahead are the soldiers?"

"Those two?" Baptiste asked. "Hell, I'd be surprised if they made it beyond the next hill. They ain't exactly cut for this country. But they'll be all right, I suppose, if they live long enough."

"Is this your only rabbit?" Jack asked.

"I snared two," Baptiste said. "Already ate one."

"Good," Jack said. "But not that I would share."

"Wouldn't expect it from you," Baptiste said. "Anything broken permanent on you?"

"Don't think so," Jack said. "Most things still bend as intended."

"I've noticed," Baptiste said, "that you have a tendency to make people murderously angry. Did you find what you was looking for?"

"Yes," Jack said.

"My sympathies," Baptiste said. "It will bring nothing but trouble."

"I know."

Jack threw a bone into the ashes and embers.

"It's clear tonight," Baptiste said, "but I can feel a storm coming. Tomorrow, perhaps, or the next day. It's going to storm something fierce. A lot of snow."

"Not a bad guess for winter."

"My joints don't lie," Baptiste said. "Better than any weather glass. We had better make for the Mandan villages rather than try the lower route."

"I aim to go home," Jack said.

"Better to spend a couple of moons in a warm earth lodge than leave your bones to be gnawed at and scattered by critters," Baptiste said. "I don't mind the prospect of an unmarked grave. It's the tiny teeth of the foxes that bother me. I've killed too many for them to let me rest."

"Foxes?" Jack asked. "Or men?"

"Them, too. My sleep will not be a restful one, I fear."

"What do you think comes after?" Jack asked.

"After death?" Baptiste asked. "Everything. Nothing. Whatever it is, we can't change it. Unless you believe in the priestly mumbo-jumbo. Do you, Jack?"

"I believe in Jesus and Mari," Jack said.

Baptiste thought he said Jesus and Mary.

"Beyond that, I'm not really sure," Jack said. "Sometimes I'm afraid there is no God, and at other times I'm afraid there is. Kind of like your fox teeth, I reckon."

"It's a powerful mystery," Baptiste said.

Jack threw another bone into the remains of the fire.

"The soldiers told a strange story today," Baptiste said. "They said that a few days after the detail left Fort Nonsense, they came upon a free trapper who was missing a hand."

"Came upon. How?" Jack asked, his interest stirred.

"In a clearing not far from the Stinking Water River," Baptiste said. "The trapper was a big man, he said, and French. One of his hands had been taken off badly at the wrist. The stub was stinking and festered."

"Which hand?"

"The left one, I believe. The soldiers reckoned it even worse luck that the trapper had lost his favored hand."

"What was this trapper's name?"

"Called himself La Bête, the beast," Baptiste said. "The soldier said they couldn't get much of anything that made sense. He was a lunatic and told a story about him and his brother getting caught stealing plews from the Nation that Has No Name. They said they were taken before this medicine woman, a fat old warrior squaw, who decided their punishment in a tongue they'd never heard before. They were bound at the wrist—that is, one left hand and one right hand bound—by the drowning chain that had been removed from a beaver trap. The chain was wrapped tightly over each wrist and then pinned with the ring that holds the chain to the spring. Then the pin was blunted by being beaten with rocks, so that it could not be opened without the aid of a blacksmith."

"So this was so tight it starved the hand of blood?"

"No," Baptiste said. "But tight enough that it could not be slipped over the hand or otherwise removed."

"Then what caused the dismemberment?"

"This is the part that gets kinder interesting," Baptiste said. "The brothers had their rifles and other possessions taken from them, but each was allowed to keep their knives. Then they were set free."

"But not from each other."

"No," Baptiste said. "They couldn't make much distance bound so, nor could they find meat. They scavenged what they could, but it wasn't enough. And the longer they spent bound together, the more they came to hate the other. It was a punishment worthy of the Old Testament."

"But they had their knives."

"They couldn't really fight, because bound as they were, mortal wounds would be inflicted by both attacker and attacked. They could not sleep for fear of being killed by the other. Their madness deepened, and soon they were stumbling without aim, sure to perish. Then something fortuitous happened—one lost his footing and tumbled down an incline over a cliff edge, taking the other with him. They fell into the tops of some trees, fell from branch to branch, and then their bound wrists became caught in the fork of a cedar tree, just ten feet from the ground."

"This was luck?"

"It forced them to undertake the only thing that would save them," Baptiste said. "Because a man abhors cutting away his own hand, the brothers agreed to use their knives on the other. It was, of course, more difficult than one could imagine. Whatever sanity they retained was lost as they hacked away at each other's hands. By the time the last sinew gave and they dropped to dirt, they were truly beasts. He didn't say what became of the brother."

Jack knew, but did not say.

"The soldiers tried to doctor La Bête, but he was having none of it," Baptiste said. "Said the only law was no law at all, and he attacked the soldiers, trying to bite them as an animal would, and had to be driven off with repeated blows from their rifle butts."

"They should have put a ball into his brain."

"They pitied him."

"Their pity was wasted," Jack said bitterly.

"What is this story to you?" Baptiste asked.

"A mystery answered."

Baptiste asked how.

"I encountered his brother," Jack said without elaboration. His lids were becoming too heavy to keep open. "It was an unpleasant meeting."

"This La Bête is surely dead by now," Baptiste said. "He could not have lasted long in such a shape, deep into madness, even rabid perhaps, and with a festering stump where his hand was."

"It would be comforting to think so," Jack said drowsily.

"Sleep," Baptiste said. "Then we will see what the morning brings."

* * *

Jack and Baptiste set out just before dawn. The sky was clear and slowly yielding its stars to a rose-colored dawn. There was no wind, and the small sounds of the wilderness carried far. Jack could hear a chipmunk scurrying across the dead leaves, water rippling in the creek below, a crow greeting the sun while wheeling far overhead. They had ridden for a quarter of an hour or so, listening to the creak of leather and the sound of their horses, when a rifle shot echoed from the hills. The report had a clear bell-like quality, and Jack reined 'Clipse to a stop.

Baptiste began to speak, but Jack held up his hand.

"Listen," Jack said.

"It ain't close," Baptiste said.

"Shush," Jack said, counting the seconds in his mind. If there was a reload and another shot, it would take half a minute. Just before Jack reached thirty in his head, the rifle sounded again.

"Hear that?" Jack asked. "It's a B flat."

"I'll take your word for it," Baptiste said.

"Which direction did it come from?" Jack asked.

"The hills can trick you," Baptiste said.

"Just take a guess and point."

Baptiste shook his head, then aimed a finger to the northwest.

"That's where I thought, too," Jack said.

"What's it matter, Jack? That's not in our direction."

Jack put a hand to his jaw. He had forgotten his tooth for a while, but it was beginning to ache again.

"It's my direction now," Jack said.

"I thought you were setting a course for home," Baptiste said.

"That sound," Jack said.

"Ignore it," Baptiste said.

"It changes things."

Baptiste took his unlit clay pipe from his pocket and put the stem in the corner of his mouth. He suggested they stop just long enough for him to have a smoke, and they could talk it over.

"The trail will go cold if I wait," Jack said. "Whoever is firing that piece is not likely to stay put. Two rounds. Hunting, perhaps. Or a fight. Either way, it's someplace you leave behind."

"Do I have to tie you to a tree until you come to your senses?"

"I am in my sense," Jack said.

"You can't be sure it's your rifle."

"I must know," Jack said.

"But will it be worth the price, Jack?"

"That's what I aim to find out," he said.

In frustration, Baptiste uttered a particularly earthy curse.

"You are one crazy and difficult old bird," Jack said, "but you have proved good enough to roam the mountains with. I wish you well. Take care of that bald head of yours."

"Farewell, Jack," Baptiste said. "I expect to see you no more."

Jack turned 'Clipse to the northwest and urged speed.

29   *The Ghost Rifle*

Medicine Owl Woman lowered the butt of the rifle to the ground, the ramrod already in her hand, ready to quickly load yet a third ball. But when she saw the bull elk fall hard on its side, she knew it would not be necessary. It had been a difficult shot, uphill, at a distance greater than five arrow flights, and she had misjudged the elevation with her first round. It had passed narrowly over the shoulder of the elk and split a branch of a juniper tree beyond. She had corrected this with the second shot, which had found the elk's lungs.

She was a tall woman, heavy with muscle, and wearing the trappings of a warrior. Her face above her lower lip was painted with white clay, except for the nose and eyelids, which gave the appearance of a skull without a jaw. A scar ran diagonally from her left brow, across the bridge of her nose, and to her right cheekbone. It was from her first fight, many years ago, when she had allowed an enemy to get too close, and he had taken a wild swing with a knife. She was lucky it was a long knife. The edge had skittered across the bony parts of her face, but had not reached her eye. Despite the blood running down her face, she had caught his arm, twisted it until it snapped, and took the knife away from him. She had then disemboweled him with it.

Medicine Owl Woman spat the ball she had held in her mouth into the palm of her hand.

There were two others standing near her, a boy and an old man. The young one made a joke about her spitting out the balls of men that displeased her, and Medicine Owl Woman whacked the impertinent young man about the head with the hickory ramrod.

"There is butchering to do," she said. "And yet you remain here hurling jokes. Go, before I lose my sense of humor."

The boy trotted ahead.

"You allow your sister's boy to disrespect his elders," the woman said. "I am tolerant, but others will not be so kind. He needs more discipline than my ramrod can impart."

"He is of his own mind," the old man said. "As are you."

Medicine Owl Woman made a dismissive sound.

"It is a big elk," the old man said. "You have made much meat."

"I missed the first shot."

"It was of no consequence," the old man said. "The result is the same."

"Is it?" she asked. "The ammunition is not inexhaustible. The price in powder and shot for this animal was double."

"A bargain still," the old man said.

"I wish for a challenge beyond elk," Medicine Owl Woman said.

There was no hurry now in reloading, so she would take her time, because the more care in loading meant better accuracy in shooting. She took the powder horn, measured her powder in a hollow bone that held just the right amount, and poured it down the mouth of the barrel. She slapped the side of the gun with the palm of her hand to make sure all the powder went down to the breech. Then she patched the ball and perched it on the end of the barrel. She used a short wooden rod to start it down the muzzle, then used the ramrod to push it home. She did this fluidly, and with only enough force to seat the ball, so she would not crush the powder. Ramming the ball home always made a peculiar hollow sound that rose in pitch, and it made her smile. Then she picked up the rifle and poured some fine powder into the pan.

Then she cradled the rifle in the crook of her arm. The familiar weight of it was reassuring. The rifle was fifty caliber, with a short barrel, a half walnut stock, and a round brass patchbox. The rifle remained as it was the day, twelve years before, when she dove into the Missouri River and recovered it from the wreck of a keelboat that had burned and sank. She had been young then, only twenty, and while the rifle had not changed, she had. She had more muscle now, but also more fat, and in deepest winter, the cold found a way into her bones. But she was not yet too old to fight, and her mind for war remained as sharp as ever, and the *Wakan Tanka* still sometimes spoke to her in visions. She had no time for husbands, and certainly not for children. She sometimes thought of taking a wife, but she found the company of most women tiresome. She had long been a *winoxtca,* a member of the warrior women's society, and she took satisfaction in serving her village.

The old man was her uncle, Shouts His Name, a shaman of considerable power in his day, but his time on earth was fading. Medicine Owl Woman was made sad by this, but was also impatient for his passing, so that he could be spared the indignities of unnatural age.

"I had a dream last night," the old man said.

"Oh?"

"It was like the old dreams," he said. "You were there, and the thunder stick you wrestled from the demon hog fish at the bottom of the river."

"There was no demon fish," she said. "Only the white man's boat."

"You know how it is in dreams," Shouts His Name said. "You see things more clearly than in the daylight world, where much is an illusion. In my dream, there was a child floating down the river, an infant, in a reed basket. I was afraid the demon hog fish would devour the child, but White Buffalo Calf Woman appeared and snatched the child from the water just in time."

"I see," Medicine Owl Woman said. "Was this child one of the people?"

"No," Shouts His Name said. "The child was of undetermined origin. White Buffalo Calf Woman brought the child to the village and told us we must care for her."

"This was a girl child?"

"Yes," Shouts His Name said. "I said that."

"No, you didn't. But go on."

"It was unclear whether the child would bring us joy or sorrow."

"Did this child have a name?"

"Not that I remember," he said.

"And what were we to do that the child would bring joy?"

"White Buffalo Calf Woman said it was out of our hands," he said. "But our lot was to care for the child even if she brought us misery."

"This does not sound like a dream, Uncle. Every child has the potential to bring joy or suffering, and the parents can do little to choose. It is an everyday mystery."

"No," Shouts His Name said. "The child does not have the fate of just the village in her hands. It is the fate of the whole world."

Medicine Calf Woman smiled.

"The next generation always carries that burden," she said.

The old man made a motion with his hand that was like parting a curtain.

"Yes," he said. "And yet no."

"Come," she said. "Let us go supervise Soils His Britches before he makes a mess of the meat. Bring the horses."

Together they started for where the boy Blue Otter was working on the elk at the summit of the hill. The woman walked ahead while the old man trailed behind, leading a pair of buckskin ponies. They were still two hundred yards away when they saw the boy stand and begin waving his hands over his head.

"There is trouble," Medicine Owl Woman said. "What is he shouting?"

"I cannot hear him," the old man said. "He is too far away."

The boy now turned to face something they could not see. He was gesturing, as if engaged in conversation.

"I will help him," the old man said.

Before Medicine Owl Woman could say no, he had flopped up onto the back of one of the ponies, the reins in his hand. There was no saddle, and the bridle was just a piece of rope that lopped around the animal's lower jaw. It took him a moment to become firmly seated on the animal's back, then he held his war club high over his head. He gave a whoop as the pony surged forward.

"Old fool," Medicine Owl Woman called.

The old man had dropped the reins of the other pony and it had ambled thirty paces away. Medicine Owl Woman looked at the pony, then back at the top of the hill, then planted her feet and raised the rifle to a ready position.

Jack rode slowly forward, his hands resting easy on the pommel, the 1803 remaining in its scabbard. He did not want to frighten the boy, he only wanted to talk. He knew the rifle he had heard not long before must be very near, but he was confused about why there was only a boy leaning over the elk doing the butchering. What was on the other side of the hill, he wondered?

"Hello," Jack said, then repeated the greeting in French.

The boy stared at him, still crouching over his work, an obsidian knife in his hand.

"Parley?"

The boy didn't speak Jack's languages, but he knew

what the word *parley* meant. He straightened and began to speak. Jack did not know what the boy was saying, but could hear the fear in his voice.

"I just want to talk," Jack said. "If only we could. I don't even recognize the sound of your language."

Jack was keeping an eye on the trade knife, which the boy was using to punctuate his sentences.

"Fine kill," Jack said, nodding toward the elk. "The rifle that claimed it. Does it make the sound of a bell?"

The boy continued gesturing.

"All right," Jack said, glancing around, trying to see where the shot had come from. The boy had already made enough progress to obscure any sign that might have helped. The shot could have come from the far side of the hill, but that would have been the most difficult to make. The ground on either side was flatter, but Jack saw no sign of the hunter. Had a white trapper killed the elk and then moved on, leaving the boy the meat? Or was the rifle carried by someone in the boy's band who had decided to remain out of sight?

"I know you're nervous," Jack said easily. "Tell the truth, I've got the jitters myself. It's pretty open up here. We make as good of targets as that elk was, but somewhat poorer eating."

Then Jack heard the sound of hooves coming fast from the other side of the hill. He reached for the butt of the 1803 in its scabbard, but the boy started waving for him to stop. The trade knife was still in the boy's hand, and he was stepping toward Jack.

"Jesus and Mari," Jack whispered. "What do I do?"

Jack released the 1803, letting it fall back in scabbard. He was determined not to kill a boy today.

He nudged 'Clipse forward, so he could see what was coming up the hill.

It was an old man with a war club on a buckskin pony.

He rode surprisingly fast, Jack thought.

Their horses met and reared. 'Clipse was several hands higher and a few hundred pounds heavier than the pony, so when he came down, hooves flashing, the buckskin toppled. The old man spilled from the pony's back and rolled on the ground, the war club still in his hand.

The boy advanced with the knife, but Jack pointed at him and shouted, "No!" The boy stopped.

The old man, blood streaming down the side of his face where he had struck the ground, got to his feet and raised the war club. Its business end was a stone that had been smoothed to a perfect oval and channeled for the sinew that bound it to the club's handle.

Jack turned 'Clipse and reined him backwards, out of reach, while drawing the 1803 with his free hand. He cocked the rifle and held it muzzle up.

"I won't kill a boy," Jack said. "But drop that club or I just might kill you."

The old man lurched forward, and Jack knew that if he managed to connect with a knee or a shin with the club—or 'Clipse's forelegs—the injury would prove catastrophic. Still, he did not want to shoot the old man, either.

"All right," Jack said. "Stop this nonsense. I'm riding away."

The 1803 still in hand, Jack wheeled 'Clipse. He was about to touch his heels to the horse's sides and race back the way he came when he was lifted from the saddle by what seemed the back of God's hand.

The rifle flew from his grasp.

He hovered for a moment between the earth and sky, his back arched and his arms outstretched, blasted by a white light as hot as the sun. He seemed made of mist and bone, of light and shade, of blood and breath.

Then he crashed to the hard earth.

His vision narrowed in the fog of imminent unconsciousness. He tried to push himself up with his right hand, but found that his arm was unresponsive. There was the sensation that a red-hot poker had pierced his back and come out his chest. Then, a moment before the world went black, the report of the rifle that had fired the shot finally came, a perfect B flat ringing in his ears.

30 *Oblivion*

Oblivion cradled Jack in its cold embrace. Time passed but he had no sense of it, locked in a dreamless and fevered sleep while hovering near death. When he did rouse, he was given water or a little soft food, of which he took little. He remembered the rifle shot that had pierced him, but little else, and he had no inclination to speak or even to ask where he was. It no longer mattered to him. He could summon no reason why it should.

Then one day the throbbing of his tooth dragged him awake.

He opened his eyes and saw only shadows, thrown by a small fire burning nearby. He was lying in an earth lodge, in a pile of blankets and robes, and there was the smell of meat cooking. He attempted to sit up, but the pain in his chest made him cry out. He fell back into the robes, suddenly aware of the stench from his own body.

"You're awake."

A male voice. Deep and familiar.

A figure left the fire and loomed over Jack.

Jack blinked, trying to make out the face. But his eyes were too blurry and the corner of the lodge too dark.

"Who's that?"

The man eased himself to the ground and sat cross-legged next to Jack.

"Don't you recognize your old one-eyed friend Quarles?"

The man pointed to the patch over his left eye.

"Quarles," Jack said.

"It has been many years since we met in St. Louis," Quarles said. "Both of us fugitives, both of us young and green. Neither of us are quite so young now or quite so green."

"You were black then," Jack said with effort. "And you remain so."

"True," Quarles said. "But we both have been free men lo these many years. I heard you were dead, more than once, and your demise became more wild with each telling. First you were killed by the war chief Lightning Crow, then you were killed by the lord of the grizzly bears, and then you were skinned alive and your lights eaten by the Nation that Has No Name."

"All true," Jack said.

Quarles laughed.

"You damn near made it true enough this time," Quarles said.

"How—" Jack started to ask, and then could not finish the sentence.

"You've been shot straight through," Quarles said. "A woman brought you to me, dragging you on a travois behind her horse. She was a strange one, dressed as a warrior, and with a face painted like a skull. An old man and a boy were with her. They made me right scared, because they were from no tribe I recognized. None of them spoke, except the old man. Half in sign language and half in English he said the woman had shot you from the saddle and captured your horse, and that she did not wish you to die but found you bothersome. Said she was in favor of leaving you where you fell, but the boy had talked her into taking you to me, because I might know what to do with a crazy wounded white man."

"Did you?"

"As best I could," Quarles said. "It was a clean shot, the ball having come out your chest without breaking a rib. But it did shatter your shoulder blade and puncture your lung. I cleaned things up as best I could, trimmed away the edges of the wound, and put a poultice on both sides that Stands in Reeds made. She's over there now, cooking buffalo steaks."

"Your woman?"

"Yes," Quarles said. "She is the sister of my wife, who drowned three—no, four—years ago. I cannot say her name. It is discouraged."

"Where are we?"

"Hidatsa village on the Missouri above the Knife," Quarles said.

"How long?"

"A month," Quarles said.

"Have to leave," Jack said.

"There are three feet of snow on the ground," Quarles said. "You wouldn't get a hundred yards before you'd end up a bloody icicle I'd have to stare at until the thaw. No, Jack, you're here until spring."

Jack muttered a curse.

"The wound," he said. "How bad is it?"

"I gave you precious little chance of survival in the first few days," Quarles said. "Most wounds like yours are fatal, and when yours began to fester I started to think about digging a grave before the ground froze solid. But I drained the pus on a regular schedule and after two weeks it did not stink so much. Kept the willow bark poultices on, front and back. Stands in the Reeds did a lot of praying and smudging sage over you. After three weeks, I didn't think I was going to have to bury you, but you didn't seem to want to wake up, either. What finally brought you around?"

"My tooth," Jack said.

"Not your chest?"

"Hurts, too," Jack said. "But the tooth drives me mad."

Quarles turned and spoke to Stands in Reeds. She came over and placed a small jug beside Jack, then gave Quarles a stern look.

"She says just a little," Quarles said, uncorking the jug.

He held the jug to Jack's lips and poured a little into his mouth.

Jack swallowed, and the bitterness was evident on his face.

"The alcohol has a bit of the poppy in it," Quarles said. "Opium. Since the steamboats started coming up river, you can get nearly any damn thing you want in St. Louis. I keep it around for pain. Beats the hell out of gunpowder for a toothache."

Jack took a little more, then he closed his eyes and let his head fall back on the robes. Quarles corked the bottle and placed it within Jack's reach. He sat there for ten minutes, watching Jack's breathing.

"Cotton to some solid food?" Quarles asked.

"Not now," Jack said drowsily. "Later."

"Are you going to let me pull that tooth?"

"Sure," Jack said sluggishly. "Tomorrow, maybe."

Quarles sighed.

"Jack, there's something else you should know."

"Hmm?"

"The woman who shot you, Medicine Owl Woman," Quarles said. "I got a good look at the rifle she used. I hadn't seen it in years, but there was no doubt about it. There's not another round patch box with a design like that on any gun I've ever seen, in the mountains or the plains."

"Yeah?" Jack was almost asleep.

"She shot you with your own rifle, the one you made in St. Louis," Quarles said. "It was the Ghost Rifle."

31   *The Middle Distance*

Jack sat atop the horse, staring at the remains of the cabin. Most of the roof had been burned away, and what hadn't burned had since collapsed. The east and north walls—the front and the side—were gone, leaving the blackened interior of the cabin exposed like the rib cage of some great beast. Only the fireplace still stood, the rough stones reaching toward the autumn sky.

Sometimes Jack would glance from the cabin to the aspens in the middle distance on the side of the mountain, now turned to gold. But then his eyes would return to the cabin, the weight of the past year unbearable on his shoulders.

Finally, he swung down from the saddle, his boots touching earth that now seemed alien to him. He walked carefully among the ruins, searching for some sign that Sky and Hawk had escaped. Here, dent and blackened, was a tin cup he recognized as his favorite. There, broken and charred, was the table where he and Sky had shared so many meals. The Dutch oven, broken dishes, spoons twisted by the heat. But there were no bones. He stepped lightly across to the far side, where part of a wall still stood, and passed through a vacant doorway.

He walked over to the door of the root cellar.

He grasped the wooden handle and swung the once-heavy door open, now as light as cork. The door crumbled into pieces as it came to rest, leaving a swirl of dust and ash to hang in the afternoon light.

The domed top of a human skull shone like a pearl in the gloom.

Jack walked carefully down the earthen steps and crouched beside the skeleton. There were other bones, a rib cage covered in some tatters of blue cloth. There were arm bones and a hand, and a single-shot pistol nearby. It had been fired, and its action was now rusted together, the hammer forever fixed to the frizzen.

Gingerly, Jack picked up the skull. It was light, like a hollow gourd. His heart in his throat, he turned the skull in his hands to look at the face. It was intact, with no obvious sign of violence. One of the upper front teeth was chipped, from the childhood accident.

"Sky," Jack said.

His chin dropped to his chest and he wept, cradling the skull.

Because the skull was not blackened, he knew the fire had not reached her, but it had probably taken all of the air from the cellar. He did not know if she had fired the pistol before or after taking refuge. He hoped it was before, and that the ball had found its target. If after, then she had suffocated while someone likely held their foot on the cellar door, and she may have fired into the door trying to escape. But the door was in too poor of a shape to yield any clues.

When no more tears would come, he placed the skull outside on the ground, on a spot where the pine needles were thick, the vacant eyes pointed toward the aspen. Then he went back down into the cellar, took off his coat, and began to gather more bones. He lifted the rotting blue cloth that bundled the rib cage, and found his ledger book where he sketched his ideas and other things while sitting at the table. She had placed the book inside her dress. The book was intact, and uncharred, although the cloth boards seemed stained with blood.

Tucked behind Sky's skeleton he found that of Hawk. Sky had protected him as long as she could. He was glad, at least that they had not died alone. He searched the ground below, looking for some sign of the child that Sky carried, but found nothing. He knew there should be small, delicate bones, a tiny bird-like skull, something. Perhaps she miscarried sometime before the fire, Jack thought.

The last thing Jack found in the cellar was the small crock that held the bread starter that he had taken from the Yost's wagon. He undid the bale and moved aside the top. The starter, still grey and lumpy, had apparently survived.

With all of the bones he could recover spread out on the bed of pine needles. Jack sat down next to them and took up the ledger book, leafing through the pages. He found his diagram for the automatic loading mechanism, and many other inventions. But the pages he paused longest over were the ones that he would never allow Sky to see. These were the pages she had tried to look at on that last perfect day, and he had stopped her. She had complained that his visions seemed more real to Jack than she did, and Jack had stopped her from turning the page.

Jack stared at the picture before him.

It was a pencil sketch of Sky's face, her serious eyes as he remembered. She was on the dozen pages that followed as well, mending clothes, fleshing a skin, crouching to tend to something cooking in a pot over the fire. There were many studies of her face, some of them done while she slept, others from memory. On the very last page was a full-length sketch of Sky, nude, sleeping atop the robes in the loft.

Jack built a cairn of red rocks out behind the cabin and placed the bones of Sky and Hawk tenderly inside. With these he placed a candle taken from his saddlebags, to light the way. That was Basque tradition. The other was to leave bread, but Jack had none. So he took his finger and dipped it in the bread starter in the crock, and smeared some inside the cairn. He had not decided to take the crock with him when he left until that moment, when it occurred to him that the yeast in the starter represented the only living thing he could carry with him from the cabin.

He covered the top of the cairn with a heavy slab of red rock.

Then he said a Catholic prayer, in French, for Sky. It was the *Je Vous Salue Marie,* one that he remembered in its entirety from childhood because it was so short. Jack got through most of it, then had to take a breath before uttering the last line.

"... *maintenant et à l'heure de notre mort.*"

Now and at the hour of our death.

Jack said an *amen* and then took one last look at the aspens. It would be the last time he ever saw them, he knew, because it would be too painful ever to return. The autumn sunlight and the middle distance would never again be his. The path for now, he knew, led forever into darkness.

32 *The Natchez Mermaid*

"Professor Ashburn," the steward said, knocking on the cabin door.

Hamlin lurched from the bed to his feet. He was still dressed, except for his shoes. The card game had not ended until dawn. When Hamlin left the table, he had been playing for thirty hours straight, but he had taken from the fool planter from Memphis some five hundred dollars. That was more than a year's wages for a common laborer. Cards had not been part of the plan, Hamlin was just sitting to be sociable, but when the planter, Doherty, proved both enthusiastic and inept at poker, Hamlin could not resist the kill.

In the darkened cabin, and in his sleep-deprived state, Hamlin stubbed the little toe of his left foot on a chair leg. He hopped about while the pain shot like electricity from the insult.

"Professor Ashburn," the steward asked through the cabin door. "Are you all right?"

Hamlin limped over and opened the door. The sunlight stabbed him in both eyes.

"Why the devil are you making such a racket?" Hamlin asked. "Can't you see I'm trying to sleep?"

"Sorry, sir," the steward said. "But it's nearly noon."

"That's the middle of the night for me, son," Hamlin said.

"You gave me instructions that I was to make sure you were up by lunchtime," the steward said. "Don't you remember? Your niece and nephew are already at table."

Hamlin paused.

"Oh, yes," he said. "Of course. Are we on schedule?"

"Somewhat ahead. We will lower the gangplank at St. Louis by four o'clock."

"Thank you."

Hamlin found a dime in his pocket and pressed it into the steward's hand.

"Thank you, sir."

Hamlin shut the door and went to the basin on the nightstand. He poured some water from the pitcher. He splashed some on his face, then peered at his reflection in the round mirror behind the basin. He would have to shave quickly and carefully, break out a fresh shirt, and run a brush through his hair, but he could make himself presentable within a few minutes.

"Where are you going?" a woman mumbled from beneath the covers.

"To lunch," Hamlin said.

The woman sat up in bed. Her long dark hair fell limply over her bare breasts. Her yellow dress was crumpled on the floor beside the bed.

"Am I to stay?" she asked.

"You must leave, discreetly," Hamlin said. "Wait a few minutes after I have gone, then slip out."

"You have not yet received what you paid for."

"The spirit was willing," he said, "but sleep won out. Perhaps another time."

"Tonight?" the woman asked.

"I would not want to keep you from your friends at St. Louis, my dear," Hamlin said. "Busy yourself elsewhere on the boat. We will resume our acquaintance on my next run down the river."

The woman stared dully at him.

"That girl," she said. "She ain't your niece."

"Her feelings would be crushed to hear you talk so."

"Are you giving her the old what for?" the woman asked. "Do you like 'em young? Some men do. The younger the better."

"You are a rose yet in full bloom, my dear," Hamlin said, walking over and sitting on the bed. "There is no need to be jealous. But I won't stand for this kind of talk. If you persist with this slander, I'll be forced to take measures."

"Measures?" the woman asked.

Hamlin produced the single-shot pistol from a pocket and placed the barrel against her temple.

"Measures," he said.

The woman was too frightened to speak.

"Do not prove that I have misplaced my trust in you," Hamlin said. "Disembark as planned, do not speak of me or my wards to anyone, and I will see you again in a month or two. It's either that or you will never see anyone in this life again. Do you understand?"

The woman nodded.

Hamlin lowered the pistol.

"Now help me on with this clean shirt," he said. "There are too many buttons and not enough time."

Hamlin took a seat at the table and ran his hand over the clean white tablecloth to admire the weave. April was sitting across from him, her shoulders back and her hands in her lap. She was wearing a cheerful yellow dress, with ribbons to match in her dark hair. Gus was slouched to the side, an arm across the back of his chair, looking bored in his starched white shirt and tasteful blue jacket.

"Sit up, Tom," April said.

Gus did so. He was a head taller than April now, and the same height as Hamlin. But his chest was broader and his biceps larger. Hamlin attributed the boy's growth to regular meals.

"How are you feeling, Uncle?" April asked, a sharpness in her voice. "Your eyes are a bit red."

"I'm fine, my dear."

April looked to see that nobody was near, then leaned across the table.

"What were you thinking?" she asked. "What have you drilled into us from the very beginning? Don't deviate from the plan. And here you are playing poker all night and taking some ignorant planter for all the money he has on him."

"The opportunity presented itself." Hamlin shrugged.

"This smells of trouble," April said. "The planter will

have stewed all night and will have convinced himself that he was cheated, whether you played crooked or not."

"I never play crooked at cards," Hamlin said.

"Then you're not content to leave it at that," April said. "Flushed with either whiskey or the tumescence a pocketful of gold can bring, you drag one of the whores who had been watching the game up to your cabin?"

"Just a bit of fluff," Hamlin said. "And, that's my personal business."

"It's not when it endangers the play," April said. "We've spent weeks setting this up and you're about to spoil it because you can't keep your ego in check. And by your ego I mean your prick."

"I knew what you meant," Hamlin said.

"How much did you tell her? Or how much did she guess?"

"Enough of that," Hamlin said. "Others will wonder about the unpleasantness."

"Just a niece pouting because she did not get the bonnet she wanted," April said, leaning back and squaring her shoulders again. A tear came to her eye and rolled down her check. "There," she said. "That should do it."

Hamlin smiled and pulled a five-dollar note from his vest and pushed it across to her. April took it and dabbed her tears with a handkerchief.

"Thank you, Uncle."

Gus sighed. Since he had finally grown to match his age, there never seemed enough for him to do; the game had worked better when others could believe he was the much younger brother, but his height and deepening voice now made that impossible. He was also bored of

April and Hamlin arguing. There was only a month to go before the end of the agreed-upon two-year period, and the closer the time came, the more erratic was Hamlin's behavior. He was drinking and gambling more, and generally taking risks that might ruin them all. It was as if he would rather the three of them land in jail than go their separate ways.

"Stop it, both of you," Gus said. "You are playing each other, not others. I say we end this one. We have a five-hundred-dollar payday, which is more than enough to set up for the next play."

"But we've put so much work into the Natchez Mermaid," April said.

"We can save it for another time," Gus said.

"That's easy for you to say," April shot back. "Next time, you sew the damned monkey's head onto a catfish."

"Shush up," Hamlin said. "We'll play this out as planned."

They fell silent as a pair of men who had been a few hours at the card game passed by. They congratulated Professor Ashburn, who with an easy smile attributed his good fortune to beginner's luck. Then a tall, awkward man of about forty, dressed in somewhat better-than-respectable clothing, came and asked if he could sit with them. He had a sad face and round eyes and ear lobes that dangled like pears on the branch.

"We'd be delighted, Mister Bagley," Hamlin said.

"Please," April said. "Sit here, between me and my uncle."

Bagley muttered his thanks and took the seat.

"Have you considered my offer?" Bagley asked.

Hamlin affected a pained look.

"I have, sir," he said. "And I am sorry to disappoint."

"But why?" Bagley asked. "Is the offer not enough—"

"It is not a matter of money," Hamlin said. "I have dedicated myself to the advancement of knowledge, and I believe this specimen deserves proper study at the academy."

"Could not knowledge be advanced with the creature staying in its native land?"

"It is difficult to compete with the sheer volume of scientific talent in Paris," Hamlin said. "If we were in need of funds, then perhaps we would consider it, but our family is really quite comfortable. We have tried to accommodate your curiosity as best we could, with the private viewing. Were you satisfied with your sketches?"

"It is difficult to draw by the light of only a few tapers."

"The creature does not react well to light," Hamlin said. "It lives in the deepest parts of the river, in ledges and pockets far below the surface of the water. We fear sunlight would kill it."

"That risk would be unacceptable."

"I'm glad you understand," Hamlin said.

"I have been pondering the problem," Bagley said. "I propose a permanent abode, a great glass tank in the darkness of a good-sized cavern my family owns on some property at the bluffs near the edge of town. Illumination would be provided by lanterns only. Do you think that would be detrimental to the health of the creature?"

Hamlin pursed his lips.

"It is difficult to answer," he said. "But as I said, the advancement . . ."

"I double my offer," Bagley said. "It would be better to keep the mermaid here, where she could educate thousands of paying visitors, rather than give her over to foreign experts."

"The French Academy has no equal."

"Then let them come here," Bagley said.

"Perhaps," Hamlin said. "But let us not talk business over lunch."

"Uncle is right," April said, putting a hand on Bagley's forearm. "Let us enjoy our luncheon and one another's company. All this talk of business and natural science has made my poor head hurt."

"Sincerest apologies," he said.

Bagley was mesmerized by April. His eyes widened when he looked at her, his nostrils flared slightly, and his ears with their giant lobes reddened. It amused April that she had this effect on him, and although she found him old and plain and dull, her attention was necessary to sell the mermaid story. Bagley did not know it, but the need he sought to fill with the mermaid was his desire for April herself.

April smiled and squeezed his arm.

"Do you fence?" she asked.

"Why do you ask?"

"Because your muscles are so firm," she said.

"Well, I did in my youth," Bagley said.

"I knew it!" April said. "Do you hear that, Tom? Perhaps Mister Bagley would give you a lesson or two."

"That would be most kind of him," Gus said.

Then there was some motion at the entrance at the side of the salon deck, a man rushing past the stewards, and homing in on the table where Hamlin and his proteges sat, like a hawk descending on a rabbit with talons at the ready.

"Ashburn!" the man rumbled.

He was so mad that he was shaking.

"Why, Mister Doherty," Hamlin said pleasantly. "It is good to see you again."

"You are a swine, a filthy pig, a porcine pretender in a brocaded waistcoat!"

All eyes in the salon turned to see the commotion. A steward had Doherty by the arm, but could not move him from the spot.

"Whatever do you mean?" Hamlin asked.

"You are a filthy card sharp."

There were gasps at nearby tables.

"We had a perfectly friendly game of poker last night."

"You cheated me out of five hundred dollars."

"That is a serious allegation," Hamlin said, rising from his chair. "Let us take a stroll out on the deck and work this out. I think perhaps that you may have simply had too much wine last night."

Doherty pushed him back down in the chair.

"I wasn't drunk," he said. "You were cheating."

Hamlin delivered his next sentences calmly, and in a voice low enough so that the other tables could not hear, but with a face so cold that it could have been made of stone.

"I never cheat," Hamlin said. "You are a bad poker player and should never wager money on the game. I suggest you retract your slander or be prepared for the consequences."

"Consequence away!" Doherty hissed.

"Very well," Hamlin said, his voice returning to its natural and theatrical volume. "I am sorry for this unpleasantness, Mister Bagley. I hope you will excuse me for a moment."

Bagley was silent and slack-jawed.

In Bagley's sad eyes, Hamlin saw the prospect of selling the Natchez Mermaid fade. April had her hands to her mouth, as if with fear, but her eyes burned with anger. Gus was shaking his head.

Hamlin rose wearily.

"Will there be violence?" Bagley asked.

"No," April said. "Uncle is not a violent man."

"Come," Hamlin said to Doherty.

"Where?"

"I will fetch your money," Hamlin said. "I play only for enjoyment and the opportunity to exercise my understanding of probability. The money is of little importance."

"Uncle!" April cried. Her alarm was real, because it was a rule never to return the spoils.

"There, there," Hamlin said. "Do not be concerned. We are all friends here."

"I am not your friend," Doherty said.

"But I am yours," Hamlin said. "You will understand that one day. Come to my cabin, and we will make the matter straight between us. Wealth amounts to little when compared to the love of our fellow man. Would a card— what was the term you used?—would a card *sharp* so willingly return money taken at the table?"

"I don't know—I mean, I don't think so."

"Of course not," Hamlin said, putting his hand on

Doherty's shoulder. "If only we had the wisdom of Solomon at times such as these, all would be clear."

Gus scooted his chair away from the table. *Solomon* was the code word for making an exit as quickly and quietly as possible.

"I have just remembered a letter that must be written," he said. "Pardon me."

"Of course," April said. "And Mister Bagley, would you excuse me? All of this excitement has caused . . . well, I must go the necessary. You will wait here for me?"

Bagley looked at her blankly.

"You will wait here?" she asked again. "I should be sad to return and find you gone."

"Yes," Bagley said. "I will wait."

"Good," April said, smiling.

Outside, the spring sun was pounding down on the river as if meeting an anvil, the light scattering into a million diamonds across the undulating tops of the murky brown water. It was April 1837, and the twins had only a month left in their agreement with Hamlin.

"All of this work," April said. "Only to miss our chance at real money because Holly's pride got in the way. Damn him. Gus, you go see if the old man needs help with his friend. Don't let Hollister kill him. Thrashing, but no more, you understand?"

"I know what to do," Gus said.

"I will go dump the damned mermaid into the river," April said. "We can't leave it behind and it's too hard to carry in a hurry. We may never get another chance at this game, but that can't be helped now."

"We should find an easier play," Gus said. "This one is too complicated."

"I agree," April said, thinking of how Bagley had looked at her. "Now, go on. You know the Solomon rule, we must be quick. But Gus, if Doherty is getting the best of the old man, wait a moment or two before stepping in, won't you?"

33 *Rendezvous*

Jack was so drunk he could not read the cards he held in his hand. He covered first one eye with his hand, and then the other, to try to bring the blur of red and black into focus, but it was no use. He rested his right hand on the butt of the single-shot pistol tucked into his belt and leaned back.

"I'll be damned," he said. "I am blind drunk."

"What's it going to be?" his opponent demanded. "You drawing or what?"

"Or what," Jack said. "I feel good about this hand."

Jack couldn't remember the last time he had eaten or slept. But his capacity for alcohol and for gambling kept him awake far after most men would be slumped unconscious in some corner. He also retained the ability to talk, in complete sentences, and without slurring his words. The tolerance was an annoyance, because it did not hinder his remembering. But this night, he knew he may have now found the limit of his tolerance. Still, Jack kept his tin cup of whiskey close, taking liberal swallows.

The tavern was a stained and torn tent, with one side rolled up to allow customers easier access. Overhead,

Jack could see the midnight stars through a ragged hole in the canvas. The rendezvous was where the *Siskadee Agie*—Crow for Sage Hen River—meets Horse Creek. It was a pleasant spot, quiet for most of the year, until the fur companies and the traders and the trappers converged on it at about the time of the summer solstice and turned it into a rustic bacchanalia. Nothing was free, but everything was for sale. Even in the middle of the night, the revelry continued, with drunken singing and an occasional gunshot echoing down the midway between the rows of trader's tents, shanties, and lean-tos.

His opponent was a small man named Buzzard with a tawny beard that flowed down over his chest like a bib. He was a trapper, like most of the white men at the rendezvous, and he had a year's worth of pay in his pockets and was desperate to throw some of it on the upended whiskey barrel they were using for a card table.

"Stranger," Buzzard said, "you're too drunk to play."

"Is my money on the barrel?" Jack asked.

"Yes. Twenty dollars in silver."

"Then I am not too drunk to play," Jack said. "Get on with it, because you are in danger of boring me."

Buzzard asked for two cards. The dealer flicked them to him facedown.

The dealer was one of the traders that came to rendezvous to sell supplies needed for the next trapping season and bad whiskey for immediate consumption. He had set up a tent in the middle of the rendezvous camp, offering a comfortable place to drink and gamble. When things were slow, he dealt cards for tips.

"Raise," Buzzard said. From his pocket he produced another ten dollars and threw the coins on the barrel.

Jack laughed.

"You seem damned confident," Jack said.

"Are you in or out?" Buzzard asked.

"Oh, I'm in," Jack said, matching the money.

"All right, gentlemen," the dealer said. "Moment of truth. Lay your cards down."

Buzzard spread his out, faceup.

"Two pair," the dealer said. "Queens and Tens."

"My," Jack said. "I don't know if I can beat that."

"Show your cards," the dealer said.

Jack slapped them on the barrel.

"Full house," the dealer said.

"Damn you to hell," Buzzard said.

Jack laughed demonically.

"Most assuredly," Jack said. "I am going to hell, but I'm taking your money with me."

Jack clawed the money from the barrel and shoved it into his pockets. He drained the last of the whiskey in his tin cup. Then he spit something out of his mouth into the palm of his hand. It was a rattlesnake head.

"Well, would you look at that," he said. "It explains the curious aftertaste."

"That's what you expect with Taos Lightning," the dealer said. "I have some stuff that came from Kentucky in back, but it ain't cheap."

"What is a snake head among friends?" Jack asked. "But let me win some more money from my friend here and I just might buy some of that good Kentucky bourbon. What do you say, Buzzard, another hand?"

Buzzard stood.

"I'm all tuckered out," he said.

"Chance to win your money back," Jack said.

"I need some sleep," Buzzard said. "So do you."

"The sleep of the dead awaits," Jack said. "But not just yet. Play me just one more hand, if you have the eggs for it."

"Are you saying I don't have the balls to play a drunk?"

"Let's take a break, boys," the dealer suggested.

"No," Jack said. "I'm saying you don't have the balls to play *this* drunk."

Buzzard reached across the makeshift table and clenched Jack's shirt front in his grip. Then he jerked Jack forward, upsetting the barrel, and sending cards riffling to the dirt.

"That's it," the dealer said. "Game's closed until morning."

Jack laughed.

"What's so damned funny?" Buzzard asked, still clutching Jack's shirt front.

"This," Jack said.

The Damascus blade came from below to rest beneath Buzzard's chin, the tip hidden beneath the patch of beard that covered his throat. The man looked down at the blade and released his grip on Jack's shirt.

"Don't kill me," Buzzard said.

"I can't think of a reason not to," Jack said. "I am so drunk it would hardly be murder. That requires intent, and I can hardly form a coherent thought. It would be manslaughter under the influence of spirits, at best."

"Don't kill me, and I'll play you another hand," Buzzard said.

"Ah!" Jack said. "A reason to allow you to live."

"You have one hot knife," the trader said. "That's bad for business."

Jack sheathed the Damascus.

"Not my business," Jack said.

Jack told Buzzard to pick up the barrel and gather the cards so they could play.

"Aren't you afraid of the enemies you make?" the trader asked.

"I am afraid of nothing," Jack said. "Chief among the advantages of being irredeemably damned and knowing it is the elimination of fear. Whether hell or oblivion awaits, nothing I do will alter my trajectory in the slightest."

Jack paused.

"But I do try to keep children and innocents out of my field of fire."

"I thought I knew all the trappers this side of the Powder River," the trader said. "Stranger, what did you say your name was?"

"Mister," Jack said, "You can call me whatever suits you."

"If you say so, Hot Knife," the trader said.

Three hours later, Jack stood and raked his winnings into his pockets. He swayed slightly as he did this, ignoring the wicked looks of the man he'd just relieved of most of his year's wages. Jack could not remember the man's name, but he had disliked him from the moment he had taken the stool Buzzard had occupied. He had a pinched face that reminded Jack of a rat, and from the first hand he had decided to ruin him.

"Pleasure playing pasteboards with you," Jack said, tipping his hat.

"I am done in," the rat-faced man said.

"You accusing me of cheating?"

"No," the man said. "It was unwise of me to gamble."

Jack paused, an irritating pang of conscience developing.

"I would have felt better having lost my fortune to a highwayman," the man said. "At least then I would have somebody else to blame."

"There's an idea," Jack said.

"To get robbed?" the man asked.

He no longer looked so rat-faced to Jack.

"To do the robbing," Jack said, digging a hand in his right pocket. He brought out a handful of silver and threw it on the barrel head, and then added another to it.

"Reckon that will buy your traps and other truck for the coming season."

"Why?" the man asked.

"Don't ask why, just take it," Jack said. "And don't gamble no more."

Jack walked out onto the midway, his mind still fogged with whiskey. The sun was brightening the east, and the traders began dousing the torches and lanterns. There was still plenty of drinking and gambling going on, and a fair amount of fighting, but the camp had calmed somewhat.

Then Jack noticed a man walking ahead, a bald man well over six feet, and he had his left arm around the waist of a young Shoshone woman, half dragging her along so that her moccasins barely touched the ground. The man had a wiry black beard and dark eyes and a set of Roman beads with a wooden cross hanging from around his neck. The cross swung from a strip of zig-zag Arikara beadwork, in red and white.

Jack stopped short.

"Hold there," Jack called, his mind clearing.

The bald man stopped.

"You're too small of a man to be giving me orders," the man said in a heavy French accent.

"Perhaps," Jack said, placing his hand near the pistol in his belt. "Perhaps not. Let me see that cross you wear."

"Why?"

"I knew somebody that had one like it once."

The man pushed the Shoshone woman away. She stumbled and fell in the dirt, her black hair pillowing about her head. Jack saw that his left arm ended at his wrist. The stub was covered by a leather cap that was studded with brass tacks.

The bald man laughed, menace in his eyes.

"Who the hell are you to even be asking me these questions?" His good hand reached into a pocket and came out wearing brass knuckles. "You think that children's toy in your belt scares me? Before I'm done with you, I'm going to make you wish your mother had drowned you at birth."

"No, La Bête," the Shoshone woman pleaded.

"Shut up," the man said.

"They call you the beast?"

"I am La Bête."

Jack stood still, his hand still near the pistol.

"Tell me about the cross."

"It's a pelt," the man said.

"A pelt?"

"A plew, a prize, a trophy," he said. "I keep as a reminder of something I once did. How did you know the squaw bitch I took it from?"

"She was my wife."

Jack pulled the pistol with his right hand and filled his left with the Damascus toothpick, falling into a fighting stance.

"Do you want me to tell you how she died?"

"I know how she died," Jack said. "Unafraid."

Jack cocked the pistol.

The man spat.

A crowd of trappers had begun to form in a circle around them, summoned by the sound of an imminent fight. Bets were placed, with the odds favoring the one-handed man.

"Do you want me to tell you how your brother died?" Jack asked. "He was on the floor, trussed up like a hog, and I drove this blade down the side of his neck into his fucking heart. He died afraid."

The man roared his anger.

"Shoot him," the woman urged.

The man took half a step in her direction and then kicked her under the chin with a boot, sending her sprawling. Then he wheeled and came at Jack, swinging the brass knuckles.

Jack moved back, allowing the knuckles to catch only air. He leveled the pistol at the man's head and pulled the trigger, but at the instant the gun fired the man put the stump of his left wrist over his face. The ball embedded itself, smoking, in the leather and wood of the cap.

"Now you're cooked!"

The man drove the stump into Jack's face, and he could feel the brass tacks tearing into the flesh over his cheekbone. Jack dropped the gun and staggered back, silver spilling from his pockets.

The man rushed him, head down, like a bull.

Jack tumbled backward, but kept his grip on the Damascus.

The man advanced and Jack stabbed the man in the right foot, the blade going straight down, through leather and flesh, to embed itself in the hard sole. The man yelped and drew his foot away. He dropped the brass knuckles and grasped the blade and tried to pull it free, but could not. He limped around in circles, howling like an animal.

Jack snatched up the brass knuckles and tossed them beyond reach.

Then the man stopped trying to remove the knife from his foot and scrambled after Jack, trying to reach him with his hand.

"Come on," Jack taunted, staying just out of reach. "You can do better. Ah, there you almost had me. Try harder."

The crowd urged him on.

"That's right," Jack said. "A little more."

The man's face was made terrifying by rage, the eyes unfocused, his teeth bared. His hand was bleeding from trying to pull the Damascus from his foot and, in the flailing effort, grasping the blade instead.

Jack picked up the pistol from where he'd dropped it. Holding the pistol by the barrel, he brought the round grip down on the man's bald head. It made the sound of bunging a barrel. The man rolled over with a heavy sigh, his eyes rolling up to show only the whites. His feet were quivering.

Jack tucked the spent pistol back into his belt.

Using both hands on the hilt and a foot on the ankle, he pulled free the Damascus. Then he slashed the man's throat, ear to ear. Jack wiped the blade on the man's trousers, then sheathed the knife.

"Cut his throat as if he were a hog," somebody said as bets were settled.

Jack reached into his pocket and gathered a handful of coins.

"Here," he said, throwing the silver to the ground at their feet. "Take this and give me some peace."

The crowd—trappers and traders, the Shoshone woman, members of some other nations—clawed at the grass and dirt for the coins. After the crowd had drifted away, Jack knelt down behind the dead man's neck and untied the knot holding the beadwork. He closed his eyes and held the beadwork and the cross in his palm for several long minutes. Then he slipped them into his pocket, rose, and went off in search of more whiskey.

34   *The St. Pete*

April stood on the balcony of the Planter's Hotel, her hands on the iron rail, looking out at the landing below and the Mississippi beyond. It was the finest hotel on the river, at least in Missouri, and she relished having the means to stay there. Although Hamlin's mistake had cost them an opportunity for real wealth, the five hundred dollars he had won at cards would provide leisure for a few weeks, at least until it was time to begin work on the next scheme. Gus was with her on the balcony, his hands in his pockets and his shoulders against the wall. He did not like heights, not even that of a third-floor view.

"What do you think the matter is with Holly?" April asked.

Gus knew but he saw no point in stating the obvious, even if she could not see it.

"He's the same as he ever was," Gus said, "since the time he bumped you on the dock at Alton."

"That seems so long ago," April said. She walked over to a small, round table on the balcony that held two glasses and a squat bottle of Kentucky bourbon. She uncorked the bottle and poured. "Look at how far we've come in so little time."

"Sometimes it doesn't seem so far to me," Gus said.

April asked if Gus wanted a drink. He said no.

"What do you mean?" she asked. "Why doesn't it seem far to you?"

April raised the glass and parted her lips, the bourbon sliding down her throat like fire. She liked the sensation, even though she knew Hamlin would not approve if he smelled it on her breath.

"Are we any closer to satisfaction?"

"We have some fine things," April said. "We eat tolerable well. Old Granger is still dead."

"We are no closer to knowing who we are."

The wind fluttered the yellow ribbons in April's hair.

"It's like Holly said," she said, taking another sip. "We are who we want to be."

"We can't do this forever," Gus said. "Enough people on the river already know our faces that it makes business difficult. A few more mistakes from the old man and we're going to end up in jail."

"You've talked about jail since you were small," April said. "But we have yet to see the inside of one."

"But we have come close."

"Close doesn't count," April said.

She shaded her eyes with her hand.

"Look," she said, "there's a new boat at the wharf. It's small, but all shining and new. I can't make out the name from here."

"It's the *St. Peter*," Gus said. "It's a western rivers boat, commissioned by the American Fur Company.

John Jacob Astor's outfit. Some of the officers are at the bar downstairs, filling their bellies with whiskey. It's against the law to trade in liquor with Indians on the upper Missouri beyond Fort Leavenworth, so spirits will be in short supply. Each man is allowed only a small amount for personal use."

"That would be a powerful hardship," April said.

"When our agreement with Hamlin expires," Gus suggested, "we should strike out on our own. The old man has become a hazard."

"He taught us all about the game."

"We owe him a debt," Gus said. "But it is time to pilot our own lives."

"You may be right," April said. "But Holly is the only man close to us in our entire lives that has not betrayed us. That is worth something, is it not?"

"There's a season for learning," Gus said, "and one for gratitude. We have been tutored and have been appropriately grateful. Now is the time for the next season of our lives."

"Why, Augustus," April said, "I believe the poetry books and the private tutors have had their desired effect. That was spoken like a gentleman. Come, let us descend to the dining room. It is nearly supper time. Holly will be waiting for us."

Downstairs, they found Hamlin sitting at a table near the bar, talking to a middle-aged man in a blue suit who was smoking a fat cigar.

"There you are," Hamlin said upon seeing them. "I'd like to introduce you to the master of the *St. Peter*, Captain Pratt. Sir, this is my niece and my nephew, Kalista and Kallikrates."

"Fine names," the captain said. "Your parents were admirers of the ancient Greeks?"

"It would seem so," April allowed, irritated that she had new names to remember. She avoided approaching Hamlin too closely, lest he smell the liquor on her breath. "They would read us Homer for our bedtime stories."

"Late parents, unfortunately," Hamlin said. "Both taken by the smallpox before their time."

"My condolences," the captain said. "Were they not given the cowpox vaccine?"

"Sadly, no," Hamlin said. "My sister's husband was an ardent adherent of Swedenborg, you see."

"Ah," Pratt said. "Superstition is a disease of its own. No offense meant."

"None taken," April said. "The experience so soured . . . Kallikrates and myself that we have become confirmed atheists. Isn't that right, Kal?"

"Right as rain," Gus said. "We are disciples of reason now. Why, I understand the federal government in Washington is even arranging for the Indian tribes to be vaccinated, to spare them this scourge."

"Only the civilized tribes in the lower states," Pratt said. "No vaccines have been sent yet to the nations along the upper Missouri, except for a small amount that sank with a keelboat."

"Captain Pratt has been giving me the most fascinating account of his new boat," Hamlin said. "It's a side-wheeler built in Pittsburgh and has two boilers and special high-pressure engines."

"But supper, Uncle?" April asked.

"Supper can wait," Hamlin said. "Come sit with us."

April and Gus drew chairs up to the table.

"I believe I saw your boat, from my balcony, shining white among the other dull craft at the wharf," April said. "It is quite impressive."

"It is only one hundred and nineteen tons," Pratt said. "But she is trim."

"Now here's the part that will be of most interest," Hamlin said. "Tell her who commissioned the boat."

"John Jacob Astor?" April asked.

"Very good," Hamlin said. "He is the richest man in the world."

"Astor commissioned the boat, but he has since left the American Fur Company," Pratt said. "The company, however, is still the largest business enterprise in the United States."

"And Astor built it all with furs?" Gus asked.

"The old pirate also smuggled a lot of opium," Pratt said.

Gus laughed.

"The steamboat will end the days of the keelboat on the Missouri," Pratt declared. "When I was young, a keelboat would require twenty men, winching and dragging it along with heavy cordelles, on the journey upriver. It once would take a season to reach Fort Union. We will be there in a matter of weeks, even with regular stops to offload supplies. Downriver will be even quicker, and we will carry more furs on our decks than could a fleet of flatboats."

"But hasn't the market for beaver become soft?" April asked.

Pratt looked amused.

"How do you know that, my dear?"

"The newspapers, of course."

"Beaver is not as popular a hat material as it once was," Pratt said, "but many other furs remain lucrative, such as muskrat and fox. There is also a great demand for bison hides. They are an excellent material for making belts to drive machinery."

"Fascinating," April said. "A brave new world, is it not? What far corner is yet unreachable to us now?"

"The Rockies," Pratt said. "There are still places in the mountains that no white man has seen."

"Kalista, that's enough," Hamlin said. "Do not interrogate the captain so."

"I take no offense," Pratt said. "She is a bright young woman."

"Not bright at all, just curious," April said. "Uncle, I am famished. Perhaps you could rendezvous with your new friend after supper?"

"I'm afraid not," Pratt said. "I must gather my officers soon and return to the boat. It was a pleasure passing the time with you, Mr. Stavros. I wish you all a very good night."

The captain tugged at the bill of his cap.

On the way into the dining room, April feigned a coughing fit. She put her hand on a table, as if to steady herself, and mumbled to Gus to bring her something strong to ease her throat. Gus started to flag down a steward, but Hamlin produced a silver flask from inside his jacket.

"Here," he said. "Just a quick nip."

April took a bit more than that.

"Thank you, Uncle," she said, handing the flask back

to Hamlin and putting the back of her other hand to her lips. Once seated in the dining room, April leaned close to Hamlin and whispered in his ear.

"Do not give us names without telling us the play first," she said. "It was hard enough figuring the angle without having to remember classical names. And Holly, I'm not sure that Greek was the way to go with this one, whatever the play was to be. He seemed unclear on what the names meant."

"A deficiency in his education," Hamlin said. "The American Fur Company is rich beyond imagination. An opportunity will arise."

"How?" April asked. "They are headed upriver in the morning."

"We could work something out in a few hours," Hamlin said. "The weight on Pratt of having to make a timely departure is useful. Image a valve or some other critical part of these high-pressure engines disappearing. If we could produce one, the reward would be commensurate with the need."

"That's an idea," Gus said.

"But not a good one," April said. "You just like it because it involves something mechanical. The real money is to be made in manipulating emotional need."

Hamlin gazed at April for a moment too long, annoying her so that she put a hand to her brow.

"This is a one-night game," Hamlin said. "No weeks of preparation, no romancing the mark, less chance of things going wrong."

"Are we to rely on common criminality, then, to vandalize or steal this needed piece of hardware," April said.

"Where's the fun in that? So, which one of us wields the hammer?"

"I will," Gus said. "It's not just the officers who will over indulge tonight. The crew will, too. The watch will be light or non-existent. I will sneak aboard and perform the required task."

"No," Hamlin said. "There's another duty required. You must keep an eye on this Captain Pratt and see that he doesn't come within a thousand yards of his boat while the necessary business is being done."

"Then you, Holly?" April asked.

"Then us," Hamlin said.

April sighed.

"I will wield the hammer," Hamlin said. "And while you stand lookout, you can come up with a story to sell the item back to Pratt. Consider it an opportunity to show me what you've learned during your apprenticeship. You grow tired of my schemes. Here's your chance to stretch your wings, and see if you really want to fly."

"I did not say that."

"But the two years are nearly up," Hamlin said. "It must be on your mind."

"We have discussed it, Gus and me," she said. "But we have made no decision."

"Ah," Hamlin said. "It is good to take care in such matters."

"Even if we ask to stay," April said, "you are under no obligation."

"No," Hamlin said. "I'm not. But I rather enjoy your company."

"And if we decide to end our association," April asked, "what about you? What will you do?"

"Manage as I did before," Hamlin said. "Which is to say, I will manage quite well."

Shortly after ten that night April and Hamlin strolled down to the landing, arm in arm, a casual family outing. The wharf was packed with steamboats, from the smallest of packets to the floating hotels that made the weekly runs to New Orleans and back. The *St. Peter* had lights burning along the upper deck, but the lower deck was dark and quiet. It was a simple matter to slip from the dock onto the stern of the boat, and then disappear in the shadows.

"Be still a few minutes," Hamlin told April. "Once we're sure nobody is about, we'll proceed."

"This is a foolish plan," she said. "Do you even know which part to remove?"

"In theory," Hamlin said. "The engine cannot operate without a governor, a device that looks like a spinning toy that controls the admission of steam into the cylinder. Or so I think. We take the governors for both engines, and we've left her motionless until a replacement is found."

"Won't someone hear the hammering?"

"No hammering," Hamlin said. "The loosening of a nut, the pulling of a pin, and the device is detached. I have the tools needed in my coat pocket."

"I can't believe they left the deck unattended," she said.

"Likely drunk somewhere, as I said."

The air coming from the river was cold, and April shivered.

Hamlin put his arm around her.

She stiffened.

"If anyone should come," he said, "then we will appear as just a pair of lovers who sought a private place for an intimate moment."

"Is that what lovers do?" April asked.

Hamlin removed his arm.

"Yes," he said. "That is what they do."

He removed his jacket and offered it to April. She swung it around her shoulders, clutching the lapels, her forearms crossed over her chest.

"Your tools are light," she said. "I can hardly feel them."

"April," Hamlin said. "There is something you should know."

"Can't it wait?"

"No, I think not," he said. "It's about the way I feel about you."

"I like you just fine, too."

"No, it's more than that," he said. "At least for me. There was a reason I bumped into you on the dock at Alton. Yes, I was looking for a protege. But there was something more. I've been drawn to you since the moment I first saw you, even in rags and with hunger pinching your face."

"Drawn to me."

"Yes."

"As in romantically."

"Yes."

"Well, that explains much," she said. "The way you

look at me, especially these past months. It is like the way I see other men look at women, as if they were items in a store window they were thinking of buying."

"I do not want to buy you."

"It seems you already have," April said. "These last two years, everything Gus and I have is because of you. It's only because of that bump on the dock that things turned out as fine as they did. Otherwise, we'd still be wearing rags and hunger."

"You would have made your way," he said. "A better way, even."

"I think not," April said.

"You underestimate yourself."

"No," she said. "I know exactly who I am."

"April, I am besotted with you," Hamlin said. "It has gotten worse as you have grown to be a woman. I cannot sleep, I take no pleasure in food or drink, and all of my energy has been spent in trying to find a way to tell you how I feel."

"I am not yet sixteen," she said.

"Many women marry by sixteen."

"I do not love you," she said. "Not in that way."

"In time," Hamlin said. "Don't you think, that in time, you could come to love me in that way?"

A memory of Granger stinking and heaving on top of her stabbed at her mind. Her left hand strayed to the yellow ribbon around her neck. The bone-handled straight razor hung between her breasts.

"In that way?" April asked, strangely detached.

"In the way of men and women."

"So, you would like to play these lovers' games in the shadows with me," April said, a finger beneath the ribbon. "That is why you've been off your play, or worse, devising non-existent plays to get me alone and keep Gus occupied. There are no tools in the pocket of this coat, Holly, are there?"

"No," he said.

"The play was on me," April said. "You lied to me as you would a mark you were trying to turn. I knew none of this made sense. Now it does."

"Do you feel nothing for me?"

"You are the nearest thing to a father I have known," she said. "I now see that I've been foolish to think of you as such. You are old enough to be my father, and more. Just as you've lied to me, I've lied to myself. I thought I genuinely meant something to you, but I was just a challenging piece of fluff."

"Don't," Hamlin said.

"Why not?" April asked. "It's what you want, isn't it? Why should you care how it is delivered?"

"Lower your voice," he said.

"What is the going rate for high-quality trim?" she asked. "We can start the negotiation there, with a discount for familiarity. Or should I charge extra because the relationship borders on the incestuous? Do men have those fantasies about their daughters?"

Hamlin slapped her.

She uttered a cry, and the coat dropped to the deck.

For a moment April thought of producing the razor and giving it work, but then she caught herself, realizing she could not kill Granger twice. Her fingers left the ribbon at her throat and she gave a start, filling her lungs with the cool night air.

"I won't have you talk that way," Hamlin said.

"You," April said, "won't have me at all."

In the darkness, they heard someone call out.

"Who's there?" a rough voice asked.

Hamlin and April were like statues.

"Billy?" the voice called. "Have—"

The question was interrupted by a rattling cough.

"Have you come to spot me?" the voice asked, followed by more coughing. "I've been feeling so poorly I must have dozed off. I couldn't hold down my supper. Now my head feels as hot as the *St. Pete*'s boilers under full steam."

Hamlin slowly reached down and retrieved the coat, then grasped April's hand and led her toward the dock. She clutched his hand, feeling the warmth of his palm, the strength in his fingers. It was the feeling of safety, and that's all she had ever wanted to feel with him. But she knew that had now ended.

"Billy?" the voice called after.

35 *A Nation of One*

The boy called Blue Otter sat shivering bare-chested in the cold outside the lodge, unsure of what to do. It was snowing, and sometimes the north wind drove the flakes into his eyes, which made them sting and water. He was glad for that because it hid his tears.

The lodge behind him was dark, as were the other dozen in the village. Never in Blue Otter's eighteen years had he seen a winter where every lodge in the village was without the familiar and warm firelight in the top half of the tilted cone, above the *ozan* inner lining, and smoke drifting between the flaps at the apex. Dogs were milling about the camp, and there were a few horses tied to a line behind the lodges, but there were no human beings moving.

Blue Otter looked up at the winter sky, and it seemed the stars themselves were falling from the cloud-shrouded sky. He cried out, and asked *Wakan Tanka* what was the purpose of such misery on earth. If this had been one of the old stories, Blue Otter said, then White Buffalo Calf Woman would have appeared and explained the meaning to him, or perhaps Coyote would come stealing, with his sly smile, and laugh at the folly of human beings. But this was no story and there was only Blue Otter, alone, in a dark village with a winter night approaching.

When he finally rose, he had to break free of where his knees had frozen to the ground and brush a mound of snow from his bare head and shoulders. He had left his robe behind in the dark lodge before him, not believing he deserved comfort. But now he was shivering and he knew he must either move or freeze to death in his grief.

Blue Otter entered the lodge and slid past the *ozan*. Light and snow fell into the lodge from the smoke flaps above. Without the fire that usually burned within the circle of stones, the lodge was as cold as the world outside. The old man was slouched near the fire stones, his eyes open and his face and hands covered with sores.

The boy started to reach for the buffalo robe that covered the old man's torso, but he stopped before touching it.

"Forgive me, Grandfather," he said. "You will need that for your journey."

Blue Otter walked over to where Medicine Owl Woman was propped up on a willow backrest. Her eyes were closed but her face and hands were covered with the same bumpy, liquid-filled sores.

"Aunt," Blue Otter said. "I must now go or else I will be forced to join you and Grandfather on the black road. But you will meet many going to the west. The plague has come up the river and swept the valley. They say Mandan and other nations are but shadows, just as our nation exists only now in one. Our name shall be heard no more, because it can only be spoken to other members of the nation, and I am now alone."

The boy went to the lodgepole from which hung Medicine Owl Woman's shooting bag. There was a deer-skin tunic below, carefully folded, and a fringed and beaded rifle case resting on it.

Blue Otter put on the tunic, then slung the shooting bag across his chest. He picked up the rifle case and opened the flap and reverently slid out the rifle, the one his aunt would tell stories about recovering from the deepest waters of the broad river. The rifle was as he had always remembered it, solid and polished and deadly. He opened the round, spring-loaded lid to the brass patch box and saw it was filled with enough linen for a dozen shots. From the weight of the shooting bag, he knew it carried at least that much powder and shot.

"Thank you, my chief," Blue Otter said to the dead woman. "The rifle will bring me food and victory. Both are necessary for life, but only one for death. You have your coups and your captured horses now."

Blue Otter left the lodge and went to the ponies. He untied six of the seven, slapping each on the rump so they would run and perhaps find a place to winter. The black horse that Medicine Owl Woman had captured from the crazy white man ran madly into the storm, eyes wide and great bursts of steam issuing from his nostrils.

Blue Otter slipped a war bridle over the head of the seventh pony, the fleetest of all, a yellow dun called Sage. Then he climbed up onto the pony's back and rode through the village for one last time. He walked Sage to the edge of the village and then, once the last lodge was behind him, he turned the pony's nose to the south, intent on leaving the Elk Valley of the Yellowstone far behind.

36   *The Oregon Trail*

Jack sat atop a rock on a promontory overlooking the spot where, a few hundred yards below, the Oregon Trail crossed the North Platte River. Behind him rose the massive Red Buttes, banded pink and red, and a scattering of scrubby green trees on top. The buttes were well known to the trappers, because they marked the boundary between the Lakota and Shoshone nations. It was late July and the river, no longer fed by snowmelt and spring storms, was shallow enough to cross.

He watched as a train of twenty wagons approached the water, the wagons pulled by oxen, with some men on horseback riding nearby herding cattle. He could see women and their bonnets in the wagons and children riding or walking and many dogs running alongside. There were other trains ahead, and some coming up behind. As they neared the river, the trains spread out, trying to find the best place to ford. The river bed here was rock and sand, which made for a good crossing, but if they ventured too far and tried a spot where the channel was too deep, they would turn their wagons into boats.

Jack had not seen such hubbub since leaving St. Louis.

He spent the afternoon watching from his rock outpost, taking occasional drinks from a jug of whiskey beside him. He tried to count the number of people he saw passing, bound for either California or the Oregon Country, but he became bored and gave up when it exceeded a hundred in an hour. The spectacle of migration made him melancholy, although not so much that he wanted to come down from his rock and interact with any of the travelers. If he did, they would question him about what dangers were ahead, and he would tell them the truth.

When the jug was empty Jack left it atop the rock, swung up onto the saddle of his mule, and rode away. The mule had no name, or at least none that Jack knew. He had bought the mule at the rendezvous but he had been drunk, and he did not now remember what her name was. He kept meaning to come up with a name, but after a few weeks it seemed pointless. She was strong, and smart, and easier to care for than a horse. When he fell from the saddle, which was often, she would wait stubbornly nearby until he woke.

Jack did not know where he was going next, and did not much care, as long as it wasn't east. He could follow the spine of the Rockies north, to Canada, where the trapping and much of everything else was controlled by the Hudson Bay Company, or he could venture south to the Arkansas, beyond which was Mexico.

In the end he allowed the mule to decide.

37 *The Grackle*

The skiff buried its bow in the muddy bank as the boatman lifted the muddy oars out of the water. Gus jumped out and pulled the boat up a few feet. April was sitting in the middle seat, in a new hat and cheerful yellow dress, her back straight and a carpet bag at her feet.

"Here we are," the boatman said.

"What is this place?" April asked.

The boatman laughed. He wore his wide straw hat at a jaunty angle, and the frayed brim quivered with mirth.

"Anywhere," he said. "You said you wanted to be anywhere but St. Louis. Well, *ma chérie,* this is it. Welcome to where the haunted and hunted come to escape."

April looked over the collection of ramshackle buildings, some of which were built right out over the river, and wrinkled her nose.

"It smells," she said.

"Smells like the river to me," the boatman said, taking in a deep breath. "Let's see now, there's fish and mud and kind of a crawfish smell that comes this time of year. It's morning, so there's still a hint of mist the sun hasn't burned off yet."

"You can smell that?"

"I was born on the river. I could smell my way back home, blindfolded."

"Does this place have a name?" Gus asked.

"It's called Vide Poche," the boatman said. "That means empty pockets."

April took a five-dollar note from her sleeve.

"That's more than I asked for."

"Take it," she said. "And if anyone comes asking about us, you tell them you took us someplace else. Across the river."

The man nodded.

Gus took April's hand and helped her out of the boat, then put a boot against the bow and shoved the skiff back into the Mississippi. The oars dipped back into the water and the boat was swiftly away.

"What now?" Gus asked.

"I don't know," April said. "But I knew we had to get away."

April nodded at the largest and cleanest building, a tavern that had a sign hanging over its door that depicted, in fading paint, a large black bird. Hand lettered over the bird was, THE GRACKLE.

"There," she said.

"What's the story?"

"No story," April said. "Not this time. Maybe not ever."

Gus opened the door to the tavern and allowed April to step inside first. Then he followed.

"Get your muddy boots off my floor," a woman called from behind the bar. "Where were you brought up, a barn?"

"Yes," Gus said.

The woman smiled.

"There's an iron just outside," she said. "Scrape 'em off and then you can come back inside."

The woman was in her middle thirties, her face lined but not tired. Her long blond hair was gathered with a green ribbon and hung down her back. Her shirt was plain cotton but there was a green silk scarf around her neck.

She was the only person in the tavern.

"We're closed," the woman told April. "Our business comes when the sun goes down. Who is it you're looking for?"

"No one," April said.

"My guess is that you'd have been looking for a father, maybe, or an older brother who didn't come home last night," the woman said. "That's most of the strangers we get at this hour. Even then, we don't get many children."

"We're not," April said.

"And I'm Queen Victoria," the woman said. "Look, I know you're all gussied up, and probably pass for older, but I know people. Had to learn since I was about your age. You're sixteen?"

"Yes," April said.

Gus came back inside.

"And your brother is seventeen?"

"No," April said. "We're the same. Twins."

The woman came out from behind the bar.

"Give me names," she said.

"I'm April, and this is Augustus."

"Last name?"

"Rapaille," April said. "Or at least that was our mother's name."

The truth felt strange on her tongue.

The woman put her hands on her hips and stared at April.

"There's a family by that name up in the big town," she said. "But you say that was your mother's name. What about your father? Did you know him?"

"No," April said. "But we're told his name was Aguirre."

"Uncommon name," the woman said. "Knew somebody, once, who was called that. Had an unusual accent. Was like a lit fuse around here for a spell. But it was a long time ago."

April suddenly found it difficult to catch her breath. She put her hand out and grasped Gus's forearm.

"Oh, Jesus Christ. What have I said?"

"Nothing," Gus said.

"Come in and sit down," the woman said, leading them to the bar. She poured April a mug of water, but April pointed at the whiskey instead.

"Really?"

April reached into the pocket of her dress, produced a half eagle gold piece, and slid it across the bar.

"That will buy more than whiskey," the woman said.

"I hope it will buy answers."

The woman took two glasses down from the shelf, took a bottle of good bourbon from the top shelf, and uncorked it. While the woman carefully poured two drinks, April saw a newspaper folded on the bar, the *Missouri Argus*. By instinct, she unfolded the paper and devoured the headlines. There was a story about Martin Van Buren, who had been sworn in as president in March, another about the financial panic that drained the New York banks of gold and silver earlier in the year, and the smallpox epidemic that had killed tens of thousands of Mandans and other tribes on the Upper Missouri. The disease was believed to have been spread by sick passengers or crew on an American Fur Company steamboat.

The woman pushed the glass of whiskey toward her.

"The papers never interested me much," the woman said. "But I always keep a few around. It keeps the men who don't like conversation while they drink longer at the bar."

April smiled and folded the paper.

"What about you?" the woman asked Gus.

"I read," he said defensively.

"No," she said. "Do you want a bourbon?"

"I don't drink," he said.

"Good lad," the woman said.

The woman lifted her glass.

"You can call me Chelley," she said. "Everybody does."

April and the woman clinked glasses. The girl took a long, slow drink, and then put the glass down.

Gus looked skeptical.

"What are the chances we would walk into this joint and find somebody who knew our father?" he asked April. "It never happened in St. Louis, or anywhere else, for that matter."

"Everybody in St. Louis knew your father," Chelley said. "He wasn't exactly shy."

"Use your talent for probability," April said. "All the times we were in those fine hotels and getting to or from the boats or fleecing some poor jackass out of his cotton money, did we ever once mention our real names?"

"No," Gus said.

"There's your answer," April said.

Gus grudgingly allowed she might be true.

"Was our father a good man?" April asked.

"You remind me of him," Chelley said.

"The way we look?"

"The way you act," Chelley said.

"But was he a good man?" April asked.

"Jacques Aguirre was good at things," Chelley said.

"Yes?"

"Guns, cards, fighting," she said. "He was good at all of those."

"You're avoiding the question," April said.

"How do you define a good man?" Chelley asked. "Someone who doesn't hurt others? That's inoffensive at best and cowardly at worst. A man who says his prayers in church every Sunday? The book of books says to go to a closet to pray. A man who hungers for nothing? That man isn't alive, he's dead."

"Then how do you define good?" Gus asked.

"He treated me well," the woman said. "Many did not."

"Were you and he . . ." April began.

"No," Chelley said. "But it wouldn't have meant anything, darling. I'm a whore. Oh, don't look so shocked. It was my choice, and I discovered I was good at it, when I was just a little older than you. Why give it away when you can bank on it? Saved up enough money and bought this place. So there you have it."

"Did you know my mother?" April asked.

"We didn't run in the same society, dear," she said. "But I knew of her. Everybody did, and what happened. Or at least part of the story. She went away and nobody knew what became of her, either."

April took another drink.

"I know what became of her. She died in childbirth."
April stared into the bourbon.

"Did he break her heart?" she asked.

"In more pieces than could be counted."

"I should like to kill him," Gus said.

"He could be already dead," April said.

"Jacques?" Chelley laughed. "I don't think so. He clung too tightly to life."

April frowned.

"If not dead, then what?" she said. "He disappears. Vanishes, with no trace left behind. That sounds to me like somebody who doesn't want to be found. Who would know where a man like that went?"

"You mean, who could guess? Just about anybody who walks into the Grackle. They are looking over their shoulders for one reason or another."

"No," April said. "Not guess. There must be a man— or a woman, perhaps—who knows."

Chelley stared at April, watched as her eyes seemed to focus on something distant.

"Perhaps," Gus said. "But how would we ever find that person?"

"Question," April said. "Whose business in town is it to know the movements of its citizens?"

"Sheriff Brown," Chelley said.

"Not a sheriff," April said. "There would be some kind of jail record, newspaper stories, something written left behind. Who else? Someone who could keep a confidence."

"A priest?" Gus asked.

"I think not," April said. "None of the priests I've known could keep their mouths shut. Let's add another wrinkle. Who would be trusted by everyone? Who would be in the position to offer advice, or some kind of help, in desperate circumstances? Someone who would have a reputation powerful enough that others would not dare to question the instructions received from them. Chelley, is there a hero in town?"

"A hero?"

"A war hero, perhaps," April said. "A politician."

"And an explorer," Chelley said. "There is only one. Governor Clark."

"Of Lewis and Clark," April said.

"Yes," Chelley said. "He was territorial governor of Missouri. In charge of all the Indian agents west of the Mississippi."

"He must be old," April said.

"Nearing seventy, I suppose," Chelley said. "Seen him a few times. Not in here, of course, but in the city. All the quality flock to him. He's a hard man to see unless you're from a fine family or are some lunatic interested in the tribes along the Upper Missouri."

"And what do we ask this Clark?" Gus asked.

"We ask him if he, or any of his agents, knows what happened to our father," April said. "We will use our considerable powers of persuasion."

Gus frowned.

"If your mother died in childbirth," Chelley said, "and your father is dead or lit out for only God knows where, then who brought you up?"

"Animals," April said. "Pigs and wolves."

"Sister," Gus said. "I don't think we should be so free with our story."

"It isn't a story," April said, motioning for Chelley to

pour more bourbon. The woman did, for each of them. "It's the truth. We were given to one family, and then another. Then we ran away. It's been three years ago now."

"That's enough," Gus said.

"So how is it that a sixteen-year-old girl walks into my bar with a five-dollar gold piece to throw down?" Chelley asked. "How have you two been shifting for yourselves?"

"Confidence games," April said. "But we're done with that now."

"Things got too hot?" Chelley asked.

"In a way," April said.

"Anybody looking for you?"

"No," April said. "At least nobody with the power of arrest."

"Damn," Chelley said. "And I thought it was going to be a dull morning. Never thought I'd hear of Jacques Aguirre again, much less have his children walk through my door."

April finished the second bourbon and asked for another.

Chelley pushed the gold piece back to her.

"The first two were on the house. But you should stop now. You don't weigh hardly anything, and another would knock you right off that stool."

"Maybe I want to be knocked off this stool."

"No, you don't," Chelley said. "Not really. Why did you come here?"

"We were looking for a place to hide for a spell," April said.

"You found the right place," Chelley said. "Vide Poche remains in shadow at noon."

April smiled.

"Do you run an honest joint?"

"Honest, how?" Chelley asked. "My whiskey is not watered down, the cards and dice are straight, and the girls upstairs either refrain from robbing the customers or are shown the door. That's honest. But our patrons? Pirates, poachers, and profiteers to a man."

"So, there's a brothel upstairs," Gus said. "And you're the pimp?"

"I'm the madam. There's a difference."

"How?" Gus asked.

"I don't beat the girls, for one."

"Teach me," April said. "Show me what you show the girls."

"You don't want to be a common whore," Chelley said.

"No," April said. "I want to be an uncommon one."

"You could make bank on that," Chelley said.

Gus said no, he would not watch his sister sell herself to strangers.

"She wouldn't," Chelley said. "The real money is always to be made in selling the promise and not the act."

April's face glowed with epiphany.

"No more confidence games," Gus said.

"Not at all, my dear Gus," April said. "What Chelley says is true. I will be a tulip bulb."

"What the hell are you talking about?" Gus asked.

"It's all in this book," April said. "I read it—oh, I don't know, last year maybe. It's called *A Memoir of Popular Delusions* and it's by a Scottish writer named Charles Mackay. He talks about a lot of things in the book, haunted houses and the poltergeists and other things people imagine, but the thing I remember best is the tulips. Two hundred years ago in Europe, tulip bulbs became the most expensive commodity in the world."

"Tulip bulbs," Chelley said. "As in the flower?"

"Yes," April said. "It was a madness. A single tulip bulb was selling for ten times what a skilled laborer was making. The mania did not last, of course, but if it's not tulips, it's always something else."

"Why would anybody pay that much for a flower bulb?" Gus asked.

"Because people convinced themselves that they were worth it," April said. "People speculated on them the way people invest in the stock market now, on the promise of some future profit. We don't need to run confidence games. People confidence themselves. All I have to do is be myself and remain forever on the promise of a return. We will be selling tulips on speculation, and our bulbs will never be planted."

Gus shook his head.

"I'll not have it," he said.

"It's not your choice," April said pleasantly.

Gus stared at his sister with a look of horror and sorrow.

"I'll not be witness to a family quarrel," Chelley said. "Take it outside. But do not lay hands on one another."

Gus led the way, pushing the door a little too hard so that it banged. April followed. They walked to the middle of the muddy lane. April folded her arms while Gus threw his hands in the air.

"We've never been separated," he said. "We have been together since before the moment we were born. We were raised in a barn, like animals, with only each other for company. We survived because we were together. Granger could not kill us, and Holly could not ruin us. I have always let you choose our path. But I will not stand idly by while you sell yourself, or the idea of yourself, to strangers."

"So it is strangers to which you object?"

"No," Gus said. "That's not what I mean."

"It's what you said."

"You know damn well what I mean," Gus said, spluttering with frustration. "You could always do this, turn any argument inside out so that you could win on rhetoric and not logic."

"Rhetoric?" April asked, her face flushed with anger. "Talk, you're the one who is just all talk. You speak of Granger and Holly as if you shared the burdens in equal measure. Well, I am here to tell you that you did not. My burden is mine, and it is time that I profited from it, because the world does not reward a woman unless she hides her smarts behind a compliant smile. I will smile all the way to my ease."

"It will mean your death," Gus said. "Have you not witnessed how poorly men treat the cyprarians—"

"The word you reach for is Cyprians."

"—dammit, Sister, you know what I mean."

"It might well mean my death," April said. "A jealous lover, the misfortune of disease, the hazards of drink and dope. But Brother, the way I see it, there's not a hell of a lot to recommend life. We're born, there are some things in between, and we die. The things between are just fluff. Some of the fluff is pleasant, like books, and some of the fluff is unpleasant, like Granger, but most of the fluff just does not matter. I will choose my fluff while I can."

"There is something broken in you," Gus said. "I love you in spite of it, but something broke in you when we were children. You must not do this. I will not watch as you kill yourself in this way."

"You cannot stop me," she said.

"No, but I can do something worse," Gus said. "I can leave."

38   *A Third Thing*

Night Bird sat in the back of the dugout canoe, paddling lazily, mostly allowing the current to push her downriver. It was late afternoon of a summer's day, and she glided among the shadows that clung to the south bank. She was wearing clothes that made her an ambiguous figure, a floppy leather hat and a man's cotton shirt that was much too big for her, so as not to invite the kind of attention that follows a woman traveling alone. She had plenty of supplies in the canoe, including one of the 1803 rifles that had been taken from the soldiers. Around her neck, hidden beneath the shirt, was her father's Jefferson Peace Medal.

The week before, when she had heard the sickness was approaching the village, she had gathered what she needed and slipped away in the middle of the night. There were those who said the plague was an unlucky spin of the great wheel of life, others who said that it had been sent by the Christian god to punish his unbelieving children, and some who said it was the manifestation of an evil spirit that went voraciously from village to village. Night Bird believed the smallpox was connected to the whites, because it had spread from their outposts along the river to the nations, just as it had in generations past.

She did not know how long it would take for her to reach St. Louis, but time now did not pass in the way it had before; there seemed both too much and too little of it. What she did know was that if she continued to follow the flow of the water, she would eventually find St. Louis.

Her dreams had deserted her in recent months, and she could no longer summon power from the sleeping world. When her dreams deserted her, she had known a change was coming, but not the nature of the change. She had lived then as other human beings do, with each day an unread page in a book whose title was unknown. She found the experience unpleasant, and hoped one day the dreams would return, but she feared they would not. The last power dream she had was a violent and lustful dream of Jack Picaro. She found no comfort in remembering the dream, only a growing unease.

She rehearsed in her head the speech she would give when she finally met her grandfather. She could not quite imagine the kind of palace he might live in, but believed it must be a variation of the ugly wooden box-like houses the white men placed in and around the forts they had built along the river. In her mind's eye there was a council fire in the middle of some kind of great room, with Clark on a kind of throne, and lesser white men arranged on either side. She would be announced and enter the room, her chin high, and she would begin by saying that she was the daughter of Standing Wolf. She would say that she carried a message from the center of the world, and she would enumerate the many insults, injuries, and indignities that her people had endured because of the captains Clark and Lewis. It would take an hour or more, she thought, for the speech to be given. When she came to the end of it, she would say that she had not yet delivered her message in full. Then she would kill Clark, preferably by stabbing or some other way that required her to get very close to him, and she would drop the knife or gun or whatever she had used on the ground. Then she would wait with arms crossed above her head until the subchiefs tore her to pieces. She did not quite know why she would hold her arms crossed in such a fashion, but the image pleased her.

She was indulging this daydream, only occasionally dipping her paddle in the water, not so much for propulsion but for steering, when she heard something monstrous coming around the next bend. It was a cacophony, a kind of metallic chugging sound she had never heard before, mixed with the hissing of air and the sound of water churning without stop. A smudge of smoke hung over the trees beyond the bend.

Night Bird knew what it was, for the tales had passed from village to village, but still she was unprepared for the sight of the steamboat. With its bow breaking the water in a wide V before it, the machine seemed to be in perpetual lunge from the water, ready to swallow those before it, as in the story of Jonah and the whale in the white man's book. It was painted white, with red trim, with a low-slung cabin and railings and windows and doors, and she could see men milling about. There were all manner of goods piled on the boat's low-slung leather deck, crates and boxes and piles of things she could not identify. On either side of its body was a large wheel, painted red, propelling it down the river like the churning feet of a duck. On the side of the drum-like thing that covered the top of the wheel, in red letters, was YELLOW STONE.

Once it had rounded the bend and she saw it from the waterline all the way to the top of its stacks, it seemed like such a monster that she had trouble catching her breath. She knew the boat was like other things in the white man's world, a contraption of metal and wood, and yet it was that and more. She slid the canoe beneath the overhanging branches of a willow tree and remained still while the boat passed. When it was gone, the wash threatened to capsize the dugout, and the stench of oil and smoke stung her nostrils.

Night Bird had considered herself schooled in the ways of the world, but her encounter with the steamboat left her shaken. Had she not been hugging the bank, the boat would have run right over the dugout, smashing her and the canoe to bits. This caused a sick feeling in her stomach, because she had seldom encountered things that had caused this type of fear. There was the grizzly bear, which was the lord of the mountains, and there was the lightning, which was lord of the sky. None could stand against either. To these she now added a third, the steamboat.

39   *Dapple*

Bent's Fort overlooked the Arkansas River like an adobe castle. At each corner was a tower with a swivel gun that had command not only of the river, but of several hundred yards of the Santa Fe Trail, as well. Shining pink in the noonday sun, the fort reminded Jack of some of the centuries-old structures that dotted the countryside around his hometown of Carcosa, in the Basque country of northern Spain. Those ancient structures held the ghosts of the past in them, and their walls carried the names of families whose lines had long since perished. But this pink castle, situated on a swatch of grass on a dusty and heavily used trail, throbbed with life. A huge American flag fluttered on a mast above the fort, a little the worse for wear from sun and rain, and Jack counted the number of stars.

Twenty-six.

Jack dismounted and led the mule toward the entrance of the fort. Everything he owned was on his back or on the mule. He carried a long rifle in the crook of his arm, a .45 caliber with a full stock in the Kentucky style, that he had won on a throw of dice after a chance encounter with an emigrant bound for Oregon. He did not care for the gun, thinking it unwieldy for the west, but it had taken plenty of antelope, so at least he had not gone hungry. On his belt was the Damascus toothpick, and behind the mule's saddle was a meager bedroll and a bag that carried his ledger book and the small crock containing the yeast starter from the ruins of Hell's Gate.

He was sober, because he had drunk up the last of his whiskey on the plains somewhere below the South Platte. He knew there would be plenty of spirits inside the fort. The pasture beyond the fort was dotted with several dozen lodges, and Jack recognized them as Cheyenne and Arapaho. The tribes brought buffalo hides to the fort for trade, which were then pressed, bundled, and loaded on wagons for points east. Buffalo hides were now the most common item of the fur trade, and the fort was the center of the most powerful cartel on the southern mountains and plains. It was called, after its owners, Bent, St. Vrain, and Company. The fort was the only permanent white American settlement on the Santa Fe Trail between Missouri and Mexico. The trail approached the fort from the north, then split around it like a wishbone, joining again on the south side. On either side of the fort were heavy wagons and big two-wheeled carts and oxen and picket lines of horses, and tents here and there, travelers and traders pausing for a few days' rest in relative security.

Jack knew where the trail began to the north, because he had passed there on a keel boat fifteen years before. It was along the river in the far northwestern corner of

Missouri. The trail ended at Santa Fe, in Mexico about three hundred miles to the south, a place he had never seen. But if you were traveling up from Mexico, Jack reckoned, you'd think the trail began at Santa Fe and ended in Missouri.

Near the fort, on the south side of the trail, the Arkansas River wove a crooked bend beyond a marshy area. Jack could see the tops of some great cottonwoods leaning out over the river, and through the branches he could glimpse the dull brown water, flowing in an eventual easterly direction.

Fifty yards or so from the entrance to the fort, Jack approached a Mexican boy who was sitting on a stool, tending to a small cook fire, near a picket line of horses.

"Morning," Jack said.

The boy glanced at Jack's long hair, dirty beard, and filthy clothes. Then he looked away, trying to avoid eye contact because he was afraid Jack would ask for some of the pork tamales he was preparing to fry up. The boy looked up at the sky and then shook his head.

"Es mediodia," he said.

"Could be," Jack said, in Spanish. "Time's a bit different this far south. Would you know what month it is?"

"It is the last day of August," the boy said.

The boy looked puzzled.

"Do you not know the time for travel has begun?" he asked. "The heat of summer is over. It is time to get on with business."

"I haven't had much business to attend of late," Jack said.

He told Jack his accent was foreign sounding.

Jack allowed that everyone said so.

"Your Spanish is too hard for me to understand," the boy said. "It makes my head ache. Let's speak English."

"Very well," Jack said.

"My name is Santiago Chavez," the boy said.

"Pleased to meet you," Jack said. "You can call me Picaro."

"My father and uncle are inside the fort, for supplies. We're on our way to Missouri to buy cloth and other goods to bring back to San Patricio." The boy was obviously proud of his role in the endeavor. "We will buy wagons at Westport Landing to carry the goods back. The wagons will be sold, too, when we reach home."

"Sound plan," Jack said. "Have any trouble on the trail?"

The boy considered the question.

"No," he said. "But I am not the one to ask. It is only my first trip. My father has been coming for fifteen years, as long as I have been alive. Before that, my grandfather and his father before him brought goods up from Mexico City on El Camino Real. Both routes have their dangers, but my father says this north route crosses the wildest country. If we are not worrying about water, we are watching out for Indians. This is all Comancheria, to the great bend in the Arkansas."

"Comanche," Jack said. "It's a nation I've not encountered."

"Me, neither," the boy said. "Not yet."

The boy looked thoughtful as he sprinkled some spice on the pork.

"How do you make a living?" the boy asked.

"I'm a free trapper, or was," Jack said. "I see there's little use for that around here. It's all buffalo and no beaver. Before that, I was a gunsmith. Now? I'm not sure what to call myself, except drunk most of the time."

"You do not seem drunk now," the boy said.

"No," Jack said. "But drinking is what I'm fixing to do. I'm going to get stinking drunk. But I need someplace to picket my mule and my possibles for a few hours, maybe even overnight. There'd be a few coins in it for you."

"Do not insult me," the boy said. "I do not seek to profit from those less fortunate than myself. You look as though you should keep your money and buy new clothes, or pay to have washed the ones you own."

"I stink, I know," Jack said. "But I haven't been near other people in weeks. The mule doesn't seem to mind."

"My father says that liquor robs a man first of his senses. Then it robs him of his family. Finally, it takes his life."

"Don Chavez is a wise man," Jack said.

"Then why don't you stop?"

"Because I have little sense and no family."

"What about grandchildren?"

Jack laughed.

"It seems I appear older than I am," Jack said. "I am not yet forty."

"It is all the hair," the boy said. "But still, that seems old to me."

"It did to me, too, when I was your age."

The boy nodded. The pork sizzled in the skillet.

"Do you still know how to work on guns?" the boy asked.

"I have tried to forget," Jack said, "but cannot."

"Then perhaps we could help one another," the boy said. "My father has given me an old *pistola* to carry, for when we are forced to fight the Comanche. But it has become unreliable."

"Unreliable how?"

"It misfires often," the boy said.

"Are you loading it correctly?"

The boy glared at him.

"Let me take a look," Jack said.

From the things beside his stool, the boy produced a flintlock pistol with a tapered barrel, a bulb at the end of the butt, and intricate scrollwork on the lock. The engraving showed a lion, reared back on its hind legs, roaring.

"Spanish," Jack said. "I know these guns."

Jack took the ramrod out and slipped it down the barrel to make sure it was unloaded. Then he cocked the hammer, listening carefully to the sound of the action. He declared the spring good.

"When it misfires," Jack said, "does the pan flash?"

"No," the boy said. "The cock hangs."

"Ah," Jack said.

"What?"

Jack reached into his bag over his shoulder and pulled out a tool that was a combination screwdriver and pick lock. In a moment he had removed the screws holding the lock in place.

"Here," he said, using his finger to point to the tumbler and sear. "The sear screw is ill-fitted and there has been so much wear, here, that sometimes it prevents the hammer from tripping. Look at this burr. Have you a file?"

The boy found a horseshoe file in a wooden box that contained odds and ends.

"That's big," Jack said. "But I think I can make it work if I hold the sear against it with my fingers rather than the other way around."

"There's a smith in the fort," the boy said.

"Smiths don't loan tools," Jack said. "And they don't work for favors."

Jack worked carefully, pinching the sear between his thumb and index finger, and often checking his work. Finally, after twenty minutes, he reassembled the lock. He aligned the sear screw and then, using the tool, slowly drove the screw into the threads, exerting enough pressure to make the threads bite and straighten the screw. Then he screwed the lock back into the pistol and worked the trigger and the hammer, feeling and listening.

"There," he said. "This repair should last the journey. Use it in health."

"I am grateful," Santiago said.

"Is that your only weapon?"

"My father and uncle have fine guns," Santiago said. "But this is all they have given me. It belonged to my grandfather."

"It is a fine old piece," Jack said. "But it is unsuited for defense on the trail."

"Why?"

"It is a smoothbore," Jack said. "And although it is a good-looking pistol, many rounds have passed down the barrel. I would be surprised if you could hit a dinner plate at twenty yards. Tell me, have you practiced? That is about its accurate range, is it not?"

The boy nodded.

"This weapon is only good for close in, just beyond arm's reach," Jack said. "It is also heavy and cumbersome to hold. It is a pistol to keep beside the bed, for protection against doorbreakers."

"My father and my uncle said it was sufficient."

"How many fights have they been in?"

"A few," the boy said. "Well, none."

"Then listen to someone who has been in many," Jack said. "You would be no match for an iron-tipped arrow shot from the bow of a seasoned warrior. What you need is a long gun, in a light or medium caliber, and with a weight that won't tire you. You need something that will reach out at least two hundred yards with accuracy, or more, to give you a fighting chance. Do you understand?"

"I do," Santiago said. "But why do you take such an interest in me?"

Jack smiled.

"Because you are a serious boy of philosophical bent," he said. "This is the best conversation I have had in . . . well, for longer than I can remember. I have forgotten how much I enjoy talking, and I would hate to think of my new conversant friend coming to harm."

Santiago nodded.

"I will watch your rifle and your things and your mule, but only until dawn. That's when we must be on the trail again. Do not still be drunk at that hour."

"If I am," Jack said, "I will crawl out to sleep beside the mule."

The boy smiled.

"What is her name?" he asked.

"Mule," Jack said.

"She must have a name," the boy insisted.

"What do you suggest?"

"Dapple," Santiago said.

40 *Lieutenant Clark*

The end of July was stifling in St. Louis and that made it easy, because just about every window that could be opened was, to let in some air. Gus had been watching the house on Broadway Street from the shadows beneath an elm tree in the yard of a home just down the street. Hidden in the shadows, Gus and April had watched as one by one the yellow lights in the home of Meriwether Clark, the famous explorer's son, were extinguished. All of the windows in the upper story were wide open, and the curtains seemed to breathe with the night wind, sometimes fluttering outside. On the ground floor there were fewer windows, but they were open, as well, but not as far. Gus studied the home, trying to determine in which of his son's rooms William Clark lay dying.

April had presented herself three days before at William Clark's home, in a new yellow dress, and with a story about how she had been sent with greetings from an old Virginia family, the Smiths. April thought there were enough Smiths everywhere that if you showed up and claimed you were a friend of the Smiths, who knew your family back when, then you were likely to be admitted rather than turned away. She knew that people would routinely put themselves at some degree of risk rather than seem impolite. Gus had objected to the plan on the grounds that it was deceitful, but April said she would only claim to convey a message, rather than assert membership in the family. Gus had also wanted to know what the message was.

"Anything," April had said. "How about, remember the old pear tree which so cheered Grandma Smith when it blossomed? Of course, you do, everyone knows that story. Well, a wind storm came along and knocked it down. But you know what was found among the roots? A rusty old pen knife with your initials! Here it is. Could it be yours?"

Nine times out of ten, April said, people will say they recognize it.

"And we're in the house," she said, "for the price of some initials scratched in a piece of trash, but we are also in the confidence of our subject."

But at William Clark's door, April was told by a maid that the governor had become unexpectedly ill and had been taken to his son's house. Then the maid began to cry, and said she feared the governor would not recover.

Knowing time was short, the plan was changed to something more to Gus's liking. It would be a straight-forward plan, with Gus sneaking into the home at night and asking the old man directly, if he was still sensible enough to answer questions. April would stand watch on the street outside. If anything seemed amiss, she would alert him.

After the last candle had been out for thirty minutes, and with a waxing gibbous moon above, Gus crossed Broadway in his bare feet, hopped over the short iron rail fence, and went to the partially open window at a corner of the house. He slipped his hands beneath the sash and lifted. With a series of creaks, the window rose. He waited a few seconds, and then pulled himself up into the window and over. The polished oak of the floors inside was smooth and cool on the soles of his feet.

The house was so quiet that Gus could hear only his own breathing.

Gus found the staircase and went quickly upstairs, finding himself in a long hallway with closed doors on either side. The floor here was painted wood, which did not feel as good as the oak. On the other sides of the closed doors he could hear sounds of snoring. He walked cautiously down the hall, pausing briefly at each door, until he neared the end and discovered a door ajar. It would make sense, he thought, to leave the door to a sick room partially open, so as to not disturb the patient in coming and going, or to better hear if they called.

Gus moved slowly to the door, listening carefully.

He could hear no sound.

He turned sideways and, squeezing past the door and the jamb, entered the room. Enough moonlight was streaming through the open window that he had no difficulty making out the interior. In the bed was an old man, sheets pulled up to his chin.

The old man's eyes were open.

Gus closed the door. He walked across the room and took a seat beside the bed.

"How do you fare?"

"It no longer matters," the old man said.

"Are you Captain Clark?"

"It will be forever Lieutenant Clark," the old man said. "I was promised a captain's commission but never received it. Who are you?"

"Aguirre," Gus said. "My name is Aguirre."

"Ah," Clark said. "Have you killed Standing Wolf? Have you brought back the peace medal?"

Then Clark began to cough, and Gus became afraid someone might hear. There was a pitcher of water on the night table, and Gus poured a glass half full. Clark took it and swallowed some, with difficulty, then handed the glass back.

"Whiskey," Clark said. "That's what I need, not this warm bathwater."

"What ails you?"

"Age," Clark said. "The body fails. The heart falters and stops."

"Who do you think I am?" Gus asked.

"Jacques Aguirre," Clark said. "Your profile is unmistakable. You came to me in the middle of the night, just as you have now, but it has been so many years I feared you were dead. So you do not have the peace medal?"

"I am not Jacques Aguirre," Gus said. "That was my father."

The old man sighed.

"Tell me about my father," Gus said. "How did you know him?"

"He was a gunsmith," Clark said, waving his hand. "He came to rob me one night and I offered my help instead. You surely know this story."

"I do not," Gus said. "What kind of help did you give him?"

"A letter of introduction," Clark said. "For Ashley's One Hundred."

"Explain," Gus said.

"The expedition to the Upper Missouri," Clark said impatiently. "The fur trading venture. General Ashley and Captain Henry. I wrote a letter to Henry asking him to find a berth for your father on a keel boat."

"So Ashley or this Henry could say what became of him?"

"If they were above ground, yes," Clark said. "But Ashley died in March of pneumonia. Andrew Henry has been dead these six or seven years."

"What kind of man was my father?"

Clark smiled.

"A man unafraid. He had an unusual accent, something from the Old World. I don't remember which country."

"Thank you," Gus said. "There must be someone connected with the expedition who remembers what happened to him. Can you remember anything else?"

There was a sound on the street below.

Gus stood and looked out the window.

April was in the street, waving her arms.

"Solomon," she hissed.

"I must go," Gus said.

"Stay," Clark said.

Gus heard footsteps coming up the stairs.

"I cannot. But I wish you well on your coming journey."

"You don't understand."

The old man reached out and grasped Gus by the arm. His grip was surprisingly strong.

"Your father," Clark said. "You will not find him by the name Aguirre. The letter of introduction used another name."

"Yes?" Gus asked.

The footsteps were coming down the hall now.

"Solomon!" April shouted from below. "Solomon!"

"The name," Gus said. "Tell me."

"It was . . ."

"Yes?"

"Rascal, rapscallion. Not those, but something like it. I don't remember. But his rifle."

"What about it?"

The footsteps were outside the room. The light of a candle shone beneath the door.

"Father?" a male voice came. "Are you having nightmares again?"

Gus started for the window, but the old man's grip tightened.

"The rifle he made," Clark said. "It was unusual. Made to kill a ghost."

"Yes?"

"Accurate beyond reason. And it made a sound."

"How do you mean?"

"It rang like a bell when fired."

The door opened.

Clark released his grip.

Gus shot through the window, the curtain billowing behind him, and for a moment it seemed as if he were suspended in space, with April watching from the street below. Then he landed on the roof of the porch below, rolled twice, and fell into the top of an apple tree. He managed to grasp a branch and dangle for a moment before he dropped to the ground, his bare feet touching the grass.

"Come on," April said, already running.

Gus shot across the lawn, leaped the iron fence, and joined her.

In a moment they were in the shadows around the corner of one of the houses on the opposite side of the street. Gus could see Clark's son looking out the open window of his father's sickroom, puzzled at the commotion below.

"That was close," April said.

"I thought he was going to catch me."

"He?" April asked. "There was a woman who approached the house not long after you entered. She wore a floppy hat and a cloak and carried something in her hand that shone in the moonlight. She went around to the back. I thought she belonged to the household and the candle was hers."

Gus shook his head.

"Did you find Clark?" April asked.

Between gulps of breath, Gus said yes.

"What did he say?"

"I need you to shut up and listen."

"To hell with you," April said.

"He knew our father," Gus said.

"How?"

"He wrote a letter of introduction."

"Under what name?" April asked.

"The old man doesn't remember."

"Then how does that help us?"

"That's what I'm trying to tell you," Gus said. "He doesn't remember the name, but recalls a rifle that our father carried. Something he made. He said it made the sound of a bell when fired."

April thought for a moment.

"There can't be another like it."

"No," Gus said. "Somebody is sure to remember it. That is how we find our father."

41   *The Peacock*

Jack threaded his way through the crowd to the board plank that served as a bar at the far end of Bent's Fort. The men—trappers or traders or soldiers—grudgingly gave way, most avoiding eye contact, some holding their noses as he passed.

"Whiskey," Jack said as he reached the bar.

"Money," the bartender said.

Jack took a coin from his pocket and put it on the plank. He didn't know how much money he had left, but it tugged at his pocket as if it were a pouch of rifle balls.

The bartender, a squat man with gray hair and bulging eyes, picked up the coin and examined it. It was a half dollar, with a bust of Lady Liberty on one side and an oddly canted eagle on the other.

"What's wrong?" Jack asked. "Don't you take American money here?"

"We take anything," the bartender said, "as long as it's real."

The bartender put a tumbler on the plank and sloppily poured it half-full of whiskey from an earthenware jug.

"No change?" Jack asked.

"That's four bits' worth," the bartender said.

Jack leaned his elbows on the plank and looked down at the amber liquid. He picked it up with his right hand, brought it to his nose, and inhaled. It was whiskey, all right, and as he had remembered, with no snake heads or other foolishness. He was about to bring the tumbler to his lips when there was a piercing bird-like scream.

Jack put the drink down.

"What was that?"

The bartender laughed.

"Peacock," he said.

Jack turned, and beyond the crowd, out in the courtyard near the fur press where they compressed the buffalo hides into tight bundles for transport, a peacock was strutting. Its body was a brilliant blue in the sun. As it walked it cocked its head from side to side, the crown spread wide. Its tail, with feathers carrying a multitude of accusing eyes, followed behind.

"Why on earth are there peacocks here?"

"It's what the old man—that's Mr. William Bent—wanted," the bartender said. "Had some idea he could raise peafowl, or so he said. But I think he just likes to keep 'em around as pets. They're as good as watchdogs, and they don't bite."

"I have never seen one before," Jack said.

"There's a bonus for your fifty center," the bartender said, then turned to another customer.

Jack stared down at the drink for a minute or so more. The peacock screamed again, and this time the crowd of men around him turned and laughed at the bird. Finally Jack pushed the drink aside and turned.

"What's wrong with that, mister?" a trapper at his elbow asked.

"Nothing," Jack said.

Three hands reached for the tumbler at once. Jack did not see who won it, because he had turned and walked back to the courtyard. He watched the peacock for a long time, fascinated by how colorful the bird was. It was as if some storybook from his childhood had come to life. Peacocks were among the treasures given to King Solomon. In Greek mythology, the peacock carried the eyes of Hera's slain bodyguard, Argus. But Jack did not know what the peacocks meant to him personally, except that they were beautiful.

After ten minutes or so, the bird scurried across the courtyard and into the shadows along one of the side galleries. Jack looked around him, as if seeing the world for a second time. He heard the ringing of a blacksmith's iron coming from the rear of the fort, and he made for the sound. There, he found stalls with merchants selling every kind of merchandise that could be made at the fort or freighted in. There was also a barber in a fenced area just beyond the courtyard.

Jack bought a bath first. He washed in a tub that was barely hidden behind a thick wooden fence. Then he paid for a shave and a haircut. He bought a clean shirt, one of blue cotton, and threw the old one in the fire used to heat the water. His old trousers and the well-worn belt, with the Damascus blade and sheath, would have to remain. But he found a hat that suited, one of tan felt with bead-work and a turkey feather already stuck in the band. Then he went to the blacksmith and paid too much for a mountain rifle of .54 caliber that had been stamped Traylor &

Sons, St. Louis. Jack had not known the maker during his time in Missouri. The rifle was percussion, with an octagonal barrel, and a walnut stock. Jack would have sneered at the workmanship in years past, but he now recognized value in utility. Jack bought a tin of the little caps the rifle required, and three pounds of cast lead balls, enough for a couple of hundred shots. He paid far more than the rifle and the ammunition were worth in the states, but on the trail the gunsmith could ask as much as the market would bear.

His pockets were light when he left the fort.

Jack found Santiago sitting on the stool, with his father and uncle nearby.

The boy looked at him without realizing who it was.

"Santiago," Jack said.

"*Señor* Picaro? You are . . . so different. Papa, this is the man I told you about, the old man who asked me to watch his mule and repaired the *pistola*."

Don Chavez grinned. He was a big man, broad across the shoulders, with a well-tended beard.

"He does not look so old to me," Don Chavez said in Spanish. "What is he? Five years older than me?"

"That seems about right," Jack said.

"Oh, he speaks Spanish," Don Chavez said.

"He does not speak it so well," the boy said. "There is some difficulty with his accent. But he understands it. Allow me to translate to English, if you will."

"What does he want?" the uncle asked. He was younger than Don Chavez by a couple of years. He was a small man who deferred to his older brother, and his speech was clipped, as if he were afraid to say too much.

"Nothing," Jack said in English. "To collect my things and thank Santiago for tending the mule."

"Dapple," Santiago said.

"Yes," Jack said. "Dapple."

"You did not get stinking drunk," Santiago said. "What happened?"

"I changed my mind."

"So you are going now?" Santiago asked.

"I am," Jack said.

"Where?"

"The Valley of Lost Souls, perhaps," Jack said. "It is not far from here, I understand. It sounds like a pleasant enough place to pass autumn."

"That is in Mexico," the uncle said. "There is a settlement along the Purgatory with a few gringos, but they married well and have legitimate land grants."

"I won't be putting down roots," Jack said.

Tio Chavez shrugged.

"You have a new rifle," Santiago said. "It is wise to have two. But you must have spent all of your money."

"Nearly so," Jack said. "But I won't be needing two rifles. With your father's permission, I'd like to leave my old gun here with you. It is of a length and caliber that will suit you, I believe."

Santiago spoke hurriedly to his father.

"How much?" Don Chavez asked.

"It is a gift," Jack said. "I would be pleased if the boy accepted it."

Jack walked over to the picket line and began to saddle Dapple. He worked carefully, speaking often to the mule, and was nearly finished when the father called to him.

"Señor," he said. "You have been in the wilderness for some time?"

"I've been in the mountains," Jack said in Spanish.

"English, please," Santiago said.

"Sixteen years in the mountains," Jack said. "Around the Missouri and the Yellowstone Rivers, mostly. Not long on the plains. Just sort of followed my mule down here."

"You have been in many fights?"

"What do you mean?"

"With bad men," Don Chavez said. "Indians. Bandits."

"I've been in my share of scrapes," Jack said. "Some with people from the nations. Some with whites. Bad men come in all stripes, and I suppose I have to count myself among them."

"So you have killed?"

Jack paused.

"Yes, but none that I'm truly proud of," he said. "Why this interest in combat?"

"Do you have an interest in employment?" Don Chavez asked.

"With you? Why?"

"We are merchants," Don Chavez said. "We know our business, but the trail is full of challenges. Robbers, Indians, wild animals. In the past we have employed men like yourself, men who know the smell of gunpowder and the flash of the knife. But this season there was too much competition. Others pay better."

"So, you want me to kill for you?"

"Only if necessary to protect us," Don Chavez said. "We are still five hundred miles from Missouri. Another month on the trail. This is the most dangerous part for us because others see us with only our horses and they know . . ."

"That you have silver and gold to buy goods," Jack said. "Coming back down the trail, your wealth is in the wagons. Easier to rob you headed to Missouri than on the way back home."

"You understand precisely," Don Chavez said. "Santiago is but a boy, and my brother Domingo is small and not so brave. And to tell the truth, I have no stomach for fighting."

"I will take you to Westport," Jack said. "But no farther into Missouri. And I will not accompany you back down the trail home."

"I understand," Don Chavez said. "There will be no drinking."

"I'm not thirsty."

"So, you agree?"

"I agree," Jack said.

"But I have not told you what your pay will be."

"You're trusting me to keep you alive, if I can," Jack said. "I'll trust you to pay me fairly. Besides, I like the boy."

"Good," Don Chavez said. "The Valley of Lost Souls was no place for you, *señor*."

42 *Orphans All*

"We think you may have known our father," Gus said. "Jacques Aguirre."

April was standing back, watching from what seemed a respectful distance as Gus spoke to Decatur Jones. They were in the Yellowstone House, a popular tavern in a limestone building not far from the courthouse in downtown St. Louis. Jones owned the tavern and they knew that, as a young man, Jones had been part of the Ashley expedition. Everyone said so. If anyone would remember a man with an unusual accent and a remarkable rifle, it would be Jones.

But April had convinced Gus that they should not wear fine clothes to visit Jones, but that they should dress as they were, orphans, and they would leave out the parts of their story that included murder and confidence. They had to gain Jones's trust, she said. As April listened to the conversation, she was annoyed at the clumsy way Gus was handling himself, but she managed to maintain her innocent smile.

"I've never known anybody by that name," Jones said.

Gus said he may have known him by some other name.

"This is nonsense," Decatur said. "I don't know anyone named Aguirre. What other name would he have used?"

Gus said he didn't know, but that Governor Clark—God rest his soul—had indicated as much.

"You were admitted to see William Clark," Decatur said. "While he was ill and nearing death at the home of his son, Meriwether Clark. And you were allowed to speak to him."

"Well, no," April said before her brother could speak. "Gus was not exactly admitted."

Gus allowed he had come in the middle of the night, and that Clark had spoken of wolves and peace medals, and had mentioned a rifle that rang like a bell. He said Clark had talked of a letter of introduction.

"What was the name used?" Jones asked.

Gus said Clark could not recall.

"And he spoke of a rifle that rang like a bell?"

"Yes," Gus said. "He was very clear about that."

"The ghost rifle," Jones whispered.

Jones called for his bartender to bring whiskey.

"Can I have one, too?" April asked.

"No," Decatur said. "But you can have some bread and cheese."

After the food came, and Jones was swirling the whiskey in his glass, he began to speak.

"I knew your father as Jack Picaro," Jones said.

April asked him to spell the last name.

He did.

"Picaro," Gus said, the name strange on his tongue.

Picaro, April thought. *Of course. A rough and some-*

times dishonest character of low standing, but appealing, whose episodic adventures are the stuff of fantasy. She didn't pay attention to much of the conversation after that, because her mind was unspooling all of the examples she had read, from *Don Quixote* to *Moll Flanders.* The hero's quest, whether noble or comic, was always doomed.

When they were once again outside, after Jones had talked about the man known as Jack Picaro and his ghost rifle, April could not shake the feeling that she was trapped in some kind of dream. Gus spoke to her, and she did not hear him.

"April," he said, again. "What is the matter?"

She mumbled something he couldn't make out. Her eyes were on the faces of the people passing in the street, men and women and children, all going about their business unawares.

"Tell me," Gus said.

"Life is absurd," she blurted. "Look at them, they have no idea."

"You mean life has no meaning?"

"It would be better if it had no meaning," April shrieked, drawing stares. "It is worse than meaningless. It has a meaning, and that meaning is a burlesque. We are mere parodies of human beings, orphans all, engaged in folly that we think has substance, when truly that substance is laughter for the gods. If there were any gods, which I don't believe, so that makes it ever so much worse. For whose amusement? What is the show for? Whose dream is this?"

Gus grasped her by the arm.

"Don't," she said.

"People are watching," Gus said.

"Or course they're watching," April said, her fingers inching toward the yellow ribbon around her neck. "They must watch, they have no choice."

Gus grasped her wrist with his free hand.

"Let me go," she said.

He drew her to him in an embrace.

"Don't," he said.

"The only thing there is fluff," she said. "You're born, you died, there's fluff in between. That's all we have. Our mother is dead, our father fled from us, the world is indifferent."

"We have a chance of finding our father now."

"For what?" April asked. "To pursue him in the hope of making hearth and home complete? Will he have changed? Or will he reject us once again?"

"It does not matter what he wants," Gus said.

April took a breath, calming a bit.

"You still want to kill him," she said.

Gus was silent.

"Leave me out of this," she said. "Abandon me, like he did, only for what? Justice? Revenge? None of it will change the years. No, dear brother, I will chase only fluff from here to the end, and may God make it quick."

43 *Gravity*

April was leaning with her back against the bar, a tumbler of bourbon in her right hand, and a wicked smile on her face. The Grackle was doing a good business for so early on a Friday evening. There were the usual gamblers and losers at the tables along the far wall, the drinks were flowing, and Chelley was sending a steady stream of customers upstairs.

"You doing okay, kid?" Chelley asked.

"Hand me the bottle," April said.

"You sure?"

"I feel great. I want to feel better. Give me the bottle."

"Maybe not tonight," Chelley said. "I expect a real player later on, a regular John Jacob Astor, and you're going to want to be straight for him. He'll expect you to be all blushes and moonbeams. If he smells bourbon on your breath or gets a whiff of poppies, the show's over."

"The show isn't over until I decide," April said, the fingertips of her left hand brushing the yellow ribbon around her neck. "Besides, what man really knows what he wants? This rich prick will want what I say he will. By the time I'm through with him, he'll hand over his last nickel just to touch my hand. Now, hand me the bottle."

Chelley shook her head, but took the squat brown bottle from its hiding place beneath the bar.

"How much of this have you had already?" Chelley asked, holding the bottle up to the lantern light. "I swear there was more yesterday."

"Just give it."

"It's your funeral, sister."

Chelley uncorked the bottle and offered it to April, who took it in her left hand and drew it to her lips. April closed her eyes as the bitter liquid passed her lips.

"That's enough."

April swallowed and brought her hand up, a thumb catching a drip from the corner of her mouth.

Then she opened her eyes and handed the bottle back to Chelley, who corked it and decided to find somewhere different to hide it.

"Where's your brother?" Chelley asked. "Haven't seen him around in a few days. He's good for business. The gamblers like him. He knows how to deal a deck of cards."

"Don't know," April said.

"You don't know?" Chelley asked. "You two are like peas in a pod."

"I won't think about him tonight," April said, angry that Chelley had brought up Augustus. "Just leave me alone, will you?"

"Whatever you say, sweetheart. Just take it easy."

"Easy," April said, enjoying the spreading feeling of unfeeling. "That's just the way I like it."

April laughed.

"The Romantics," April said. "Now, they had the right idea."

She began to recite Coleridge, but Chelley stopped her.

"Not that again," she said. "I've heard it a hundred times."

"And will a hundred times more. *Weave a circle round him thrice*."

April picked up the tumbler of bourbon from the bar and took a deep slug. Then she stopped, a puzzled expression on her face. She suddenly could not feel the arm or the hand that held the drink. The tumbler slipped from her hand and shattered on the floor, the bourbon splashing the hem of her yellow dress.

"I'll be damned," April said.

Then her eyes fluttered, her knees buckled, and she surrendered to gravity, collapsing to the floor.

44   *Crossing*

Gus stepped off the gangplank of the packet steamboat *Ithaca* onto the wharf at Westport Landing. The wharf was really a ledge of natural stone that projected out into the water beneath some high cliffs, near where the Kansas and Missouri Rivers met, but it provided a solid footing for the constant flow of traffic to and from the boats.

He made his way through the crowd and what there was of town, which was mostly a few blocks of half-finished wood frame businesses fronting the river, and a few complete houses behind.

Gus was carrying no cases or bags, and his clothes were coarse, like that of the workers struggling to finish walls and roofs before winter came. But in his pocket was a modest sum of money taken from those who had been foolish enough to play a few hands of cards with him. He never took all of their money, or humiliated them by commenting on their play, but he always took enough for his needs. His need, at present, was to buy a trusty rifle and the other supplies for the journey ahead.

For the first time in his eighteen years, he was happy.

He felt free.

He knew that Westport Landing, in 1840, was the place to enjoy that freedom. At the western edge of Missouri, facing the vast unorganized territory, the choices seemed unlimited. Continuing upriver would take him to the northern plains that were hard against the Rockies. The trails that branched from Westport Landing would lead him to the Oregon Country, to California, or to Santa Fe in Mexico. When he had started out, he was sure that he was bound for vengeance, to seek out his father on the Upper Missouri.

It was a pleasant afternoon in late fall, with plenty of sunshine and just a hint of chill in the air, and the trees on the bluffs overlooking the landing had turned to shades of gold, red, and orange. Gus could see oak and maple, elm and mulberry. He stood and stared for a minute or more before a passerby jostled his shoulder and brought him out of his reverie.

"Watch it," Gus said.

The man turned. He was covered in trail dust, cradled a large-caliber rifle, and had a tan hat with a turkey feather in the band. He was about forty, and his face was lined from years of wind and sun. He was bound for the *Ithaca*, which was already building steam to back away from the wharf.

"Got a boat to catch," the man said in an accent Gus couldn't place. "But don't stand still, son. You'll get run down."

Keep reading for a special excerpt . . .

THE GHOST RIFLE
By Max McCoy

Descended from a long line of ramblers and rogues,
Jack Picaro came to America to seek his fortune.
But after killing his best friend in a drunken duel, the
apprentice gunsmith flees westward, leaving behind
his children, Gus and April. As Jack ventures up the
Missouri River, he finds an unspoiled land where a
man can live free—and also be attacked by
an Arikara war party. His rifle stolen in the bloody
skirmish, Jack sets out alone to reclaim it.
His wild escapade ends in a fight to the death
with a legendary Crow warrior named Standing Wolf.
So begins a fateful epic search across the last frontiers
of the untamed West. From the muddy banks of the
Mississippi to the shining peaks of the Rockies,
Jack Picaro will leave a trail of clues for an abandoned
son, Gus, to find him: a famous gunsmith
who will make history with a weapon of his own
design—and forged a legend that would be
passed down for generations.
This is the story of . . . the ghost rifle

***Look for* The Ghost Rifle**
on sale now where books are sold!

1   *Bloody Island*

Jacques Aguirre was hungry. He was always hungry, even when he had just eaten, and if he wasn't hungry for food, he wanted whiskey, or the thrill of laying money on the turn of a card, and always the attention of women beyond his station. There were other hungers that ebbed or rose according to his spirit—a fascination with clever objects, a thirst for respect, the yearning for freedom— but his essential condition was ravenous.

Even now, as he stood with a heavy dueling pistol in his right hand, muzzle to the stars and the flint ratcheted back, he could not untangle his whiskey-soaked mind from his hunger; his thoughts wheeled back around to food, and the shortbread pies filled with sweet black- berry jam that he had eaten as a child at the sturdy oak table in his grandfather's great stone house across the ocean.

"Ready?" Aristide Rapaille called.

"Always," Jacques said, drunkenly overconfident.

"Then point your piece at the ground," Aristide chided.

"Ha," Jacques said. He lowered the pistol and gave his friend a sly grin.

Aristide was standing twenty paces to the side, his arms folded in Gallic disgust, his stylish boots planted wide in the sand and mud on the banks of this narrow island in the middle of the Mississippi. Even standing in muck, he had the air of a patrician, and his face with its fine features seemed always to be privy to some hidden joke.

It was not yet spring, but no longer winter; on this first Thursday of March 1822, the island was cold and the willows rippled in the midnight breeze. Beyond the willows and other scrub trees, at the river's edge, the water swirled past, driven by spring rains. The moon was climbing the southern sky, nearing full, blocking out the nearby stars, rendering the island and the river beyond in a muted and surreal palette.

The moon reminded Jacques of an unblinking cat's eye, seeing all but moved by nothing. The thought—and the whiskey in his gut—made him laugh.

"Will you be still?" Aristide scolded.

Aristide turned his head to look at his uncle. The moonlight gleamed and rippled on the slick beaver felt of his high hat. The hat had cost an ounce of gold, weeks of labor for the average tradesman, and was fitting for an individual of Aristide Rapaille's position—son of one of the wealthiest families in St. Louis, friend of former territorial governor William Clark, and owner of the most expensive, if not the best, gun shop in the city. It was at the shop, on Chestnut Street just around the corner from the St. Louis County District Court and Jail, where his friend Jacques spent twelve hours of every day. The difference in stations between them was a scandal for the Rapaille family, for Jacques was not just an employee but an indentured servant.

"Are you ready, *tonton*?"

The uncle, Guy Rapaille, was holding the pistol at an awkward angle, in order to examine the lock in the moonlight. Rotund and bespectacled, with an expensive hat that rose even higher than Aristide's, the uncle was having second thoughts about having challenged a man less than half his age, and far below his class, to settle a manner of honor. Unlike the Rapailles, Jacques had no hat, or fancy vest, and instead of a fine coat with bright brass buttons, his was plain dark cotton with bone toggles.

But here, on Bloody Island, their clothes mattered little. Many before them had come to this broad sandbar between the Missouri and Illinois shores—where dueling had long been outlawed—to settle personal differences. Local attorney Thomas Hart Benton had killed Charles Lucas, another lawyer, here just five years before, settling in honor (if not in truth) which one was the liar.

As Jacques was the challenged, the right to choose weapons belonged to him—and of course he chose pistols.

The pistols had not been made at the shop, which specialized in the new short-barreled, large-caliber, half-stock rifles favored by the free trappers who ascended the Missouri River in search of the finest beaver pelts, from the coldest and highest places in the unimagined West, from which Aristide's hat was made.

The pistols were a boxed pair, made in London by Manton, in .51 caliber with 10-inch octagonal barrels. The stocks were walnut and the furniture was silver, and they were loaded with balls that had been cast from lead taken from the mines in Washington County, a day's ride to the southwest.

"Are you having difficulty with your piece?" Aristide asked.

"Of course, he has difficulty," Jacques called. "Just ask his wife!"

"Please," Aristide said. "No more. This is an affair of honor."

"He has no honor," the uncle said. "Look at how he has mistreated your poor sister, Abella. He should be ashamed, but instead he cracks wise. How can you befriend such a person? He is a jack, a knave—no more than a *picaro*, a rogue."

Jacques had heard the term thrown at him before, across the gambling tables in the dark dens along the Mississippi below the city, or from the wealthier patrons of the shop when he was so bold to address them directly, and from Sheriff Brown when he cautioned Jacques against his libertine ways. He rather enjoyed the sound of *rogue*.

"I am unsure of the flint," the uncle said.

"I loaded the pistol myself," Aristide said. "The flint is seated well, and the pan is primed."

"Might you not have allowed your affection for your friend—"

"No, Uncle."

Jacques muttered and cursed in the language of his childhood.

"In English or French, if you please," the uncle snapped.

"I do not please," Jacques said.

"Nobody can understand that guttural argot," Uncle Guy said. "It is not Spanish, but it sounds Gypsy."

"I am not Romany," Jacques said. "I am Basque, from the ancient city of Carcosa. My native tongue is Euskara, and if you had heard my grandfather sing the ballads of love—well, you would never mistake Euskara for Romany again—or perhaps some lesser language, like French."

"Your impudence will be your death," the uncle said in French.

"Perhaps," Jacques replied in English. "But not tonight. Would it be satisfactory if we traded pieces?"

The uncle conceded that it would.

Aristide went about the careful business of swapping the guns, one at a time, turning his shoulders to the moonlight to ease the work. Standing twenty yards away, in the direction of the skiff that had brought them to the island, was Dr. Mason Muldridge, hands clasped in front of him, watching silently.

"This would be simpler, Uncle, had you a proper second," Aristide said, as he handed over the new piece, butt first. "Our good doctor seems ill-suited to such a venture."

Muldridge stared, but said nothing. He had been pulled from his bed and the arms of a well-earned sleep by drunken and frantic pounding on his front door, expecting to attend to some calamity, perhaps the loss of a limb. Because he could not refuse his friend Rapaille, he had made it clear he would take no part other than to care for the injured or pronounce the death of one of the principals.

"Well, it's good that old Muldridge is here," Jacques said. "After this is settled, I could use a shave and a haircut. That was your profession before, was it not? A barber?"

Muldridge took a pinch of snuff.

"This is all forbidden by the Code Duello," Muldridge said. "Never at night."

"Galway rules or Kilkenny?" Jacques taunted.

Muldridge's nose twitched.

"The latter allows nights and every other Easter, seconds to be chosen from among the finer bordellos, and coffee and beignets at dawn."

Muldridge sneezed mightily.

"Leave him alone, Jacky," Aristide said.

"If this were proper, the combatants would be gentlemen," the older Rapaille said, squinting to inspect the pistol's lock. "I lower myself to right a wrong."

"You only lower yourself to make water."

"Jacques!" Aristide chided.

"But does he not look like an old woman?"

"Just what I would expect from a drunken peasant."

"I am drunk," Jacques said. "Blessedly and enthusiastically and dangerously drunk. But, my sir who is almost my uncle by virtue of my brotherly friendship with our beloved Aristide, my birth is as noble as your own. Ah, I see you are confused. Should I speak slower? Allow me to make it plain: In the Basque country, my family are aristocrats, lords of the land, masters of the sea, and I was their prince. It is only through an unfortunate series of miscalculations involving certain games of chance that has resulted in my temporary servitude. But rest assured, I am your peer, if not your better."

The older Rapaille snorted.

"My better?" he asked. "Surely this bootlick jokes. He cannot even vote."

"Please," Aristide said. "We are all of us Americans now. Let us remember the Declaration of the Rights of

Man and to not bring the prejudices and ignorance of the Old World into this new one."

Jacques smiled grimly.

"It seems not all Americans are as equal as others," he said. "It is true that I cannot yet vote, although I am counted as a free man. My status enrages me. And do not forget, my dear friend, that the Rights of Man gave birth to the bastard Corsican, dead but still stinking on St. Helena. Let us all be done with Bonaparte."

"We have the Bill of Rights," Aristide said.

"Ever the optimist," Jacques said. "Why should we expect Americans to fare any better? In time, these declarations too shall be perverted from an instrument of freedom to one of bondage and chaos. But here, standing on an island between and beyond the states, we are truly equal, and I am about to cast a leaden and irrevocable vote with the most democratic of ballots."

The uncle blinked back fear.

"Stand well clear, doctor," Jacques said, waving a hand at Muldridge. "Your skill as a surgeon might be required before the night is out, and it would be a shame if an errant ballot found a home in your breast."

"I beg you," Muldridge called as he stepped back a few more yards. "Stop this lunacy."

Jacques laughed again, turned, and threw a rude salute to the moon.

"Let us wait," Aristide offered. "Next month Jacky will have completed his term of service and will be a free man. In that month he might sober up enough to regret his loutish behavior and offer a proper apology."

"And allow him to ruin other young women," the uncle asked, "like a dog in rut?"

"Now you call your own niece a bitch," Jacques said.

"And my sister," Aristide cautioned.

Jacques did not hear the uncle's protestations, for he was suddenly awash in guilt for this last bit of cruelty. His affection for her seemed genuine. But how was he to know? He remembered the last time they had embraced, a fortnight ago, in the shadow of the old Spanish tower that overlooked the river. Abella was a pale and lissome girl, with black hair that cascaded down to her thin waist, with trusting eyes and kind hands, skin that smelled of vanilla, and a mouth that was ripe to be kissed.

"Jacky!" Aristide called once more. "Stay awake!"

Jacques looked up.

"Is the challenged ready?"

"I am," Jacques said absently in Euskara. He was still thinking of Abella, for she had promised to meet him again tonight, beneath the Spanish tower. He was glad the moon was full, because it would better illumine her graceful form.

There was a muttering behind him.

"I am ready," he said impatiently. "I am eternally ready."

"In French, if you please." Jacques laughed.

"I do not please," Jacques roared. "I am never pleased! I am hungry, as God is my witness, and I starve for life. Let us get on with it, so that I may continue my pursuits—of good whiskey, blind luck, and bad women. For God's sake, Ari, hand me the flask from your pocket for courage before your uncle's lack of wit and paucity of charm forces me to use my pistol on myself."

Aristide warned him about further insults.

"Does he never shut up?" Uncle Guy asked. "All he does is talk. A torrent of words pour from his mouth, equal parts bile and self-aggrandizement, but not an iota of wisdom."

Jacques waved him off.

"Will you not offer an apology?" Aristide inquired. "This whole business can be avoided."

"I will not accept," the uncle said.

"And I will not offer," Jacques said. But at the edge of his mind there was a softly formed thought that perhaps he should, that he should not always be so ready to court trouble, that the uncle was right, every word in his head tumbled unchecked from his mouth.

"Very well," Aristide said. "Is the challenger ready?"

"I am," the uncle said.

"Then take your ground," Aristide said. "The challenged has chosen the weapons and, and as required by the code, the challenger specifies the distance. How many yards, *tonton*?"

The old man began to speak, then hesitated.

"You must give a distance," Aristide said gently.

"Thirty yards," the old man stuttered.

"Why not a hundred?" Aristide asked. "The result will be the same."

"You will now each count off fifteen paces, in opposite directions," Aristide said. "Then you will stop and turn to face your rival. The signal to fire will be when I drop this." Aristide produced a square of white silk. "No shooting into the ground or the air is permitted, nor is any advance or retreat. You must stand your ground and exchange shots. If, after the first exchange, neither party has received a ball, then the pieces may be loaded and the signal repeated. But in no cases will more than three exchanges be allowed. Understood?"

"Yes," the old man said.

"Of course," Jacques said.

"Then take your ground."

Then the men stepped away from one another, counting as they planted each foot in the sand.

"Un," Uncle Guy said.

"*Bat!*" Jacques returned in Euskara.

"Deux."

"*Bi!*"

"Trois."

"*Hiru!*"

"For God's sake, gentlemen," Aristide said. "Be good enough to count in the same language."

"Four." This, in unison.

Jacques reached fifteen first, and he turned as the older man continued, a bit unsteadily.

"Fifteen," Uncle Guy said, finally, and turned cautiously.

"Very well," Aristide said. Then he held out his right hand, the silk square, undulating in the breeze, at shoulder height. The combatants raised and cocked their pistols.

Aristide released the square, and his uncle fired before it had touched the ground. Jacques saw the shower of sparks and tongue of fire from his opponent's pistol. The scene was frozen for an instant in his mind, as when a flash of lightning captures a lingering moment, and by the time he heard the sound of the blast, he felt the air ripple as the ball nipped at his right shoulder.

Outraged, he placed the moonlight-gilded sights of his dueling pistol on the uncle's nose and flicked his finger forward to set the trigger. Suddenly, he was sober.

It would take only a few ounces of pressure from his right index finger to reduce the dotard's head to mush. But his hungers did not include bloodlust, so he shifted his aim to the top of the uncle's beaver hat and squeezed the trigger. The pistol thundered and bucked in his hand, and he watched with satisfaction as the ridiculous hat wheeled wildly into darkness.

The old man dropped his pistol and clasped the top of his head with both hands, as if to make sure his skull remained intact.

"Nicely placed," Aristide said.

"Thank you, my friend."

"Are we done?" Jacques asked.

"No," the uncle said. "Reload."

"Very well," Aristide said tiredly, and took the pistol offered by Jacques. Carefully he tamped down fresh powder and patched ball, primed the pan, and handed it butt first to his friend. But as Jacques grasped the handle, Aristide would not release his hold. Blood, as black as ink in the moonlight, was running down Jacques's wrist and dripping to the sand.

"You have been hit," Aristide said, letting go of the pistol and calling for Muldridge.

Jacques cursed.

"Did you not feel it?" Aristide asked.

"No," Jacques said. "Not until now."

Jacques suddenly felt the weight and awkwardness of the pistol and wanted to be done with it. He slipped the weapon into the outside pocket of his coat, then removed the jacket, noting the hole in the sleeve.

"Take off your shirt as well," Muldridge directed, suddenly competent.

Jacques lifted his left arm while Aristide helped pull it over his head. Because Jacques was a working man, his dress was simpler than that of Aristide; not only was he disallowed a shirt with separate cuffs and collars, he could not afford one, either. The shirt had to be given a little tug, because the fabric of the right sleeve stuck in the warm blood coating his elbow and forearm. There was a light sheen of sweat on his chest and on his ribs, betraying a fear of being shot at that whiskey could not smother. From a silver chain around his neck swung a curious piece, a milled and polished brass disk that was some three inches across, with four curved arms in the center. The design was odd, like that of a cross with curiously lobed ends, facing left. On the outside was a row of teeth punctuated by indents around the rim, with another circle of teeth and indents nestled inside.

"What is the medallion?" Uncle Guy asked, staring at the disk.

"Let me conduct my examination, for God's sake," Muldridge said. He gently touched Jacques's shoulders and turned him gently this way and that in the moonlight, his face inscrutable in concentration.

Jacques could not see the wound, but was alarmed by the amount of blood.

"Well?" Aristide asked. "How bad is it?"

"It will leave a scar," Muldridge said.

"So does amputation," Jacques said.

"For God's sake, doctor, how bad is it?" Aristide pressed.

"No bones broken, or damage to the biceps," the doctor said. "Your arm was bent, holding the barrel of the pistol upright, when Monsieur Rapaille fired. The ball passed through the fabric and gave you a nasty bite. It will leave a scar, nothing more. Keep it clean and pray that it does not fester."

Jacques nodded.

His left hand fluttered upward and instinctively grasped the brass disk dangling from the chain around his neck, his thumb skimming the teeth, as he muttered thanks to both Saint Ignatius and the chthonic goddess Mari.

"Is it a religious symbol?" Guy asked with suspicion. "It resembles Ezekiel's dream of a wheel within a wheel."

"Exactly," Aristide said. He knew the truth, that the pattern in the disk was the *lauburu,* the ancient four-headed cross of the Basque people. But he wanted to deflect his uncle's questions. "It is some pagan symbol, which Jacky's people revere. But such strangeness cannot be accounted for. Best to leave it alone, rather than court the devil."

Uncle Guy crossed himself.

"You are a lucky fool," Muldridge told Jacques. "You mocked me until you needed attention. What if the ball had shattered your arm, or ruined your hand? What kind of living would you have made then, unable to run a nut or turn a screw? What would an apology have cost you? If your life means so little to you, what about that of the girl, Abella? What of her life?"

"You speak out of turn," Jacques said.

The doctor pursed his lips, holding the words back.

"Then this affair of honor is over," Aristide said quickly. "The challenger has drawn substantial blood. I assume this is enough to represent satisfaction?"

"It is," Guy said, his relief evident.

"I have grown tired of this," Jacques said as Muldridge bandaged his upper arm with a strip of cloth ripped from his ruined shirt. "Now that we are all Americans again, let us return to the public house beneath Tower Hill. We will toast our fine adventure casting ballots of lead on Bloody Island."

2   *The Landing*

Aristide put his back into the oars as the skiff drew near the end of Lucas Street, where the ground dipped gently to the river's edge. This was the broad levee, where the steamboats docked, took on firewood and offloaded passengers and goods, and made repairs. It was edged by storehouses and workshops and businesses decorated with columns and capitals, whitewashed walls, and broad vaulted windows where an occasional candle burned.

The skiff was an eleven-foot boat of the kind that fishermen up and down the river used, with a flat stern and a snub bow, and coils of rough hemp rope in the bottom. They had found the boat tied beneath one of the lesser docks and had borrowed it to make their way to Bloody Island, for it had just enough seats for the dueling party of four. They had been halfway across the river when they discovered the boat leaked; it wasn't enough to cause an immediate concern of sinking, but was enough to swell the coils of rope and damp their boots. So on the way back, Aristide—who was clearly the only viable candidate for rowing—rowed now with purpose, both to cut across the current in order to round the shallow bar that

guarded the deeper channel along the levee, and to
reduce the amount of time they would have to spend with
their toes sloshing in the Mississippi. But Aristide, facing
the stern, was having a difficult time steering the boat,
because the required maneuvers seemed backward.

"Aller à droit!" Uncle Guy cried out. Then, *"A gauche!
A gauche!"*

The wooden bottom of the boat scraped over the sand
and gravel of the towhead. There was a chill wind on the
water, and it seemed to grow suddenly colder as the boat
slowed.

"Pull," the uncle said.

Aristide did, and the boat resumed its forward motion.

"Snag!" Jacques cried.

With a groan the boat lurched up on a submerged tree
trunk, pivoted wildly, and then was free. Aristide pulled
one oar handle and pushed the other in an attempt to
make a line again for shore.

"My God, Aristide," Jacques said. "Have you never
rowed a boat before?"

"Not at night or with people shouting directions or
with a head still singing with rum. If either you or my
dear uncle can do better, you are welcome to try."

"No, thank you," Muldridge said from the stern.

"Thank you, Doctor," Aristide said.

The boat was now heading roughly in the right direction, but the faster current in the channel was sweeping
it downstream.

"Faster!" Jacque shouted, then laughed.

Aristide cursed and pulled harder.

"Ah," the uncle said as the levee neared.

Then the boat crossed the eddy line to calmer water,

and Aristide lifted the oars from the water as they glided toward a dock. It wasn't the dock they had taken the boat from, but it didn't matter to them.

Uncle Guy rose from his seat in the bow and reached a hand out to grasp the dock. He missed, then caught a plank on the second try and pulled the skiff in close.

"There are steps," Aristide said, nodding at some stones rising from the water to the top of the landing. The boat was close enough that the others could now reach across the gunwale and help pull the skiff along, and soon the bow bumped into the stone steps. The uncle grabbed the end of a coil of rope at his feet and tied a careless knot around a piling, while in the stern the doctor quickly tied an expert clove hitch.

"I am done with this leaky tub," Uncle Guy said, stepping shakily out of the boat and up onto the steps. He kept one foot too long in the skiff, and the imbalance drove one side of the boat dangerously close to the water. Jacques was behind him, with his rough coat over his shoulders, and he put both hands on the old man's posterior and pushed him up. As the uncle finally gained both feet on the steps, the skiff righted itself with a jolt, and Jacques fell, losing his coat, laughing. He was up in a moment, however, but forgot his coat, for he was warm yet with drink and the excitement of the duel. He put one boot on the gunwale and lightly jumped for the steps. But he did not see that his right boot had become entangled in a loop in the rope Uncle Guy had hastily uncoiled to tie up with, and it tripped him just as he made the steps.

Jacques fell heavily on the steps, and as he did the dueling pistol that had been in his right pocket clattered to the stone. Whether the gun had been cocked when he put it in his pocket, or whether the jolt had drawn the hammer back just far enough, Jacques would forever ponder but never know. What was certain was the flash of flame and the crack of thunder as the gun discharged, its barrel pointed back toward the river.

"Jacky?" Aristide asked. "What a peculiar joke."

Jacques glanced back and saw his friend Aristide looking at him with surprise, standing with his hands out as if Christ crucified, his shirt smoldering from the burning patch and a dark-as-ink stain spreading from his right side. Their eyes met, and the last emotion that Jacques ever saw on his friend's face was disappointment. Then Aristide buckled and he pitched into the Mississippi, the motion carrying his body away from the skiff.

Silence descended like a thunderclap. The night wind was suddenly cold on Jacques's bare chest.

"Ari," he said.

Jacques tore off his boots and dove from the steps into the river, swimming madly, calling his friend's name when his head bobbed above water. Aristide was floating facedown, but as the weight of the tail of his coat slipped to one side, he turned, his hair swirling in the water around his face. Jacques thought he should be able to reach Aristide in just a few strokes, but the farther he swam, the more distance there seemed between them.

Then Aristide's body slid beneath a downstream dock, where a dozen silent keelboats were moored. If there were watchmen on the keelboats, they were either passed out drunk or asleep, for nothing moved on their decks. Then the moon was shrouded by some low clouds, portending rain, and it was darker now than it had been on the island.

Jacques stared at the darkness beneath the docks, thinking of the snakes that were surely coiled in the driftwood and tree branches and other trash that collected there. A fear of those hidden places gripped him, and he could not bring himself to search beneath the docks for Aristide's body. Jacques sobbed as he swam back to the skiff, calling for Uncle Guy and the doctor to help search.

Muldridge, who was still sitting in the stern of the skiff, shrugged.

"The river has him now," he said.

"There must be something to be done," Uncle Guy said, but his uncertain tone betrayed his words.

"Not until dawn," the doctor said. "And even then, our task will be to find the body. Such a wound was surely fatal, and if he did survive the gunshot, he would be insensate and drown. His body will likely be carried far downriver."

Jacques pulled himself dripping up onto the bottom step, where the sulfurous stench of black powder lingered. Out of habit, his right hand went to the brass disk around his neck. It was still there. Then he sat and pulled his knees up and rested his forehead on his folded arms. He had killed his best and only friend by accident, but it made Aristide no less dead.

"What have I done?" he asked.

"You have committed murder," Uncle Guy said, "and for this you will surely hang."

"But it was an accident," Jacques said. "You saw so yourself."

"I saw no such thing," Uncle Guy said. "My back was turned. I only heard the shot. When I did look around, I saw my nephew Aristide murdered."

"Then you, good doctor," Jacques said. "You must have seen."

"My view was blocked by Aristide's back," Muldridge said. "I know only the result."

Jacques turned back to Uncle Guy.

"Please, friend's dear uncle," Jacques implored. "The pistol fell from my pocket when I tripped on the rope you carelessly dragged behind you. This you must know to be true."

"You were drunk and should have watched your step."

Jacques found himself suddenly without words. The silence that followed was excruciating, an indictment unspoken, a judgment implicit. Shame and guilt were unfamiliar emotions, and as hot tears spilled down his cheeks, his stomach churned so that he thought he would retch.

"We should summon Sheriff Brown," Muldridge said.

"Yes," Jacques said resignedly. "It must be so."

His life had been changed in an instant. No longer would he have Aristide to drink and laugh with, to throw dice and play cards with, to be the brother that blood had never given him. The sheriff would come and he would spend some weeks in the wretched jail in the courthouse downtown and eventually there would be a trial and even though he might be acquitted of murder, he would always be guilty of taking his friend's life.

"Let us not summon the sheriff yet," Uncle Guy said.

He was standing on the dock above them, his dueling pistol held loosely in his hand.

"What do you mean?" Muldridge asked.

"Why go through a trial when we have the means to dispense justice immediately? Trial by jury is unreliable.

We understand perfectly the guilt of the accused. Let us not allow his fate to be decided by a dozen chosen from the rabble who are no better than the accused. It would be better to be done with this *picaro* here and now."

"Aristide's death was an accident," Jacques said. "This is murder."

"Guy, he is right," Muldridge said.

"Stand clear!"

"Where am I to go?" Muldridge asked. "The boat is not large."

"Let him do it," Jacques said. "It is no more than I deserve."

"At least allow me to make myself small," Muldridge said, scooting to the bottom of the boat and doing just that.

"Quit whimpering," Jacques said. "I will mount the steps and stand on the dock, facing the firing squad of one."

Uncle Guy hesitated.

"No," he said. "Allow the doctor to pass instead."

Jacques shrugged.

Muldridge rose and clamored forward, exited the boat, then quickly ascended the steps to the dock.

"I am alone now," Jacques said, "waiting for my own Charon to lead me from this dreary coast. But that would be you, dear uncle of the dead, would it not? You will kill me and then—what?—throw my body into the boat and push it into the current? Both Ari and I will be missing for a few days, and then one will be found, and eventually the other, and it will seem that we had a contretemps that turned unexpectedly violent, with results mortal to us both."

"Why do you still talk?" Uncle Guy asked. "Even at the point of a gun, you continue to spew your thoughts at us as incautiously as if you had sneezed with a mouthful of wine."

Jacques shrugged.

"The truth is, I had not considered yet what to do beyond killing you."

"You should," Jacques said. "I have presented you a nearly perfect plan."

"Nearly?"

"The doctor," Jacques said. "What of him? Can you count on his silence?"

"Muldridge is our family doctor," Uncle Guy said. "A man of discretion."

"Please," the doctor pleaded. "Leave me out of this."

"Ah, it is too late for that," Jacques said. "You will allow Uncle Guy to murder me without benefit of judge or jury? Even if you think I deserve it, there will be uncomfortable questions from Sheriff Brown and others. You will keep silent during questioning? Can you lie convincingly? Will your palms not sweat and your eyes not twitch knowing that giving false testimony is one of the most serious of crimes itself?"

"Shut up," Uncle Guy shouted. "Just shut up."

His shout echoed back from the walls of the warehouses. Somewhere, a dog began to bark, and then another. Soon, a chorus of angry canines rose toward the night sky, and a few more lights appeared in the windows of the trying-to-sleep river town.

"There is my jury," Jacques said. "A jury of dogs. They deliver their verdict, and it seems not to be in my favor.

Proceed, Uncle Guy. Even you can put a ball in my chest at this distance."

"You talk to buy time."

It was true. Even though a part of him longed to be punished for the accidental killing of his best friend, the greater part sought to live. Jacques knew that if he kept talking—and kept Uncle Guy answering—the greater his chances were of either talking his way out of his own murder, or seizing upon some small advantage that would allow him to escape.

"Give me the medallion," said Uncle Guy.

"You have a sudden interest in paganism?"

"I would deprive you of comfort at the moment of your death."

"Oh, you think it valuable, don't you?"

"What is it, then?"

"Come closer," Jacques said, beckoning. "Press the muzzle against my bare chest and pull the trigger. I long for justice and the forgiveness of that long sleep that awaits. You can take the disk and study it at your leisure when I am dead." He was hoping to lure Uncle Guy close enough so that he could make a grab for the pistol's barrel and wrest it away.

"No, you come up here."

"Very well, Uncle."

Barefoot, Jacques slowly climbed the steps. His pace was as slow as if he were ascending the gallows. At the top step, he looked up at the night sky. The clouds were so thick now that he could see no stars.

Then he stepped onto the dock, finding his footing with careful toes.

They were only ten feet apart, but in the darkness,

they were just shadows to one another. Jacques's back was to the river, and the rotund shadow that was the uncle blocked his path to the landing. Jacques could not see it, but he sensed the hammer of the pistol was cocked and that Rapaille's finger was on the trigger. He only hesitated, Jacques knew, because his old and tired eyes were unsure of his target now that the dock had been deprived of moonlight.

He heard the uncle take two steps toward him, to improve his aim, and Jacques knew it was time to move or die. He crouched and lunged forward, colliding with the great stomach that preceded Uncle Guy like the prow of a ship, and they both tumbled to the rough planks of the dock while fighting for the pistol. Jacques wrapped both of his hands around the wrist that held the pistol, forcing the barrel away. The old man drove the fingers of his other hand into the soft flesh of Jacques's nose and upper lip, the fingernails stabbing him. Jacques bit one of the offending fingers, hard enough to hear a crack, and the uncle yelped in pain and withdrew his injured hand.

The doctor was ascending the stone steps, but Jacques warned him that he would be next to be bitten. Muldridge obediently sat on the top step.

Uncle Guy cursed and squirmed, but Jacques managed to twist and bring a knee up and press it against the old man's throat, forcing the right side of his face into the rough timber of the decking.

"Let go of the piece," Jacques said, surprised that he could not yet prise the pistol loose.

Uncle Guy, face against the dock, said something that sounded like "no."

"I swear I will crush your windpipe if I must. Let go, Uncle."

More sounds, but none that were words.

Jacques had more leverage now, and he brought more force to bear on Uncle Guy's neck. There was a gurgling sound, and labored breathing, and finally the old man's grip on the pistol began to loosen. Then suddenly Jacques had the pistol.

Jacques got to his feet and pointed the pistol at the uncle, who was alternately coughing and sucking in air. Jacques stepped cautiously past him, a bit closer to the dark rows of warehouses and the rest of St. Louis on the limestone bluffs beyond. With his free hand, he wiped the blood away from his nose and gums.

"Damn you," the uncle said between wheezes. "Damn your children, and all that you and they may touch."

Anger and grief expanded in Jacques's heart until it felt as if the ballooning organ would push his ribs through his chest. His head was ablaze with an unquenchable fire, and he was half surprised to find that his skull cast no light on his surroundings. The dogs keened in the distance, round upon round of hoarse cries of some pain from the beginning of the world, and Jacques stumbled backward, pushing his hands to his ears, the pistol still in his right fist.

"Aristide," Jacques cried. "Oh, Aristide!"

Then he turned and flung the pistol over Uncle Guy's head, beyond the end of the dock, and far across the dark water. It landed with a percussive splash in the Mississippi and was gone forever.

Jacques ran. The bottoms of his feet beat a tattoo on the wooden decking. He slipped, ripping his trousers and bloodying his knee. Then he was up and flying again down the dock in the dark, carrying his hunger and his shame with him. He jumped from the dock, and his feet sank into the sand and mud of the landing, bringing him to hands and knees, with his forehead touching the earth, an involuntary prostration to the crushing and sure consequences of hubris and careless action. Never again, he swore to himself, would he speak without thinking or act without sincerity and deliberation. He was fluent in four languages, and had damned himself in all; he had all the strength and dexterity a man of twenty-three could expect, and had employed these to his ruin; he had had a friend who loved him like a brother, and he had betrayed that fraternal love with fatal carelessness.

Jacques lifted his head, brushed the sand and mud from his face with a forearm, heard the dogs baying and snarling in the distant night. His right hand clasped the disk that swung from the chain around his neck, holding it tight over his heart. He rose, nearly fell again, and of a sudden, found his feet and was running toward the darkness.

Connect with Us

Visit us online at
KensingtonBooks.com
to read more from your favorite authors, see books
by series, view reading group guides, and more.

for sneak peeks, chances to win books and prize packs,
and to share your thoughts with other readers.

facebook.com/kensingtonpublishing
twitter.com/kensingtonbooks

Tell us what you think!

To share your thoughts, submit a review,
or sign up for our eNewsletters, please visit:
KensingtonBooks.com/TellUs.